VIA Folios 54

The Three-Legged One

Giose Rimanelli

The Three-Legged One

A Glossed Novel

Bordighera Press
2009

Library of Congress Control Number: 2008940161

Printed in the United States.

Published by
BORDIGHERA PRESS
John D. Calandra Italian American Institute
25 West 43rd Street, 17th Floor
New York, NY 10036

VIA FOLIOS 54
ISBN 978-1-59954-000-9

The city in these pages is imaginary.
The people, the places are all fictitious.
Only the Academic routine is based on
established investigatory technique.

for Sheryl

Roses are

planted where thorns grow

and to
Dr. Elio D'Ascenzo
of Colle del Brigante,
(Termoli, Molise) where
I wrote the first draft of
this book ages ago
lost there and found again
today:
an "essential" now in my marginalia...

Is Giose Rimanelli an Italian/American Writer?

An Introduction

Giose Rimanelli had keen insights into the plight of the Italian American long before he ever became one. The Italian living in North America served as a regular subject for his writing. In *Una posizione sociale* (1959) he recounts the life of the Italian living in New Orleans in the early 1900s and examines the lynching of 13 Italians. In 1966 he collected, edited and introduced *Modern Canadian Stories*. *Tragica America* (1968) contains his reflections of his first years in the United States. Seven years later he gave us a greater insight into the literature of Italy through *Italian Literature: Roots and Branches*. Since his retirement from academia, Rimanelli has continued writing his fiction in Italian and publishing it primarily in Italy. North America had entered his imagination long before his arrival in the 1950s. His grandfather was born in New Orleans, and his mother in Canada. We can see images of America forming in his earliest novels. Over the years that he has lived here, Rimanelli has been writing poetry and novels in English and had accumulated a number of unpublished manuscripts. Early in the 1970s he wrote his first novel in English entitled *Benedetta in Guysterland*, which was published for the first time in 1993 by Guernica Editions in Montreal, Canada, and was awarded a 1993 American Book Award by the Before Columbus Foundation.

Benedetta in Guysterland occupies a pivotal position in the history of Italian/American narrative as the bridge over the border between modernism and postmodernism, between the mythic and philosophic narrative modes. Rimanelli was writing *Benedetta* during the same time younger Italian/American writers such as Don DeLillo and Gilbert Sorrentino were beginning their writing careers. Until this novel, we could not talk about a distinctive and visible Italian/American presence in postmodernism. *Benedetta in Guysterland* filled a deep void in Italian/American literary history; that void is the cavity caused by the decay of a literary realism characteristic of the standard fare produced by Italian/American writers. For too long, those imaginations have been held prisoners by the psycho-social borders of the Italian/American ghetto. While the emphasis of most Italian/American fiction has been the Italian/American experience, most authors have been unable to gain a distance from the subject that would enable them to gain the new perspectives necessary to renew the story of Italian life in America. What Mario Puzo romanticized in *The Godfather* (1969), and what Gay Talese historicized in *Honor Thy Father* (1971), Giose Rimanelli has parodied in *Benedetta*. Through parody he has transcended the Italian/American subject by, above all, writing a book about literature through the same subject of the mafia used by Puzo and Talese. Like James Joyce, Rimanelli unites high culture with popular culture in this labyrinth of a text that reads like a map of Western civilization.

With *Moliseide and Other Poems*, Giose Rimanelli began his fifth decade of publishing and earned the right to be referred to as the Ezra Pound of Italian/American writing. Rimanelli is a man of incredible knowledge--most of it self-taught; he is also, like Walt Whitman, a man of incredible compassion, which comes from his ability to listen. These poems are, in the purist sense, echoings of the world around him, but there is a twist. In the act of responding to stimuli, Rimanelli's poetry draws attention away from itself and toward the object of his inspiration. In this way, the craftsman remains invisible, and these poems can become songs for everyone.

Moliseide has become Rimanelli's *Leaves of Grass*. He has published two previous versions, one with cassette recordings of his lyrics in the music of Benito Faraone, one of his childhood friends.

It's as though the longer he lives, the more he needs to adjust the presentation of his past. Rimanelli's wisdom lies in his ability to change the past through verse. And this change ripples back through to the present.

The collection is divided into three parts. Part One is presented in three languages; the original in the dialect of Molise is accompanied by two translations: Italian and English. These poems which form the earliest 1990 version, come at you as pastoral postcards, the struggle between the old world and the new as in "Kawasaki Blues," or pure lyrical myth as in ballads such as "Ballad of the Sorcerer" and "Ballad of the Lizard." More than anything else, the poems in this section give you a sense of what life is like in Molise: "Molise's World is made of all those things/ that fill our lives with the And the Square/ is always watching who gets married there/ because it wants finest air./ People arrive and eat, they rest and think: 'These mornings are a nectar!' to see if you make do."

In Part Two, we move away from the Molisano dialect; there are love songs, lighter verse, land travel songs. While these poems might be less didactic, they do offer lessons of what it is like to leave one's ancestral homeland and enter the wide world beyond childhood. One of the lessons taught by association and not words in this section is one found in "Molisan Nights:" "Molisan Nights hanging on the walls; of ancient houses long ago abandoned. Lianas of memories still rooted/ in the days of love that went with youth." Nothing is as it was, but that doesn't mean it can't become a song. In Part Three, we return to a trilingual presentation of 23 poems which are reminiscent of Eugenio Montale's "Xenia" poems: more meditations than songs, more chants of wisdom than contemporary tunes.

Since winning the 1994 American Book Award for *Benedetta in Guysterland*, Rimanelli had been busy catching up with the many novels, poems and stories he penned as a way of learning the

English language nearly 40 years ago. His *Alien Cantica: An American Journey* (1964-1993), published in a bi-lingual edition by Peter Lang in 1995, collected his poems written during this period in a "slangy American for my own practice."

Accademia, the second novel in what will be called his American triology, is the result of Rimanelli's more than twenty-five years of living in the American academe. The novel is to him what "Lolita" was to Vladimir Nabokov. Rimanelli invites this comparison by setting the novel in Anabasis, Nabokov County, Appalachia USA, a highly symbolic location in which myth-like events occur on streets named after Greek and Roman gods and historical events and places. Like Nabokov, Rimanelli was a well-known author in his native language before immigrating to the United States, took up residence in an American university, and worked at his literary trade in his new acquired language, English. If *Benedetta in Guysterland*, was Rimanelli's American primer, then *Accademia* is his graduate thesis, proving that he has not only mastered the English language, but that he's conquered the cultural obstacles that most uneducated immigrants never get the chance to encounter.

So much of the novel is couched in Jungian symbolism that we can't help but see the characters as archetypes. This psychological element enables the novel to reach beyond autobiography and into the lives of everyone who has ever gone to college. Rimanelli structures the novel into two halves; a male point-of-view in chapters 1-9 comes to us through Simon Dona, an Italian immigrant professor, and a female point-of-view in chapters 10-19 through his young, American born second wife, Lisa. The voice of Simon returns for the last chapter.

You don't read this novel to follow a story, but to follow the effect that intellectual development and display has on an Italian immigrant. Simon Dona becomes, for all of Italian America, a trickster who both succeeds and fails at playing his song of life in the key of intellect. Rimanelli uses this trickster character to show us how not to become intellectuals.

Although the novel opens with references to Simon Dona's family (he has two sons from a previous marriage in Italy and one from his younger wife Lisa), family life in this academic environment is all but destroyed. An extended family of friends and colleagues, a weak replacement for the nuclear family, becomes the focus of this Italian narrator's story. As Simon recalls events in the social life of the academe, he rarely mentions his offspring, suggesting that there is little room for the traditional family in this heady, hedonistic atmosphere. The novel becomes a study of the interaction of those scholars whose lives intertwine in the academe making for a richly symbolic story of parodic incest that waxes and wanes on the battleground of male-female sexuality and intellectuality. Each character lives in a self-created labyrinth constructed by social and economic opportunities accepted and denied. In Simon Dona's case, the maze is the American academe, in which he lives in a house made of glass.

Characters in the novel are all obsessed with studying, philosophizing and achieving sexual fantasies, and intellectual superiority at the expense of dealing with, the less desirable, but more stable reality of lasting relationships. Dona is a physical anthropologist who studies the Macaque species, "The most ancient species besides man." But in writing his book, Dona is actually putting forth his research the likes of Madison, a colleague turned lover who studies roaches and names her subjects after people she knows.

The novel is wrought with irony and satire of academic introspection and subsequent self-realization. Dona understands the split between public and private life; however as one who lives in a glass house, he knows he can be observed just as the caged animals he studies; the important thing is that Dona can verbalize this: "On the outside we are social saints, and inside our own glass house we are monsters, prisoners of perverted habits, voluntary suicides for the lack of sincerity with ourselves."

Dona reminds us that we all inhabit glass houses and though we may intend for our lives to be open and revealing, we are all victims of the clash between our needs and our desires, a battle between our psyches and our libidos. The results of these interactions are the clouds of doubt and self-deceit that clothe our personalities and tint our relationships. As an American academic with international impact, Rimanelli gives us a glimpse into the world of screwed up scholars, an insight that might just save us from becoming like them.

With *The Three-Legged One* once again I found in my hands another unpublished novel of Giose Rimanelli, which, after a number of readings, I realize will once again become a major literary statement. To call him an Italian American writer is to do a disservice to the worlds we find in the writings of Giose Rimanelli. Why, you could drop this man into the Antarctic and he would soon become an Italian Antarctican writer. This is to say that Rimanelli is a writer, a writer of the world he lives in, a creator of the worlds in his writing. To study any of his works is to enact a literary vivisection for it not only survives scrutiny, it changes under it. This is certainly true for Benedetta, as a liquid novel, its contents pour through most critical vessels and continue to bring new ways of reading to the fore. A most recent example is the work on *Benedetta* by the young scholar Chiara Mazzuchelli, who applies theories of gossip to illustrate how the novel further enacts its role as a missing link between the typical modern master narratives and the undermining narrative factures found in the best of what can be called post-modern fiction.

This new novel completes what will inevitably be called the Anabasis Trilogy, and remove any doubt of Rimanelli's place in American literature. With *The Three-Legged One*, Rimanelli joins the ranks of great American writers who have crafted three significant novels related by place. We have John Dos Passos USA Triology, The Swedish trilogies of Ole Edvart Rolvaag and Vilhelm Moberg, James T. Farrell's Studs Lonigan Trilogy, Henry Miller's Rosy Crucifixion trilogy, William Faulkner's Snopes' Trilogy, Willa Cather's Prairie Trilogy, William Carlos Williams's White Mule trilogy, John Edgar Wideman's Homewood Trilogy, William Kennedy's Albany Trilogy, and Cormack McCarthy's Border Trilogy.

This pastoral novel is written in a *contrasto*, a form Virgil used to capture conversations between shepherds. Rimanelli uses it to present the stories of two workers and a husband and wife. Dedicated to two stalwarts of Canadian American literature, the late Malcolm Lowry and the late Earle Birney, this pastiche of stories seems to be more knitted together than his earlier works, and one might ask if this is some kind of last ditch effort to construct a whole out of disparate parts of fiction that he had produced in English over the years. In fact, the first part, called "The Eyetalian" was written, like *Benedetta*, as a way of exercising his early English language muscles. This section, echoing the dialogues we find in Virgil's "Georgics" is a spring of sorts that recounts the arrival in Anabasis of two immigrants, one Conor "Little Fart Irisk" McCurn, a Scotch-Irish logger whose life echoes that of Earle Birney, and the other an Italian known as Skip "Clubfoot Eyetalian" Horace, who is a thinly disguised version of a young Rimanelli. The section resembles Virgil's famous ecologues and follows the reactions of each as they come to inhabit adjacent spaces in the land of Anabasis; part two "Squatters" introduces the male/female couple of Skip Horace and Lady Bee Do Abigail, through a contrasto of sorts that takes us through the summer and autumn of their shared life, and section three, "The Old Couple" consists of 35 prose-poem segments that recount the winter years of this couple as they fight off the advance of commercial development of their pastoral home in the woods.

Skip Horace is much like his famous namesake Quintus Horatio Flaccus, and curiously very much like his creator/author. Flaccus, grew up in what we now call Basilicata and after a classical education in Greece returned to Rome to serve in the Roman army of Brutus after which he turned toward literary pursuits; sound familiar? Coincidence or a rebirth? Whatever it is, it all comes together in this novel. What remains, is for this book to be published and see if it can stand the scrutiny given to the earlier works. No doubt that one of us must find a publisher for this one, and since I have made it a goal to publish my teachers: first Rimanelli, then Frank Lentricchia, then Christian Messenger and most recently Robert Viscusi, it was my hope that I could help in the publication of the final novel in the American trilogy.

So, to return to the original question of my investigation, is Giose Rimanelli an Italian/American writer? I must conclude with a resounding yes, but qualify that if he is an Italian/American writer, then he must also be an Italian writer and an Italian/Canadian writer, and when you think of all that labeling it could confuse those who need to catalogue this man's life's work, so let's just leave it as this: Giose Rimanelli is a writer of the world who must be reckoned with if one is to understand just what has happened to our world in the late 20th and early 21st century.

Fred Gardaphé, Distinguished Professor
Queens College/CUNY &
The John D. Calandra Italian American Institute

FOREWORD

These are love diaries. Written in a form almost analytical they cover the periods between 1960 and 1976. Only the notebooks bearing the dates 1973-74 constitute a deliberate narrative structure. I have made no deletions or additions in the process of preparing them for publication, save for the foot-notes and commentaries that accompany the text.

The diaries were sent to me by a colleague, the anthropologist Simon Dona, along with a novel by Robert P. Pirsing, *Zen and the Art of Motorcycle Maintenance*, and in turn I shall send it for a reading to my good pal Fred G., who is a rich man with a good taste and a gentle humour.

As a distraction from his scholarly pursuits, Dona often volunteered his services as a test pilot to Japanese and American firms, following which he published his observations and reflections in the *Road Test Annual* and the *Cycle World*. He also wrote for French and Italian newspapers which featured his signed contributions for many years.

Dona had developed an almost suicidal love for motorcycles, especially after the divorce from his second wife, Vera Jones. He had tried them all. And he had also written (in Italian) his memoirs, based on an anthropological appraisal of his selfhood and of his home town, Selimo, in Italy.

A local poet, who had reviewed the book, concluded his piece with the following observation:

> The final passages are written completely in English, nevertheless the name Selimo recurs frequently. Obviously it is the text of one of his classroom lectures as taped by a student. My ignorance of English causes me to pause in my reading, perplexed. These parti-

cular passages strike me as being the surface of a frozen lake beneath which moves an indecipherable something. These English passages are a kind of diaphragm between two realities, the one in which he lives and the one in which, perhaps some day, he would like again to live... two modes of being that reflect the duality of his soul.

Dona's soul was tortuous and innocent. Although the last pages of his autobiography clearly stressed the possibility of a re-entry into the maternal womb, i.e. world of Selimo and its environs, he still toyed with the idea of being useful to his fellow townsmen in a scholarly capacity. His epistolary gives an idea of the strong communicative ties that he had maintained with his home town. But one day a letter arrived from his close friend Elio which literally shook him up and dispelled the very idea of a possible homecoming. Elio, ensconced in his lair atop Colle Del Brigante, a jewel-case of mysteries overlooking the Adriatic, wind-battered and oozing sultriness, had practically spelt out to him that love is not the fruit of togetherness but of two separate solitudes, unfortunately. Every reunion becomes a slaughter and every separation is cottoned in melancholy. The harsh law enjoins us only to live out the illusion to the end.

Elio wrote:

"For us, my dear friend, to create and die, to resurrect and relapse, alone and exclusively is life, beyond any borders. Nevertheless, the alternating landscape that morning and twilight offer us in the desperate solitudes of night, and between bloodstained sheets, is light."

On that day, May 7, '76, after receiving the letter, Simon went to the garage and mounted his Harley. Nothing more was ever heard of him, but it certainly must have been a suicide inasmuch as he had left an updated last will behind.

After almost forty years, I have decided to prepare these tormented pages for publication in order to extract there from, along with my readers, some teachings of an edifying character.

R. Carmen Cara
Professor of Administrative Law

New Year's Day 1994
University of Anaconda
Anaconda, N.Y.

Revision:
Lowell, Massachusetts
Luglio 2008

PART ONE

SIMON'S DIARY

In order to decide I chose a different name
In order to change course I summoned the pigeons
    to appear
Then the scene changes and there is wallowing in the
    courtyard
Nuts are eaten and heads are bent over plate
Setting out towards the re-closed curtains fingers
    among the books
Than all becomes

Antonio Porta, *Cara*

... any work, any novel tells, through the events of its plot, the story of its own creation, that is, its own story... The sense of a work consists in telling about itself, in speaking to us of its own existence... The very existence of a novel is the last link in the chain of its plot: where the story that is narrated ends, is precisely where the story that narrates, the literary story, begins.

Tzvetan Todorov, *Literature and Signification*

1.

Summer had crammed the house with guests. Now it's empty-ing out. Academic life, chaotic and monotonous, is starting all over again. It's already completely programmed. But the feeling remains motionless.

Meanwhile I record the passing days, the things of yesterday and the things of today up to the point where memory makes me hallucinate. The barometer is rising but the expectation is the journey. The sun, lacking rays, is overly big. Fixing one's gaze on it is like no longer seeing. The aim is not to remember but to save what I do not know in the moment that I know what I am not saving.

I go downstairs and I see Dino still carrying his backpack. My son Dino returned to Italy on the 12th bringing Revlon perfumes for his mother, a dozen of old Beatle records for his brother Sandro, and a new tennis racquet for himself.

I go upstairs and I see Daniel seated at the piano, practicing. My son Daniel has also just returned from a visit, to his grand-mother in New Canaan, Connecticut. And he brought back with him fifty dollars neatly folded in the pocket of chic trendy suit, along with a miniscule iguana in a straw-lined cardboard box to add to his zoo.

Vera had driven him back. Her fingernails and lips were chewed up, and she looked weary and rancorous. Dino is less restrained than Daniel whom he disparagingly calls "the kid." He is two years older than Daniel and engages in all-round sports: swimming and cycling, soccer and fencing and horsemanship while Daniel is still a pollywog in a pool. Dino admittedly masturbates, he would like to have a woman and doesn't yet know how to go about it, but he will be grabbed up soon, since he's good looking and knows it. His English isn't so good, but it doesn't bother him in the least; his communication with others takes the form of an explosive sensuality. And all this repels Daniel who fancies himself a member of the master race, like his mother. This so-called brother is actually a stranger as was Sandro for that matter, whose acquaintance he had made only last summer. Nor has Daniel forgotten Sandro, his father's eldest son, a youngster savage and malign, a sly provocateur, who sported a scornful mustache in the manner of a West Point cadet.

In Sandro's eyes Daniel, "the kid," was a fat pinkish pig ling to be roasted on a spit, to Vera's horror, because through him she intuits Billie's revenge, Billie the Roman lady whose man she had walked off with wantonly and capriciously, subsequently dubbing divorce love.

Nor does Daniel forget the day he fell in the canal on Cape Cod, experiencing the first real terror of his life as drowning in the water, under the eyes of this guffawing stranger who watched him from the bridge. And even his father, the father of both of them, didn't as much as budge an inch, seated under an enormous beach umbrella, absorbed in a book. But there was really nothing to be done, the father indeed being the least concerned since he was the one really marginal to the situation. For the children, the offspring of two marriages and reared in two different countries (Sandro and Dino in Rome and Daniel with his grandmother in New Canaan) appeared to him only as intermittence of lights and shadows amid insane peals of laughter.

The only thing that still interests this old man exiled from all affections, exiled from himself, exiled from the great causes that enjoin participation, is the wild journey into the sex of this princess fourteen years his junior, on which he drunkenly feeds in a parody of incest. He's a child.

Although sex is the most unreal of fantasies, it gives one joy and repose, it is another life at the portals of death. Our sex life, however, is poisoned by social monsters, by boredom, by porno-fantasy and by lukewarm blood. Vera knows this, but she always demands more, and now. She is projected towards regions unknown, and all that is left for me is to await the new unknown. It will be a shattering event, but even that will pass. I hear the blow arriving from the rotten shrubs of our town, Anaconda, New York. It would be possible already to make a souvenir photo of it lightly over-exposed with a black and white 135mm.

This is the reason of diaries. Things, happenings are recorded or remembered because we are separated from them. We have remained alone.

2.

On the fourteenth the carpet-cleaners came. On the fifteenth the refrigerator repairman showed up. And the sixteenth saw the arrival of Anna Madison from New Orleans, and she slept in the small room.

She didn't feel like driving directly to her apartment on State Street, in the old part of town. She wanted me, or Vera, in order to forget herself.

The two women find peace in each other's company. It is a friendship built on tremors, anxieties and confidences that exclude the male and the element of struggle. Anna is much more covetous and gloomy than Vera. The lust in her eyes is always a prenatal journey promised to the crew. She is as darksome and tender as an oriental night, while Vera projects a liquid pomeridian lustfulness that sets romantics sighing.

Anna made some phone-calls, one of which was to Punks, that is Andrew, the deserted husband. But then she abruptly hung up.

"You are separate entities now," I remind her. "To what purpose?"

"I'd like to go there and burn his damn house down, with him inside it and all the shit he produces," she replied in a rattle-like voice.

"It didn't seem to bother you when you were with Punks," I point out with a seeming indifference. For when she's disparaging Punks' shit, it seems that she's also disparaging my "shit," in the sense that some of Punks' ideas are mine, which I made available to him.

But this woman has never understood Andrew, astrologically a *Cancer*. Nor has she read his only book which leaves an imprint.

He is a laboratory chemist who experiments with guinea pigs. And he's whimsical. His diagnoses are very often wrong. Only years later did his notebooks reveal that he had arrived at an exact hypothesis which, however, was considered incorrect at that time because of the lack of technical means for its verification, and because of the skepticism of his colleagues.

In his early young manhood he had published an annotated edition of Robert Chambers' book on evolution, *The Vestiges of the Natural History of Creation,* which had first appeared anonymously in 1844.

Andrew, commenting on Chambers more as historian than as chemist, also discussed the geologist Lyell whose ideas on species that had become extinct in consequence of the struggle for survival, had influenced Darwin as much as he had been influenced by the Malthusian concept of power-population, published in 1798.

Andrew's work, though based on the history of science, tries ("creative analysis") to determine whether or not biology is indeed an exact science, and whether or not it conforms to the same principles that govern other sciences. The advances made by astronomy, physics and chemistry have been amply recorded down the centuries. Biology, on the contrary, is a subject so recent and so vast that it is difficult, if not altogether impossible, to establish where and when it started i.e. where it begins and ends at this particular point in time.

Since all thought depends on the brain, Andrew questions whether frontiers exist between philosophy and biology. And since all living things are made up of molecules may it not be possible that the study of life derives its basic principles from those governing physics and chemistry?

These ideas, only seemingly hypothetical, ultimately led Andrew to the exploration of metaphysical problems. Hence it should occasion no surprise to note that his commentaries on the

Vestiges of Natural History conclude with embarrassing questions: Is it absolutely proved that fixed laws exist in the universe? And if such exist, how many of them are known by the human being?[1]

Andrew is brilliant, clever, sensuous, useless. Unfortunately, his exploration of existence is wholly directed towards the useless: for him, at least, it is a form of active boredom, the presupposition of which is a hedonistic, possibly painless, life style. The artist, as he often repeated, is an a-temporal, asexual being constantly in a state of pregnancy. And this pregnancy would define the useless better than does any other expression.

In order to pay for the Bentley, the Morgan, and the Land Rover, crouched in his enormous garage, in his spare time Andrew produces and directs short porno underground films in the New York tradition of Andy Warhol and Jonas Mekas, the costs of which are met by generous grants from a long list of educational foundations. One of them, marked by the wit and melodrama that could pass as an experiment in iconography, also bears the signature of the socio-biologist Simon Dona.

Academically, he is a physical anthropologist, the I of this Diary, better known in American university circles for the endless interpolations that his writings, based on experiments with monkeys of the Macaque species in the Philippines and in Borneo (the rhesus monkeys, such as the mandril and the baboon) offer to the old adage:

Higgamous, Hoggamous, woman's monogamous
Hoggamous, Higgamous, man is polygamous.

---

[1] Re-reading for the fourth time these *Diaries* today, February 28, 1980, and still undecided as regards their publication, I realize that Andrew Madison's comments have been nothing short of seminal. A sample of books published in the United States between 1979 and 1980 again propose the evolutionist problem discussed years before by Andrew. See the article by J.Z. Young on *The New York Review or Books*, Volume XXVII, Number I, February 7, 1980.

The film is titled *The 12th Macaque,* in part derived from the sexual theories of Tiger-Fox, Morris, Dawkins, Maynard Smith which hold that man can be divided into *one-animal men* and *two-animal men,* but it is mainly based on my own personal convictions concerning the bonnet monkey, the monkey with a crop-tail, the cap-like head, and whose hair hangs like trinkets on his wily face, who goes swimming to hunt sea-crabs and who climbs coconut trees to steal coconuts.[2]

It stresses, pretentiously to be sure, the basic differences in male-female sexuality among humans. It is naught else but a short film, made to amuse and provoke the egg heads at our university along with the wives and lovers.

Many still reproach us for it, especially the compact band of feminists whom one of our Spanish colleagues, a Galdos and

---

[2] Even as a young man Simon Dona conducted vast studies in Asia and Pakistan., in Japan., in the Philippines., in Borneo., in North Africa/and in that only European colony of nonhuman primates on the Rock of Gibraltar whose members are called *Barbary apes* who are especially large sized and tail-less. There are 12 species of macaques, or catarrhine monkeys. The typical macaque is the rhesus monkey, accustomed to high altitudes and to devastating fields and gardens. It has been largely used for medical purposes and other scientific experiments. One of the components of human blood is called Rh because it is found in monkeys. The crop-tailed macaque is very hairy and its face is bare and pink. It is found in the altitudes of South East Asia. Its nearest relative is the Japanese macaque and it is the most ancient primate besides man. Vast studies have been dedicated to its social organization and the existence of definite and transmittable cultural differences among different groups, has been ascertained. The only non-Asiatic macaque is that found in Northwest Africa, the *Barbary ape,* tail-less, and a member of the colony on the Rock of Gibraltar.

Simon Dona's studies lay great stress on the notion of one-animal man. There exists, namely, a feminine human nature and a masculine human nature and these two natures exhibit an extraordinary difference between them even though these differences often and somehow are masked by the compromises of heterosexual relations, and by moral injunctions. It would follow, therefore, that a sexual "estrangement" exists between male and female. The dispositions and the sexual desires between male-female revolved themselves in the process of mutual adaptiveness. Dona went so far as to formulate the concept that if one of the sexes is good, the other is poison

Fernan Caballero scholar, marshals and marches down from Lesbos.

Rafael Oviedo de Bernalbe generally spends his academic vacations at the Vatican library in Rome, masquerading alternatively as a Basque revolutionary and as an agent of *Pro Deo*. He is gentle, bearded and sly, gliding through the corridors with a conspirational air. When he is all by himself in his novice's cell, he plays the flute. Disappointed in married love, disenchanted with women in general, for years he has found a pondered pleasure in bird watching, in particular their copulations. Although Fernan Caballero's book, *La Gaviota*, no way refers to homosexuality among wild birds, it led him to closely study the hymeneal behavior of sea gulls, a study further encouraged by Virgil's assertion that "they can because they think they can." In fact he spent a whole summer studying the sob-like noises of sea gulls in the grottoes of the Tremiti archipelago facing the promontory of Gargano in Italy, in order to definitely establish whether or not their lamentations are due to the tragic death of the Greek hero Diomedes, as handed down to us by Pliny and Theophrastus. He came back convinced that at least eighteen percent of sea gulls are lesbian. One of his reports to the "Feathers Gaviotanos," which in some way is linked to the American Association for the Advancement of Science, indicated that one of the female gulls assumes the male role, and that the birds finally form a stable union based more or less on the type existing between heterosexual sea gulls. They go through the motion of copulation, depositing sterile eggs and defending their nest like every other couple. He found no evidence of homosexuality among male sea gulls.[3] His error,

---

[3] A few years ago a Californian couple, George Hunt and his wife, Molly, substantiated Rafael Oviedo de Bernalbe's theory in an article published in *Science*, the organ of the American Association for the Advancement of Science, in which they summarized the findings of their three-year study of sea gulls. After observing 1200 sea gull couples on the island of Santa Barbara, an uninhabited rock 40 miles southeast of Los Angeles, they concluded that "14% of

nevertheless, is to confuse women with feminism and feminists with lesbianism. Thus when he proposed that it would be *of interest to Hispanics* in *our Hall of Learning* to give a seminar on the theme *The Role of Sea Gulls Departmental and/or University Committees,* the feminists in the department reacted fiercely, wives and lovers following suit. Worst of all he had the proposal circulated anonymously.[4]

That was a strange, Vietnamized, so to speak, epoch. Violence ran along a tightrope and love was sparse and twisted, striking a

---

female sea gulls are lesbians," thereby proving with solid evidence the existence of a diffused homosexuality among wild birds.

[4] The document was denounced as "abnormal" and Bernalbe's Department, meeting in extraordinary session, approved the following condemnatory resolution:

I. The Department goes on record as strongly condemning the person or persons who attacked two members of our department in an anonymous document distributed in Departmental mailboxes.

2. The Department should employ all the resources at its disposal to ascertain the identity of the person or persons guilty of this attack against women, and to prevent the repetition of similar acts.

3. The Department expresses its respect and concern to those persons attacked in such a cowardly and unprofessional manner.

The question was also discussed by powerful national organizations. *The American Civil Liberties Union* soundly denounced racism, chauvinism and machismo in American society, and the grave discrimination against women in Academe. The *National Organization for Women* polemicizedon male society in all social sectors, including academe, for its insistence on maintaining the status quo in a moment in which we *are seeking to win ratification of the Equal Rights Amendment,* in a world in which women *are doomed to a second rate economic status of lower pay, unequal credit and inadequate job security.*

The author of this *Diary,* who at that time was called upon to voice his view on the female homosexual, declared that she is not "genetically focalized", that she does not prefer "anonymous sex", and rarely chooses the mate for a one-night stand. Her life is very similar to heterosexual life, unlike that of the homosexual male. It is the nature and the interests of the human female that gives structure to family life, and much more so that do the nature and interests of the man. The Lesbian brings the same nature and interests to the academic world.

precarious balance between morality and blasphemy. Often it was pure violence. And violence is as binding as love. There was much quarreling, and quarreling by no means precludes violence because it is already violence. The academics engaged in it with words, knowing well that a word can be as destructive as the blow of a hand. Consequently violence, be it verbal or physical, invites vengeance.

Sex had become a battle-ground, and pleasures a bone of contention between two dogs. There was much talk of sado-masochism, a perversion that was violently injected into pleasure itself to a degree so extreme that the latter became obscure, cruel and criminal.

Later we realized that everything we did out of love was no different from what we did out of hatred.

The "I" of this narrative often quoted from the Mimiambi of Publilius Syrus. *Ab amante lacrymis redimus iracundiam.* Tears redeem the lover's rage. Everybody talked, only few listened. The Academy was the mother, and to her they attributed guilt and wonder, loss and self-modesty, death and metaphor, justice and purity, intentionality and cowardice, hope and judgment, ideology and humorism, obligation and desperation, faith and malice, rite and madness, forgiveness and sublimation, pietas and ecstasy, obsession and discourse. And sentimentalism to boot. But today the reaction is harsh and uncompromising, even if it's in the hands of Matthias, the *Sagittarius,* our fraternal Vice President of the Academic Research and Publications Committee.

Now Anna, bereft of Andrew, is on the prowl for men and women, in a perennial and frustrating anxiety of eternal repose (or gratification) that she calls transcendental meditation, trying ever more to attract Vera's vague into the orbit of her shadow — with me in the center, observing and writing.

She ran a high fever at midnight and asked me to take her temperature. At 2 a.m. she comes into my room and slips into the bed. She has the chills and wants me to keep her warm. Nobody talks. Our two bodies hold each other in the darkness, pierced at intervals by sobs and nervous peals of laughter. We're on a trip now. I'm the horse, she's the carriage. And we are alone and depleted, devoid of purposes or desires. But this jumping about between the squeaking of wheels and pieces of furniture, laments and neighing, is like re-running the 120 miles that separates us from New Canaan, where Vera sleeps alone in the old bed that she slept in as a girl.

"Tomorrow," I say to Anna, "I'll phone Vera and tell her that we have done something that we have always wanted to do."

"She'll answer that the three of us should have done it together."

Only now I do realize that violence thus employed no longer has any significance: it becomes part of our pleasure.

Awake, I watch her all night, remembering Roseanne and Vera in the same bed — the 20-year old Roseanne who sleeps with a smile on her face, and Vera who sleeps and sobs in foaming protest against the insult and injury.

This house has become a railing on which sea gulls sit.

3.

Growing up in America today, the Seventies, for a woman signifies dying of orgasms.

On the following day she is in a demure hysterical state, and wants me to take her to the laboratory. The cockroaches in residence hear the key turning in the lock and pass along the news of her arrival among themselves. The darkness is suddenly pierced by the cone of light from Anna's infrared pocket lamp, revealing the oscilloscope, the cork ball, boxes of cereals, a dripping sink, moist plastic plates, still water in flower-pots, a half-rotten apple left in the open, a garbage can with a half-opened cover, dry crumbs of cat food in a yellow oval plate.

The light suddenly focuses on a pair of mahogany-colored insects on a white, wooden gangway. They are about five centimeters long and their antennae are locked in a duel.

"Professor Roeder and Doctoress Scharrer are rubbing noses," Anna explains, adding: "They are sniffing each other with their antennae, and I'm certain that they know one another's identity."

"Do you name your cockroaches after people you know?" I ask.

"I've got about 35 of them here. And even if I don't recognize them perfectly, I call them Dr. Kenneth, Dr. Berta, Dr. Michael, Dr. Dale, Dr. Noam, Dr. Louis, Dr. Charlotte, etc. They are my academicians."

"In Rome they call them *bacarozzi,* and they are not academics but religious, priests in general."

"Do you see the one over there? That's you."

I follow the cone of light as it falls on a nearby spur on which a huge male roach is bent over in a interdictive posture.

"It's almost certain that Dr. Dona will remain there for hours, probably all day and all night prohibiting access to his turf."

I laugh nervously. This lady entomologist is more fragile than I thought. Keeping one eye on the door, I interject, "Actually I don't sufficiently protect my turf, my grass meadow. My bed is a three-quarter size. You've climbed into it. Now what will you do?"

"I'm taking the train."[5]

And in fact she went to Philadelphia, looking for Morris Elliot,[6] the mandril astronomer, a *Gemini,* who lives on a river and

---

[5] At that time Anna Madison was an assistant to Matthias Freedman, professor of comparative neuroendocrinology. For decades his passion had been the study of cockroaches, "since they are tough tiny creatures that survive every kind of experimental humiliation." Freedman's grandparents, who had been destroyed in Dachau's experimental ovens, had observed in a letter to their American daughter-in-law. Ethel, that the life of cockroaches was better than that of prisoners in the hands of the Nazis. Ethel and the young Matthias sat for months in the witness' box at the Nuremberg trials which dragged on from 1945 to 1946 in order to bring the Nazi ringleaders to judgment. Matthias' eyes focused in astonishment on these big-time murderers: Goering, Frank, Ribbentrop, Kalenbrunner, Rosenberg, Frick, Sauckel, Seyss-Inquart, Streicher, Keitel Jodi, Hess, Funk, Raeder, Speer and Schirach, Neurath and Doenitz. And in a flash he understood that the study of cockroaches is the study of survival. His books on the cellular nerves and the behavior of insects are famous; one of them is a combat manual that is often found in the library of American family.

Anna Madison's studies, in sintony with Freedman's, concerned the six-footed residents of the university laboratory, numbered with adhesive tape whose movements were followed and observed on different nights of the week and then registered on a magnetic tape. Anna's interests were limited to the natural behavior of the cockroaches, to their way of communication, eating, fighting and flirting, that cockroaches rarely mate in love.

Anna's thesis, in the process of being written at the time of this *Diary,* was titled: *Cockroaches can be taught to run maze, and can even learn some things when decapitated.*

[6] Morris Elliot, together with Dr. Jeremiah Ostriker of Princeton University, and astronomers such as Riccardo Giacconi, Philip Charles, Webster Cash, and the Soviet Yakov Borisovich Zeldovich, contends that the evolution of the universe and, in particular the formation of the galaxies, has greatly depended upon a series of catastrophic explosions. Contemporary evidence, arrived at through x-rays, suggests that seismic waves derive from such catastrophic explosions

goes canoeing with Guido O. Shait, a professor of hyper-realism at our Institute of Fine Arts. He is also an actor, in spite of himself, who appears in *The 12th Macaque.* He is a sinuous and gossamer-like *Scorpio* with a curly-head of hair in the ancient Roman style, much sought after and patronized.[7]

---

initiated the formation of galaxies, andone of those waves presumably created the sun and the planets about 4.5 billion years ago. The recent seminar organized by the Harvard-Smithsonian Center for Astrophysics in Cambridge, reveals that the Einstein Observatory, which is a space ship orbited to trace a detailed map of the most distant sources of the x-rays, has determined how these seismic explosions, called *supernovas,* have gone much farther than the galaxies in which they originated. This is indicated by the survey of gas clouds outside the galaxies which contain metal atoms, presumably produced by explosions of the *supernova.*

See also the article, "Stellar Explosions Now Believed Key to Formation of the Universe", *The New York Times,* February 17, 1980.

[7] Simon Dona had written articles on behalf of his friend. One of them suggests that he harbored a deep resentment vis-a-vis his friend.

I am reproducing it here with some deletions:

G.O. *Shait is one of the American exponents of erotic hyper- realism: he can be described as a patient, ambitious, saturnine character who hankers after virtue and the absolute. He has a certain sense of humor, but for him youth begins where other seasons of youth end. He is eternally frustrated and eternally guilt-ridden and finds recompense therefrom in work. His wife/woman, however. finds it possible to experience a delayed but long experience of quiet felicity with him.*

Sensuality is at the base of his solitary, rather disjointed and esoteric life which consist of long silences, psychedelic meditation and sexual observation. He is a man of our day: he teaches drawing and painting in one of the biggest American Universities. but his real interest — aside from the teaching routine -lies in his quest for Woman, for the purpose of absolute possession.

There had been many women in G.O.'s life. However his ideal is woman in the supreme act of offering herself, which must be a total offering, whether she is a student, discovered in the lecture-hall or the horny and vaginal wife of a colleague, probably weary of the years of matrimony, whom the romantic idea of adultery makes responsive to the demand which at first Shait makes with an innocent modesty, followed by a passionate insistence and culminating with a devotion that drags in a chaotic tangle of compromises, fears and tears into his private and apparently ordered world. But, like all extreme hedonists, his demand for sexual satisfaction, for artistic sublimation, is to be fulfilled come what may. This is because passion, for him, is an esthetic and ethical ideal as well as proof and confirmation of his masculinity, ostentatiously displayed but secretly vulnerable.

His distant models are the decadents of 1830, the period in which Charles Baudelaire dyed his hair green, and the painter of lesbianism, Jules-Robert August used to represent two beauties in his paintings, one White the other Blalck, thus offering a libertine view of the Blonde and Brown motif so dear to Romanticism. In general Shait depicts two women who actually are the one and the same Woman, his ideal woman portrayed in static and ecstatic poses on which he grafts the decompositions and deformations of Time. These are the androgynous Women, who in the double figure of blonde and brunette combine, or would combine, the active and contemplative faculties, in short a fusion of intelligence and voluptuousness.

With the appearance in the Shaitian world of a married lover, a woman who leaped over the wall for a hypothetical self-discovery in a erotic ecstacy, the semi-static, platonic world of this hyper-realist becomes more glittering and activated. The new lover constitutes the sought for reciprocation and sexual performance, characterized by an extreme, real and flagellant penetration. The two figures of Women have disappeared from his paintings. They have been replaced by one woman in a posture signifying orgasm, sado-masochistic acceptance of the phallic god, the male who dominates, moulds and transfigures his victim. Each one of his paintings is a récit that finds its suspense precisely in this state of extreme chrystalliness, in its theoritcial ambivalence between nature and work, sex and society, thought and feeling, life and death.

The passage from animal to man, from nature to history, from his vegetative world in Eden to the age of work did not occur once and for always, rather, it continues to take place in every place in man's situation. The Italian writer Elio Vittorini asserts that man replaces the natural, instinctive world by the order of the world of work, but immediately after so doing he is seized with remorse, nay with the terror at the thought of having denied nature, his very animal condition. And it is in this state of repentance that he creates the "sacred", and establishes nature anew in the form of the sacred, and makes a transgression correspond to every taboo through which he has rejected her. Man constantly proceeds in fear of himself. His sexual urgencies terrify him. Saints, observes George Bataille, retreat be/lire voluptuousness. Nevertheless eroticism, that which man tries to cover and even to deny in the work-world, is an experience wed to life itself, it is a psychological investigation conducted independently of the natural end of reproduction, and for this reason it is of such fundamental importance that it is not alien to death.

There is always a cover up, naturally, in this kind of painting. For in G.O.'s mentality, as in that of the mystics, sex in prohibited and it remains exclusively in his mind: in fact to cover it up is tantamount to suggesting it and denying it simultaneously. Absent sex is worn out virility, but a virility that is always pressingly imagined and sexually sought after. The painter traverses the paths that mark the frontier between life and death as if it were a continuation of the same self-frightened earth.

G. O. s case, the Painter-Hero, recalls that Jean L the pre-Raphaelite painter. These cases could be defined as the "virility complex" since both Shait and Lorrain are endowed with a feminine sensibility marked by periods of ecstatic calm and homosexual tendencies. Sterility is the last word.

Edward Weston, a California photographer of the '30's is G.O.'s most recent predecessor. He, too, is an esoteric personage whose works are being exhibited at the

I phone Vera and right off the bat I ask her if her night has been free of remorse and regrets.

Angrily she replies, "I woke up drenched. But all I saw was a man's arms. And they weren't yours."

Another gentle Vera's phanthom fucks, I tell myself. But I am annoyed. I ask, "Did you recognize them?"

"They were G.O.'s, maybe..."

Modern Museum of Art in New York. He decapitated his women; those who had a visage were also those who had a meaning for him. Some of Shait's nudes are also faceless. The explanation of the decapitations in Weston and G.O. alike probably lies in their dual attitude towards women. Their devotion is not for a woman, but for Woman. She is powerful, frightful, hated, courted and reluctantly loved. In both artists the She entry and exit into and from their lives as inevitable as the tides. For G.O. love is carnal thing, taste, smell and naturally emotions. His brush is perfect: he loves beauty, order, harmony and an elegant setting. The woman is the spring around which his lire spins and frets. Adultery is at the base of this spring as regards the private essence of the object of his passion. It is a lustfulness that terminates in the annihilation of all lustfulness and sterility is the same as death.

I met Vera Jones and G.O. Shait the last time on February 28, 1980, Vera's birthday. They are man and wife, she divorced Simon and he divorced Phedra. Simon preferred to re-marry his motorcycle and Phedra chose to re-marry a lawyer in El Paso, Texas. And now Vera and Guido have a house in the forest, made of glass and mazes, on the very site Simon once wanted to build a house for himself and Vera. He had asked Guido to inspect the terrain and Guido had noticed that the earth there was actually sand. Citing the biblical verse Simon declared that he would never build his house on sand but Guido insisted that it was possible to build on sand. Later Guido did build his new house on Simon's lot. I had the impression that their love had also been built on sand since they now look reproachfully at each other. She still loves him, but he no longer loves her and he accuses her of being too "dependent". The truth is that he has become infatuated with another woman, still another sex, and forty-year old Vera strikes him as worn out. The house was filled with paintings of her, mostly nude. "The only thing that she gave me" said Guido, "is the most beautiful sex of my life." She repressed tears in her eyes, and a devastating sadness. She never spoke about Simon. But Guido did, and a lot. He asked if Simon had committed suicide for love. I replied, "Maybe, who knows?" "But why did he entrap me with his wife? Why did he permit it? Did he want to rid himself of her?" Tiredly, I replied that so far as I knew Simon was not a jailer. He had observed their dalliances, suffered from them, but he did not consider that he had the right to stop them. Sensualists, moreover, have no morals. Nobody makes anything of them, not even themselves.

"Guido?"

"They were strong and long. A hand was missing."

"So!" I don't know how but I get disheartened on the phone. My eyes are burning now. I'm not shedding tears, but I squeeze them shut for an instant and Shait comes into my darkness, he is luminous, observing me with his seductive smile.

Guido's girl-students, especially, adored him. He talked to them about painting in terms of Zen and exhorted them to patience, tenacity in planning, and total fidelity to art. Often he also discoursed on carnal love, but always with the detachment and melancholy air of one who is an expert on the subject but not so much as to no longer desire it or look for it.

One morning seven years ago, precisely at the beginning of the academic year, a girl, dressed only in her nightgown, climbed up to the platform on her dormitory, a twenty-four story high-rise and leaped into the void. They said that she took LSD. It was also said that she had been forsaken by, or disappointed with Professor Shait. It caused him enormous suffering, above all because the story wasn't true. "She posed for me once, but I never finished that nude. She was a strange girl; one night she stood behind the door of my studio and waited all night for me to open it. But she had not knocked and I didn't know that she was outside my door and, anyway, it's always open. In the morning, when I set out for school, I found her there almost frozen to death. I warmed her with my hands in the car. But who could imagine that she was so crazy?"

G.O. Shait is an unhappy person. He betrays friendship unwittingly, and he lies to himself just as unwittingly. He is fully convinced, however, that his presence in the world is essential while all other things and persons that dance around him are accessories. To base art on sex is wrong from the start. To use art for sex is amusing but it is illusionistic and likewise doesn't hold water from the start. To view art as an escape from individual shortcomings or physical handicaps is a forgivable fraud, as illness in an individual is forgivable. But it is enormously embarrassing when it creates illness in the other and co-involves the other, and asks the other for further forgiveness. Art and love are things that reveal themselves in a flash, but they already had deep roots in the unconscious. They last for such a brief spell that the one who picks up the pieces will be lacerated forever by a feeling of insufficiency and vindication. Such things are not my cup of tea, but they certainly appertain to Guido because he is an unhappy person.

One day, while building one of his houses, he sawed off a hand. The right eye, perfect when he's painting, did not see the saw which it was the task of the left eye to see. He was building ordinary houses out of rejects, empty tomato cans, beer bottles, and pressed cardboard. They were intimate and exotic and he sold them. Thanks to his meticulous patience G.O. had managed to achieve a respectable financial situation, accompanied by artistic distance, a melancholy raging passion for psychedelic experiences, and a never ending quest *for* sexual ecstasies sewn together by threads of mysticism. He picked his hand out of the dust and placed it on a brick. His skinny and sad-looking mastiff, Rhin-Thin-Stone sniffed it, toyed with it and then ate it in one gulp. G.O. beat the dog savagely on that rage-filled afternoon, and for twelve nights and thirteen days he lay moaning on the withered and compassionate breast of his wife, Phedra.

Over the phone I say to Vera, "Look here now, our infidelities are reciprocal."

"Have you seen Roseanne?"

"Anna's been here."

"But wasn't she supposed to be in New Orleans?"

"She was. But at this moment she's enroute to Philadelphia, looking *for* Morris Elliot who is canoeing with your 'Cropped-hand'."

She suddenly becomes silent. I know her so well: her mind runs back to episodes of the past, to things that we have done individually and which subsequently we recounted to each other because we had established a truth pat between us. This is our only freedom. It serves us as a seductive stimulus to lofty ideals, as a weapon of aggressiveness in both our public and private deficiencies, as a basis for deductive conclusions, and as a warming, coddling baby blanket. We do not have an "open" marriage, which is possible only without jealousy (which is never possible), but we insist on truth as a summons to order especially during agonizing sexual desires, and during their eventual realization, after which we tell each other about the particulars, lustrous or shabby and about our perverse fantasies. It beguiles us into wanting still to be together, scratching and martyrizing each other, which we endure because we are also proud of our reciprocal sado-masochism.

We use truth as a form of seduction above all because we know that now nobody really seduces anybody, as innocence no longer has any value whatsoever.

A phrase commonly heard among middle-aged academics, unlucky enough to have neo-phd wives who always look like 19-year olds in search of forbidden coitions, is the following:

"Well... all that is involved is an interesting interlude."

Interlude, that is, a conjugal parenthesis, an esoteric and diversifying mini-passion which neither overwhelms nor lingers for long, and which even includes subsequent tears and pardons and re-admission of the fugitives to the bourgeois cage. But this is obviously wrong because the interesting interlude inevitably leads to but one port: to separation, to halved lives, to other lives. It's a lethal, miasma-soaked game since sex experienced in this way is a swamp, period. Nevertheless we decided to continue the game and possibly to extend it up to the next day or up to the new winter. It was painful, of course. But even this is something else: it is the price to be paid and it remains absolutely *per*sonal, totally devoid of any interest to others since love's pain is real and the pursuit of happiness, in which everybody is engaged, is an illusion. But we need illusions in order to live.

At the same time will enter into a new channel, that of psychosomatic dysfunction, a form of illness that grows in the shadow of the energy contained in the illusion. The illusion will preserve us niveously, the basic dysfunction ultimately will cut off our legs. But that hath been written: so we shall wind up with a peal of laughter like those great writers who turned to humour at the close of a career as believers.[8]

"O.K. Simon," she exclaims. "I'm sorry I didn't get to see her. How was she?"

"Feverish."

"It's all Punks' fault, leaving her without a cent. "

"He couldn't help it!"

"Do you agree with me?"

"No. You women always talk about economics

---

[8] This last paragraph could induce us to think that a real physical illness was taking possession of Simon, the result of an already conscious psychosomatic dysfunction. He dealt with the subject in several clinical psychological articles in which he substantiated how a disturbance occasioned by a social or political event—such as marriage, divorce, mourning, retirement—can often be the cause of the physical illness, such as cancer, cardiacal collapse, hypertension, morbid daredevilism (the motorcycle, in his case).

In an attempt to formulate a kind of structuralist theory of the mind with these articles, Simon assumed that many physical illnesses occur immediately after a significant event has injected itself in the individual's life, particularly that event responsible for the change of his habitual lifestyle.

I think he based his findings on his familiarity with the statistical data provided by scientific articles written by the psychologists R.H. Rabe and G.W.Brown who have developed a sophisticated interview technique *for* verifying the incidents, and *for* describing the impact of disturbances on life-happenings.

A reader of Dona, Rabe and Brown, Richard Totman has just published his investigation on the subject: *Social Causes of Illness* (New York: Pantheon, 263 pp.).

after the betrayal, and it's always the husband or the lover who must pay for your frailty because he desires you, because he possesses you, because he marries you. Don't you know that Anna is tortured only by her sex? Punks showed me a list of a long series of occasional lovers whom she still visits regularly, often twice a day, every day. How is Punks to be blamed for that?"

"But he's the sex-tortured one, not Anna. And you're just like him, both understand each other perfectly," she retorted, raising her voice.

Lowering mine, I continue: "And woke up like her, right? Whereas I continue to represent the religious, familial phallus, the sharp-edged stone protecting the entrance to the cave."

"And how about Evelyn, and Roseanne," she shouts, hanging up. I'm utterly upset again, still holding the open telephone in my hand, my eyes fixed on a lecture schedule.

Now, I think wearily to myself, she'll be pouncing on me like a bolt out of the blue and demanding reparations in the form of sex and caresses for twenty-four hours, thus forcing me to neglect my work, telephone calls, unpaid bills, lectures to be prepared, shopping and the laundry. Believe it or not, Simon does everything around the house.

The Pisces Woman is a pendant on the penis. And this pendant has almost entirely devoured mine.[9]

---

[9] A note in Vera Jones' *Diary*, dated September 24, 1972, speaks of planned sexual sessions with her husband, Simon Dona. During the latter which she describes in detail, the shadow of another lover glides into her mind which, however, strikes her as something repulsive, a kind of Chinese dragon of whom, nevertheless, there is really nothing to fear.
I reproduce it here:

The sex was very good this morning. Funny I was afraid of a routine; I wasn't ever aware of that anxiety. But Simon and I now have a schedule of sort. Monday, Wednesday, Friday: lunch -long lunch hours and somehow once the routine seems to be established, a kind of deadness sets in; – meet him at the Gym at eleven to lift weights – then hours for lunch, then bed, then lovemaking but this time, almost as though he sensed what I myself was not conscious of, he suggested we have a beer, a joint and go to bed –

the breaking of the routine – so that the sex became renew, fresh. I was caressing his penis, and suddenly, with the pot making me more aware, making me alive to the beauty in everything around us Simon – his body – I suddenly felt the softness of his skin on his penis – the smoother texture – the delicacy of its surface – and as I looked at his penis as if spellbound, it grew larger – proud – so very hard, so very beautiful, and I caressed it sweetly, without violence or aggression – but only love. And he came inside me now that he was so hard – and his naturalness with me made me surprised – made me aware of how natural I am with him at times. And then he was in me – with deep secure thrusts and he kept changing the rhythm – and I enjoyed the movement of him inside me – his rhythm has variations. There was no need for orgasm. We were close – we were one – images flashed across my mind – the penis as a mushroom – agreeable with all its associations of growth and fertility but then a not so agreeable image flashed across my mind – the cap of the mushroom was transformed into the cap of a soldier – the hard metal cap on a German soldier – the bringer of death – and I wondered why my mind should make that association, and I refused it, then the rhythm of the sex caught me up again – and it was good – it seemed endless – and I never wanted it to end – it was unbelievable good, and I wondered how it was possible for me to let it become stale – to have to be jolted from routines that were never routines – to be alive with Simon in me -I adored him – and then he said, "I don't think it would be possible to duplicate this, do you?" – and I wondered if he were talking about Sonny Morebugs, the sauna professor, and the thought crossed my mind that Simon was trying to manipulate me, trying to prove something with his sexual prowess – but then I knew that was crazy not only crazy, but physically impossible – impossible in that only love and desire to be with the other – only the immediate sincere feeling – not sullied by any, any conscious ulterior routine – not divided but whole desire – love – without rationalization only such purity of emotion could give Simon the power to penetrate me – to stay inside me, thrusting with his love of me – pleasing me – pleasing himself in me – only this could give such power – and the image of 'Sonny Morebugs flashed across my mind – the looseness of his expression – the too soft curve of his wide thickish lips – and I felt as though I could not tolerate being with him – and then his face was transformed again – the eyes hollowing out – the eyeballs protruding – and he was transformed into a Chinese dragon – the physical distaste was clear. Saturday night what a mistake! I could never change my mind about Sonny Morebugs but then again, Chinese dragons are nothing to be afraid of?

Vera here is referring to a certain ennui engendered by the sexual routine and how this feared prospect might cause their constant hankering for sex to stagnate. But during the afternoon of that September 25, so important to her sexually that it made her decide to record her orgastic joy in her diary, it was Simon, as she notes, who changed the routine by suggesting that they drink beer and smoke marijuana. His colleagues in the Comparative Literature Department, especially the Italian professor Anacleto Zinghelli, recalls that this was the time when Dona had decided to resume his Latin studies, "so that I can remove myself from the routine," as he put it. He began to translate the first book of *Ars*

4.

Suddenly she's back from New Canaan, standing in the driveway threshold, looking angry and breathless, only three hours after the phone call, as if she had been literally running all the way. I notice a new dent on the car.

"What's this?"

"I banged into another car in a parking lot. I also got stopped for speeding."

With a fatherly air, I remark: "Speeding is pure, if it's intensified by terror."

"I'm not terrorized."

"Of course, you are. You've got your second ticket, one more and they'll take away your licence. And one fine day they'll also bust you and lock you up in a tiny cell without TV and without dildos, and I'll come to visit you bearing small baskets of red tomatoes along with wicked, little erotic letters in which I'll tell you all about love."

I draw closer and kiss her on the neck, chastely. She clings to me and the closeness relaxes her.

"What smells so nice, a new perfume?"

"Caron. I bathe myself in it to draw the attention of the cops."

"One of these days you'll also draw the attention of a ravine or a telegraph pole. I will weep and weep inconsolably, and bring baskets of tomatoes to place on your grave bearing the photo-

---

Amandi, scornfully defining himself (as Apollo had rebuked the poet of Sulmona, Ovid) *lascivi praeceptor amoris*. He would read from the Latin and then translate for her the different positions that a couple can assume in coition for the purpose of introducing some reasonable variety in their embraces.

graph of an angel on the headstone, and I'll declaim Andromaca's position to you."[10]

"You're beautiful Simon. Play with my skull."

"Hell no! I'll be Mercury. *Omnia solus et terunus.* All alone and thrice one. Because it is I who impregnates, generates, gives birth, devours, kills... even myself."

I make my way to the kitchen, dancing. I grab a basket of red tomatoes and carry it into the small room. Then I go out to the garden and gather some red roses, and I also take them into the room. Finally, I go upstairs to my study and I take down an acrylic painting which I myself made of her: a sweet face with an enigmatic smile, covered by enormous sunglasses. Her amulet, two fish darting in opposite directions, hang from her neck. They are reflected in her sunglasses now transformed into two enormous male members, one in a state of erection, the other in decline. I also bring the painting into the little room, and I arrange a macabre minialtar on the chest of drawers. I go into the kitchen once more and return with two candlesticks which I light in front of the painting.

"Are you crazy?"

"I've prepared the altar."

I take a red tomato from the basket and place it on the palm of her hand. Amused, she accepts it silently, examines it and then suddenly bites into it, squirting the red juice over her mild-white neck.

"I suppose that's the way you'd like to eat me, spilling blood."

---

[10] An obvious reference to *Ars Amandi* where the so-called "position of Andromaca" is described as reported in De Boccardi's *Dictionary* of *erotic literature*: "... while, on the one hand, it allows the woman to triumphantly show off all of her most ardent femininity., in total abandonment to the invisible and overwhelming wind of Eros to the point that her face bears the same expression that Bernini impressed on that of his celebrated St. Theresa and, on the other, it permits the man to identify himself, in that arcane moment, with the fabulous and homeric husband of none other than Andromaca, 'Hector, the horse-tamer'".

"No, come, let's suffer together; would you like to ?"

"In this room?"

"Isn't this the room where you brought Anna? What did you do to her?"

"Oh, I see what you're driving at. *O.K.*"

She likes to hear gruesome and macabre tales.
They form part of a ritual at the beginning of the sexual banquet.

"I bound her to the bed, hand and *foot,*" I say, "and I tickled her like that old pig Karamazov. You remember that dirty old man Karamazov, of course."

"I've never read that novel," she says, perplexed.

"Anna, however, survived," I guffawed, remembering her cockroaches.

We tumble onto the bed of the small room, already in the throes of a burgeoning anxiety. But as if we were in an empty tomb all we hear is the echo of our own laughter, a distant whistling in our ears, and the insect-like crackling of the waning wax on the candelabra.

"You also brought Evelyn here," she says. "And it is also here that you brought Roseanne. It's always here that you carry out your vendettas. Now look upon me not as your Vera but as someone else, a stranger, and amuse me. Why don't you dance for me?"

"Okay... I'm Pithagora, I'm Nijnsky... I can even dance for you... But why me?" I say in a sudden brusque tone of voice. "Why don't you dance for me? You use me, you treat me as an object. You use me and consume me. Even your dreams give you away."

"What dreams?"

"Come off it, love. You know perfectly well that your betrayals are as specific as mine. Listen, just listen to me. Why don't we try to rediscover ourselves? I mean to say... beyond this farce?"

"Impossible! We know each other *for* fourteen years. And the new is always strange, never familiar. "

"Granted. My theory about old friends holds that they are acceptable only if they have the *animus* to be new friends— generous, bright, harbor no resentments and, above all, if they are young and adventurous, those whom the French call *copain* and the Americans *buddy*. What kind of a story do you want me to tell you now, *copine?*"

"*Copine?* What's that?"

"The feminine if *copain*."

"Call me *scopina*, and tell me about the past."

"How would *you* like to hear the one about the Dwarf and the Girl with the basket of red tomatoes?"

"You, of course, are the Dwarf and I'm the Girl, right?"

"The other day, walking through a patch of woods, a girl with a basket of red tomatoes came upon a dwarf who wanted to gobble her up. Where are you going, pretty girl? To my grandmother who is ill... Oh my dear, dear girl! I who am famished come before your grandmother. Come, I'll take you to my lair and you can sleep there. No, no, Mr. Dwarf, I'll sleep with my grandmother. Her arms are tender, while yours are big and hairy. So they are, child, but they are big and hairy the better to embrace you. But you also have big teeth, Mr. Dwarf. Oh, my dear child, don't you know that strong teeth bite better? The girl didn't at all know that it was dangerous to come across a dwarf."

"But I love you, Dwarf."

"No you don't. You're about to run away, princess."

"I tell you I'm undressing, o.k.?"

I help her to undress, ritualistically, hurling one piece of clothing here and another there. We act out our sickness.

"Wait a moment," I say, "I'll put a rock record on." Since in cases of extreme depravation moralism almost reinforces the depravation, I began my moralizing tale, which amused her.

"Look here," I said, "our life is really droll, a sad joke. It's hypocritical and two-faced, a face we put on for the outside, for others, and one fixed for the inside, for you and for me. On the outside we are social saints, and inside our own world we are monsters, prisoners of perverted habits, voluntary suicides for the lack of sincerity with ourselves."

"It's not true, it's not true! But if you want to leave me, just do. Go ahead! In fact I'll leave you first, by planting a bomb in the garage."

"Exactly. Just as Anna would like to do with Punks."

But I said this laughing and it made her laugh too. Oh, these women of mine! They all have the same mentality and deep, very deep inside them, in the tiniest folds of their hysteria, they harbor an insane hatred for man, especially for the kind of man who rejected his own solitude looking for them, marrying them, torturing them, enslaving them, conditioning them and, in turn, enslaving and conditioning himself.

Moralism, how troublesome!

My mother, a Quebec Catholic, wanted me to become a priest or a missionary. And my father, a Jew without a synagogue, wanted me to be a rabbi. He had converted to Christianity to escape the sentence passed on the Chosen People to set up house and store in every angle of the world from which it then was to be expelled and thus remain permanently at the mercy of the event of Exodus. We Donas, a heraldic family of Selimo, changed our name and social station in order the better to defend our right to non-assimilation. Knowing this, I avoided synagogue and monastery alike, but in the fury of deciding I blindly ended up in the war and, of course, on the wrong side. I was saved finally thanks to the intercession of Eloi, our super protector, who had a white beard that reached down to his knees. Through his Neapolitan messenger, professor Anacleto Zinghelli, he immediately acquainted me with the sad fable about a son and a father.

A father teaches his son, still a toddler, to be more courageous. He sets him down on a step and invites him to jump, assuring him that he will catch him in mid-air in his arms. After a moment's hesitation, the child makes the leap and ends up in his father's loving arms. Now feeling plucky, tries ever more daring leaps, and he always lands safely in his father's arms. But precisely when the boy makes his last, and highest, leap, the father deliberately moves out of reach and the son falls flat on his face. At the very moment that he is picking himself up, aching and astonished, the father pitilessly makes his son aware of the truth he wants to pass on to him: "Thus you will learn not to trust a cauliflower, even if it's your father."

But Eloi, our super-protector, still opened his arms protectingly and welcomingly to me. And it was at this point that he let me know that I should grow, rebelling perhaps even against him, because at my next mistake I would most certainly be alone, without a past and without a primary trust.

After absorbing the moral of the story, I began to roam all over the world, telling myself that now I was a *scientist*. At the middle of my wandering I found myself wearing an academic cap and gown *ad honorem* one could say, precisely in recognition of those voyages I made, those researches I conducted, those books I had written, those international conferences I attended, those diplomas I had received, those medals I was awarded, those monkeys I had saved. Nevertheless death pays me a visit every fifteen years, punctually. At age twenty came the resurrection after death in the war. At age 35 my resurrection in America, after death in my native Selimo. And now, on the threshold of fifty, the new shattering blow that draws near. I am so conscious of witnessing myself dying it inebriates me with a new life.

Now there is an old man who dances in a room painted in marine colors, which has the form of a pit or a womb, as well as of a grotto where miracles are performed. The only reality is the shadow of the clown reflected on the walls by the flame of the candles. There's a knife in the tiny drawer of the night table. The old man reaches for it, feels the thin blade under his fingers, sticks it in his mouth and then removes it and hurls it on the wooden floor where she is an enormous spot of fear. She cuts her feet, traces lines of blood, the room fills up with red tomatoes, she weeps and laughs, kneels in front of him and bites him with her sharp, greedy, grating teeth, beating him with her open palms, suckling at the center of his body, sucks and swallows, after which they roll up together on the mattress, after which they roll up together in the mouldy dust under the bed.

"You're really crazy, Simon."

"How about yourself, princess?"

"I'm a wreck, a desperate one, Simon. And I'm going to lose you."

"It also applies to you, dear baby—once the primary trust is broken—that the father will catch you in his arms—life is born. You will walk alone now, and you will be more splendid than ever."

"I don't understand, I don't understand you anymore, Simon. I'm geographically confused..."

"Do you remember *The 12th Macaque?* Its message was that life, earthly and eternal alike, that of God and that of men and women, is based on two opposites: light/shadow, good/evil, love/betrayal, father/son... And the film also speaks of growth, becoming. You, too, will have to grow, suffer and die."

"Stop it, you frighten me!"

"The two of us will be losers. But the work of betrayal is identified with... "

"...with what?"

"...the work of..... redemption. Isn't it possible that we may be looking for..."

"...something definitive?"

She picks the knife up from the floor and places it against my chest. "Explain yourself once and for all time, or I'll kill you!"

"You've already done so. Sticking it inside me would only be a re-confirmation of what has already happened. "

She throws away the knife and starts to cry all over again.

"We will die of sorrow, princess. But don't worry, I'll build you the new house anyway, as promised. And I'll have G.O. design it. And when you're weary of that house too, I will become completely mute and spend my time sewing dolls and listening to Bob Dylan on the radio, or waiting for you to phone and tell me all about your lover..."

"Lover?" She arches herself, suddenly curious. "What's my lover like, daddy? Would you describe him, please?"

"He's tall and unhappy like all lovers. He's an anti-hero, but he still likes to run around the gym and lift weights..."

"Are you referring to your counterfigure, G.O.?"

"You yourself have mentioned his name."

"But you drive me to saying things, you drive me to doing things. What do you want from me?"

"One of these days you'll abandon daddy and you'll become Eve. Eve is already preformed in the Garden, and the serpent already exists in the Garden. "

"Is Shait... the serpent?"

"I haven't said it, again you yourself have mentioned him. But listen: a christologist, Mario Brelich, claims that the serpent is Chaos, i.e. the undifferentiated as such, which does not have a will of its own like a person or like God, but acts according to its internal laws. It is Evil. And it is Evil because it is the opposite of Good which is Order, light. But it does not wish Evil, because it wishes nothing. It tempts man only because man gives in to the temptations of Chaos. And the serpent, like Satan, is he who is not, the one who, at the same time, could be all. His wickedness is innate, natural to his essence, to his non-existent will. Now do you understand what Evil is?"

"I'm sleepy."

"So am I."

They swallow the pill and sleep for ten hours.

When they awake a full moon is visible amid the trees beyond the window and beyond the garden. They get down on each other with leathery tongues and fall asleep for another three hours. He is on a bridge where the brook disappears. She is now wearing the transparent tunic of dreams and is slowly waking up. Even the sun seems to be lying in wait. All that's left of the moon is a vague remembrance, stamped in the air like an empty circle.

Indeed everything is really a dream, Professor Dona. You're torturing this poor girl! But for heaven's sake, don't stop! Torture becomes her. Instead, recite the monologue to her, since she knows so little of the Bible.

"Listen, Vera, this is the monologue."

Sitting up on the bed, looking lean and stunned, he places a hand on her shoulder, after which he places his shoulder on her shoulder, and gazes at the sun through the small window and sighs. But Vera yawns.

"You've never had a wife in Vera Jones, Professor Dona. First you had a daughter, then a piece of luggage to carry here and there, to be open and shut at will, to love or reject at will. Later you had a semi-adult but sterile woman with a flat and embroidered pussy, with tiny immaculate tits who is trying to write a thesis on Spencer's *Amoretti*, who meets the circle of your friends, who is beginning to form a circle of her own friends, and who now looks at the world and desires it on behalf of self, exclusively.

"You wanted a family, Simon Dona? You just weren't made for that. After all you divorced a most virtuous woman, the woman of Rome, because she was too virtuous. And you left her with two children, alone with that burden, saddling all the blame on her mother, the deaf aristocrat. And then you took this little girls, likewise the daughter of a very rich and bitchy mother, a mother who was learned in matters of sex and would have preferred you as a lover rather than as a son-in-law. Whence the misunderstandings, rancor, brief happy life. But you are a patriarch and you have not yet realized that the *patria potestas* (see Ms. Millet, the theoretician of feminism) is under scrutiny. Marriages are financial alliances, and every family operates as an economic entity in the manner of a corporation. The family is capitalism, a concept that originated precisely in Italy with Leon Battista Alberti's *Della Famiglia,* at the base of which is *virtù,* namely the ability to control your own fortune. With marriage love becomes a contract, see Spenser. Love is no longer tragic, but domesticated.

And you, Simon, you wanted precisely to construct this capitalist corporation in the name of children and of the dowry. But you have never loved, or am I mistaken? Not even yourself. This is why you possess yourself, and this is why you possess this *poor* little girl. You have not yet wanted to understand that between you and your wife there is neither a class difference, nor a biological difference. This is what Ms. Millet's doctoral thesis tells you. In short, you are equal, each one with his or her destiny, his or her choice. Aggression and intelligence, force and efficiency are not prerogatives that are uniquely yours, and passivity and ignorance, docility, virtue and ineffectualness are not prerogatives that are uniquely hers.

You know these things, but your studies make you pretend that you don't know them. But now you must realize that you no longer have a wife, Simon, but an androgynous type of woman whom you should call LIBERA.

Read David Reuben, M.D.:

Our culture can be summed up on the word 'disposability'. The doctrine of 'use once and discard'' has infiltrated human relations. In 1974 there were 2,223,000 marriages in the United States, and 970,000 divorces. On that social frontier called California there were 159,386 marriages and 1,201,044 divorces. This does not mean that Americans are turning their back on marriage. But these figures indicate that the philosophy of 'disposability' and of 'use once and discard' has become part of the marriage game. Ever increasing numbers of men and women are disposed to consign their spouses to the garbage heap, like empty beer cans.

But you don't exactly think in these terms, Simon. You think that you have never had a frigid, subdued wife, good mother, excellent family administrator. You have never had a white pullet or a young heifer. Nevertheless you're a good guy, Simon; you're courageous, loyal, good looking, cock-centered. Only now you're in a crisis state. You've married your daughter, raping her in the park, offering her candy and making her see your member. Whereas you divorced the one who could have been the real wife after the second pregnancy, precisely because of your inability to bear the burden of a family. Or are there other reasons?

Yes, glaucoma, your glaucomic look.

You see more and want more because you know that soon you will not see at all. That's why you look, look with the eyes that remain to you, at the wet panties of hysterical little girls looking for a father. This is how you ensnared this eternal girl student, your wife, who is trying to write a thesis on Spenser. You did it with a look of yours. *Because the look is all.*

It was discovered by the feminists in France, somewhat behind in time compared to their American counterparts who discovered the zipless fuck. Sigmund Freud also hypnotized hysterics. Eve was hypnotized by the serpent. Because the look seizes, paralyzes, disarms, evaluates, penetrates.

Now, really, you're a violent type, Simon. Read *Liberation des Femmes*. It explains clearly how violence is exercised. Fathers rape their daughters in the house. Husbands calmly rape their wives in the marriage bed. Office managers rape secretaries on the moquette, the carpeting of their offices. Stable-boys rape bourgeois ladies on the straw of their stables. Doctors rape nymphomaniacs in psychiatric hospitals because they need it, as they put it. American blacks rape white women. American whites rape black women. Soldiers rape in wartime. Every act of violence is an abuse of power. Legal power, the legitimate and authoritarian power of the husband over his wife whom he views as his property. The natural power of all men over all women. The power of the dwarf over the girl with the basket of red tomatoes.

Some monologue, eh?

Vera yawns. She goes to the bathroom and, seated on the pot, she smokes her first cigarette of the day, looking as thin and worn out as Virginia Woolf at eighteen. She's reading the horoscope.

To conquer a Pisces woman is not a difficult enterprise, according to Lucia Alberti, a Viennese living in Rome. For the Pisces woman is so easily influenced, so emotional, so distant from reality. The fact that she lives in a world of her own invention makes her see in you a man of unsurpassable qualities, the richest, the handsomest, the most intelligent of the world, even if you are just a state employee with a smattering of humanistic culture. But you are not this person, Simon Dona, but the man who will come, who will tenderly touch your delicate skin, Vera, and who will talk to you about solipsism and nature, about psychedelic experiences and about Est. And I already know who he is, he has already kissed me on the mouth. He is coarse and shy, choleric and querulous, and sells himself for thirty pieces of silver because he likes the duplicitous life in which elegance is maintained and poverty shown off. Actually, he has no reason to betray me, he's simply the one who reaches out an arm and grabs. On the contrary, you Simon, have so many possible reasons for letting yourself be betrayed. You are looking for death, Simon, whereas the other is not interested in death although he, too, will die, looking for his death as an *innocent*, as do all his fellow-impotents. For your new man will be impotent, do you know that

Vera? But he will be gentle with you, indeed he will be gentle from the very start. And he will transfigure you, he will have you get a nose-job, he will have you re-dye your hair, seeking the natural root in you, he will dress you in blue jeans, he will put the generative cross around your neck, the cross of fertility: my cross. G.O. is your pre-fabricated type. The difference between him and me is this: he's gentle and I'm violent. He's shy and I'm one who walks among monkeys. You, Simon, are violent because you have the word, you have the strength, you have a penis. Why violence? The penis is violence. And the penis seeks the woman because there is a hymen to penetrate, a void to be filled, a door to be opened, a nail to be driven into the wall on which to hang a hat, a grave in which to lower the coffin, a dry earth to be fertilized, a sea to be sailed, a sky to be pierced, a moon to be walked on. The penis is the song of the penis, what else?

You are a humanistic scientist, Simon. But just like Leon Battista Alberti, at bottom, you are a misogynist. You like the company of men or to be alone, writing of your discoveries, whereas you would like the woman around you only to dry your wet feet, to fuck, to have children and to do housework, in short a woman as convenience and fate. You are frighteningly childish, Simon. Or is it all because of the glaucoma?

Of course. My love life of today is not a gift, it is not a pleasure. It's a simple and private vendetta against illness.

5.

I have always been enamoured of clouds. One of them, Anna Madison, crouches herself on my head and carries me off. I'm alone, I'm perfectly alone: yet memory continues to make something of the past surface to consciousness, and offers me the continuity of time.

The remembrance involves pot, lots of smoke, lots of laughter, lots of critiques following the screening of the film short, *The 12th Macaque*. Now the remembrance encompasses the ritual celebration in Anna's and Andrew's house on South Black Lake Road, with the usual friends, the usual professors, the couples, husbands with wives, husband without wives, wives without husbands, who are exploring and querying each other, a rattling world of divorcees, a teeming world a la Magritte, unctuous, sticky, tense as a tightrope, hysterical, made of sex and hedonism, a rather ambiguous and difficult sport of esthetic pleasure which my friends engage in with a weary arrogance.

The screening of the film was followed by some rather important critical comments, even on the part of students. But soon it became a clash of opinions between opposed and hated cliques of professors, pederasts, lesbians, supercritics, christologists and racists. Some said the film was an attack on women, others said it was a defense of women and of homosexuality. Others, still, contended that it was an attack on gossip-mongering and defective academic world. Finally a German theologian, Wolfgang Piper, as conservative as Joseph Ratsinger and Joseph Hoeffner, alluded to the film as a cynical metaphorical statement on the Roman Congregation of Rites: namely that which on February 17, 1600 condemned Giordano Bruno to be burned at the stake on the Campo de' Fiori in Rome, and which thirty-three years later tried to convince Galileo that prudence and a long life lay on the side of a geocentric model of the universe.

All expounded and defended their theses, but nobody had clear ideas, not even the two academicians who had made the film, Madison and Dona. The presentation, by the philosopher Anacleto Zinghelli, confounded ideas even more and promoted bitter resentments. Zinghelli, an authority on Manzoni and Lope de Vega, had a Jesuit past and had published a series of articles on christology which had led to his ouster from the Church as a heretic, an event which subsequently destroyed his whole life.[11]

Zinghelli, a frail, stocky man did not sit on the desk of the Lecture Center 7 but on the lectern surmounting the desk. He spoke in a strident yet booming voice and it was not exactly clear

---

[11] The 55-year old Zinghelli, today a father of two children, had obtained a doctorate in theology at a very young age at the Gregorian University of Rome, following which he left on a mission to Brazil. Although he was very devout and fervent as regards the precepts of the Holy Mother Church, he had committed an auto da fé with a little book on christology, titled: *The Hermeneutic Circle of the Gospels.* Since the '50's, when the Rev. Zinghelli was writing from Brazil, all biblical scholars, apart from fundamentalists, thought that the Gospels are not objective documentations of chronological events, but rather the result of an ambivalent play between historical events and their interpretation by the first believers. On the one hand., the contemporaries of Jesus deducted his life from their remembrances when, after the Paschal feast, they interpreted the significance of his glorification and of his awaited return while, on the other hand, their post-Paschal faith formed their interpretation of his historical life.

This same thesis was newly expounded, more forcefully and with griever consequences, by the Flemish Theologian Edward Schillebeeckx. In December of 1979 he was interrogated by the "papal advisers," and condemned for having denied the divinity of Jesus. The same "advisers" also condemned Hans Kung, professor of dogma and ecumenical theology at the University of Tubingen, for having shed doubt on the divinity of Jesus and on the virginity of Mary. They likewise silenced the French theologian Jacques Pohier, who called into the question the physical resurrection of Jesus.

In the case of Professor Anacleto Zinghelli, it was his own bishop in Rio who communicated the ex-communication to him with the words, *Roma locuta est, causa finita est,* Rome has spoken, the case is closed.

whether he was speaking in English or Italian, Portuguese or Hebrew. Nevertheless, each one of the auditors understood him in his/her own language. And many laughed out of scorn, others from disappointment.

Simon Dona or Simon Martini, he began, puffing on a long Cuban cigar: it is best that you consult the encyclopedia. It is St. Simon, one of the Twelve, as we know. He is also called Canaanite, or Zealot. He is the father of Lazarus. He is the pharisee in the house where Jesus found accommodation. He is the father of Judas Iscariot. He is Simon of Cyrene. He is Simon Magnus. His names are as many as his faces, therefore it is proper that I lecture you a little about him, otherwise you will run the risk of understanding nothing whatsoever of that terrible and sorrowful film short. You call him Professor Dona, right. And you expect him for what he is. Dona in Eyetalian means gift, and in Italy there is a saying, "Don't look a gift horse in the mouth." I, however, have been a friend of his for many years, it can be said that I saw him being born, but I have never been able to confirm even this pure factual datum. The registrar's office in Selimo, where the author's name has been recorded, is now in ashes and along with it the ledgers, the incunabula, the codices in which these mysteries are handed down to posterity. One thing I do know with certainty is that Simon's father was a fanciful character, one of those with his head permanently in the clouds, from which he took the names which he than stuck to his son. He would change his son's name every day and he would swear, while laughing, that the one being assigned on that particular day was the real one, the only one, the indestructible one. It was the same with regard to the date of birth. Simon contends that he was born on November 28, which makes him a *Sagittarius*. But his father insists that he was born on December 24, exactly at the stroke of midnight. Now, looking at him, would you say he was a *Capricorn*? Would you say that he is stubborn, obstinate, a bit of a bore, an ibex scaling a mountain in one step at a time without looking either to the right or left nor backward, tied to the earth, devoid of fantasy?

Look at his film and reply.

Oh, I know very well, of course, what you would like to tell me: that you don't believe in astrology, that it deals in fables, and that science is science and Kepler is its prophet. But I could reply with the words that Iung wrote to Freud on the distant day of May 8, 1911.

"At the moment I am busying myself with astrology, a knowledge of which seems indispensable for understanding mythology. One comes upon surprising things. I beg you to allow me to wallow in these infinities. I'll bring back some rich spoils with a view to adding to our knowledge of the human soul. I must, for a certain period, inebriate myself with magic perfumes in order to be able to completely understand what secrets the unconscious conceals in its abysses."

Now Simon Dona, or Simon Martini, St. Simon or Simon Peter, the Pharisee or the Cyrenean believes in astrology nevertheless. So true is this that he has been very careful in the choice of his friends. The first two he found when he was fishing for trout on the slopes of the Rocky Mountains, in a little stream where the water was still pristinely limpid. They had been seated on the bank with their fishing-lines for about three hours and had come up with a paltry catch, two tiny stunted fish of a dubious species and provenience. When Simon sat beside them and cast his bait into the water, the little stream suddenly began to swarm with silvery fish darting in all directions, and despite the efforts of all three fishermen they could not catch them all. It turned out that they were from Anaconda, N.Y., also professors, even if one was an illustrious and bearded surgeon, and the other an illustrious and bearded chemist who made underground movies in his spare time.

Peter was tall, hirsute, and sported a reddish beard matched by the shaggy hair on his hands. He was the director of the Ophthalmologist Clinic and his ambition was limitless. Braggart, haughty, snobbish, had been born under the sign of *Leo* and he certainly didn't hide it. The other, Andrea, was more contorted in character: vaguely homosexual, suicidal, introvert, sly, sometimes even disloyal, decisively cowardly, in short a typical representative of *Cancer* and the treacherous wickedness attributed to his zodiacal sign.

I could speak to you, similarly, about the other Ten. Of the *Sagittarius* Matthew, a trade expert specializing in tax evasion but who, nevertheless, ended up as vice-president of this University; of the *Aquarius* Rafael, the great virtuoso of the gentle flute, and of Dionisius, his brother, the favorite, who, like all the *Aries,* is somewhat fanatical but generous, impetuous, ready to take on any foe frontally, at the drop of a hat. His only misfortune is to have been born a Swiss.

And I could talk to you of fat Jack who Simon, jokingly, calls *Monsieur de Char/us,* and who in fact is a woman dressed as a man. He is a brilliant teacher of Chinese, uncertain, immodest, somewhat sticky. He is not bad subjectively, but objectively he is dangerous, a *Libra* in the pure tradition. And I could also speak about the great Carmen Cara, so incontestably *Capricorn* to the very depth's of his lawyer's soul. On the other hand, the *Taurus* Bartholomew, son of Boston Italian immigrants is an upright professor of Criminal Justice, republican, catholic, and the author of detective novels. You all know him, so you all know the limits of his imagination.

It's a great gang, as you see. But you don't know the last two. You know nothing of Tom, the *Virgo,* professor of music, who refused to heed Simon's astrological advise and died in an air crash over the Andes. And you don't really know Morris, the astronomer, a well wrought and satisfied *Gemini.* Nor do you know me, Anacleto Zinghelli, born under the sign of *Pisces:* an individual bereft of the logic, thought and brain, endowed only with an enormous pulsating belly with so many antennae and so many phalluses and also — precisely because I am a double sign — with a gigantic, odorous and clammy vagina, oh oh!.

Your reaction to this film, which wrenched my peritoneum from me, has made me furious and I would like to tear you to pieces and not only verbally.

Hence the twelfth macaque, the last arrival is missing, Guido. Guido who, as a proper *Scorpio,* rather than kissing Simon prefers to kiss his wife, Eve- Vera, full on the mouth. It is a question of Guido the obscure, the traitor who takes upon himself the terrible but irremediable burden of betrayal. Simon thunders against him, he makes fun of him, ridicules him, condemns him, transforms him into a laughing-stock, and heaps upon him the hatred that his unchanged love for Eve-Vera continues to nourish. But if Guido is a *Scorpio* to the full length of his wicked tail, he is just as much so in his good heart. Therein lies the whole drama. A drama of light and shadow, based on Simon's inability to see his shadow and the shadows of Vera and Guido, and to understand the truth, its indissolubility with light, and therefore with love. Simon's fault was precisely his hankering for love at any price, love for his twelve friends, for his beloved Guido, for Guido's paintings and for my de-sacralizing writings.

Thus, this seemingly banal story of Guido's stiffened member that conscientiously penetrates the slit belonging to Eve-Vera, suddenly is tinged with light given off by all the planets of the zodiac: it becomes emblematical, mythical, and is filled with scorpions, fish, cropped crosses and ears, bread soaked in sauce, and with *Eloi, Eloi, lama sabactani.*

This absurd story of a man who fails to understand that love is not possession, that a vagina is a great all-embracing mother, made to receive all her children, all the penises of this world, particularly the penises of traitors, this absurd story of hearts exulcerated in the crucible of academe, of penises rendered impotent by the affront suffered, takes on the color and contour of beauty, and is transmuted into a kind of aurora borealis. It becomes a conjunction of kings, an alchemic opus from which is born a deeper truth, in which the Shadow also has its role.

It is not by chance that Simon invited me to talk to you about his film inasmuch as I was born under the ambiguous sign of *Pisces*. Or is it by chance that the extremely erudite Dona invited me to talk to you about his *12th Macaque*. He suffers because of the betrayal, because of the kiss that still burns his skin, he suffers and hates Vera and Guido, and he suffers because he knows that Vera and Guido are right.

With their pact, with their embrace, and with the resultant pleasure they have expelled him from the Terrestrial Paradise. They have forced him to descend into the pits o hell, like Orpheus, to look for his Euridice-Innocence, Euridice-Capacity to love.

But you are only Simon's friends, acquaintances, apostles. You cannot see beyond your noses. You are Capricorns and Tauruses, Leos and Sagittariuses, Arietes and Libras, Geminis and Virgos, Cancers and Aquarians, and you do not see the rustling tails of Scorpios, you do not see the flashing fins of the two-fold Pisces. Among you I see only the horns of Tauruses, and the closed vaginas of Virgos, the coarse feet of Capricorn and the stupid face of Arietes, the bleating gossip-mongers of Gemini.

You see the sperm and see not the pleasure, you see the horns and fail to understand the significance of the Pact. Therefore you will condemn this film. For you *Eloi, Eloi lama sabactani* are arcane words, fruit of the mind of a madman darkened by the pain of a recent adultery. But I have not spoken for you, but for Simon, for Vera, for the Scorpio. *Amen.*[12]

---

[12] I was among the listeners. A slight fever came over me. I recalled the Horatian phrase: *Doctores scinduntur,* scholars are sundered. Zinghelli's language had been

Although No-smoking signs, printed in red, hung ubiqui-
tously on the walls, that frail and dwarfish man, the ex-theologian
Anacleto Zinghelli, looked down on his audience through the
dense grey smoke of his cigar, laughing in response to its laughter
but refusing to engage in the skirmish that he himself had
provoked by his talk.

An agricultural technician, a Black from Georgia, and known
only as Professor Harvey XX, in an extremely irritated tone, asked:
"If you, Mr. Zinghelli, thinks of *Pisces* men everything that you
have said in what is tantamount to a self-analysis, as being
equipped with member and vagina alike, as being devoid of logic
and devoid of thought, where can I ever hide this face of mine
since I was born under this zodiacal sign? It's terrible! I will have
to give careful study to ascendencies because it would be too
shameful to be forced to recognize oneself even minimally in a
subject like yourself!"

Zinghelli giggled into his cigar. "But you are an exception, of
course," he said.

Finally two robust females with flowing hair and wearing see-
through dresses, who had been sent by Matthias, grabbed the tiny
speaker and forced him to sit down in a chair next to Andrew and
Simon, who managed to look both amused and dismayed at one
and the same time.

"You've certainly tired yourself out while attempting to
destroy us," Andrew murmured in his ear.

---

outrageous, and he said things that many knew or intuited but he said them
tactelessly and—above all—without a lexicon proper to an essayist. Moreover,
and this was a very serious point, he introduced a profanity a la *Playboy* on a
subject that ought to have been interpreted linguistically and not with
psychological verbosity and not arrogantly personalized. Among other things,
everything he said was completely false. At this moment Simon Dona
immediately intuited that his friend Anacleto Zinghelli had, with unwitting
malice, introduced the palimpsests of his death.

Zinghelli shook his head in denial, and replied in Latin: "*Incertus animus dimidium est sapientiae.* Half of my wisdom is uncertain mind," he translated. And suddenly he looked sad as if asking himself, "What did I do that wasn't right?"[13]

Nevertheless the eyes of many persons in the audience sought out Guido, often fixing their gaze on Vera's ashen face.

She was sitting next to Anna and Charlotte Shark, the redoubtable lady professor of linguistics. She was known to everybody only as the cutting edge of the Feminist Movement, but she threw her weight around primarily as the brains of the academic "Inner Circle" in which the political power was centralized.

Through the radio, TV, and printed material this circle helped to program the individual along a well defined channel. In this manner, the influence of culture and ethics were restricted, psychological profiles of students and professors, as well as those of millions of citizens, were diagnosed through the computer.

The Inner Circle had also gone so far in its pretensions as to dub itself REGIME.[14]

---

[13] It was modish at that time to quote from Latin or Greek and even from Provenzale. Different academics, Dona and Zinghelli were among them, translated from Terence, Seneca, Publius Sirus and Ovid. Dionigi translated from the Greek. It was always irritating to interpolate a discussion with a Latin phrase to Latin-less academics. A favorite with Zinghelli and Dona was Publius Sirus, a mimographer of the times of Caesar and Cicero, famous above all for his gnomic utterances written in Latin iambic and trochaic verse. They found their quotations in the Cantabrigensian Codex, and then checked against the editions of Dionisio Godofredo (Basle, 1502), Desiderius Erasmus, Giorgio Fabricio (Leipzig, 1550), Giano Grutero (Frankfurt, 1604), and Pier Ambrogio Curti (Milan, 1871).

[14] Charlotte Shark was fantastically freakish, well connected in every direction, and welded a destructive influence. A naturalized American of German birth, she was the daughter of a Bavarian locomotive engineer, a radical Rightist and an un-closeted Lesbian. Rafael Oviedo de Bernalbe had imprudently exposed her with his treatise on sea gulls, and this had magnified her fierce hatred of her male colleagues, the humanists, whom she viewed as oppressors of women, and as unfair.

Charlotte studied pigeons in preference to sea gulls, convinced that one day they would be able to learn a series of symbols and through them commit

There were of course, other actors: Peter, Matthias, Rafael, Dionigi, Morris, Jack, Carmen, Bartholomew and Guido. But almost nobody knew Guido as Guido because his name had been reduced to a monogram: G.O. He was there with his wife Phedra, next to Bart and Cara, directly behind the rows of seats occupied by Anna, Vera and Charlotte. Further down, in Guido's row, sat Jack with his young chauffeur-lover, Bob, and still further down sat Dionigi, over whom his wife, Blanche, wielded a firm, heavy and be-ringed hand. Matthias and Morris, who for awhile had been leaning against the exit door opened it surreptitiously, and sneaked away.

---

themselves to speech. She followed certain theories on environmental behavior suggested by the psychologist B.E Skinner, and dismissed the more sensible analyses offered by Chomsky, a legitimate linguist who contends that human language is a specific biological system that has developed through millions of years. Hence the first rudiments of speech cannot be the result of a particular environment.

Years later the same Skinner tried to educate two pigeons, Jack and Jill. to the symbolic game of colors, with dubious results. It earned him the reproach of his colleagues. Pigeons do not have a cognitive faculty. Do sea gulls?—a gossip once asked Rafael de Bernalbe. He replied that if Charlotte Shark had adopted sea gulls in place of pigeons we might have been in a better position to justify the generous grants that she regularly received from foundations.

Charlotte had a nice appearance, but she eternally dressed as a male and wore half-length boots. She was athletic, her laughter was frank, her speech proper, and she gave the impression of having been a voracious reader. The truth of the matter, however, is that she was power-mad and vindictive to the point of hysteria. From Skinner she had learned that animals can be conditioned, and that once they have learned to execute orders they are to be rewarded. She employed the club and carrot tactic. Since those who adapted themselves to the Regime were few, her victims were many.

In the film, *The 12th Macaque,* the principal characters were dressed as monkeys, chimpanzees or humanoids, as Simon Dona had devised an allegorical and moralistic form for his subject. He derived its structure primarily from a medieval play on the seven capital sins, later embellishing it in the manner of a fabulist modelled on Carlo Gozzi, author of *The Love of the Three Oranges* (1777). Charlotte figured in it as Man/Woman, and she was assigned the role of Death.

The moderator, Sonny Morebugs, a professor of English and Finnish sauna enthusiast, (he's nicknamed King Priapus,) finally took note of Charlotte's upraised hand, and invited her to speak.

She rose from her seat and made her way to the platform in her inseparable yoke-yellow boots matching the rest of her dress. The sheets in her hand, titled "From the desk of Charlotte Shark," were also yoke-yellow and she was trying to impose some kind of order on them. Meanwhile she had begun a kind of monologue with herself, without ever casting a glance at the audience. She labelled the film "a comic operetta on hedonism," with a particular emphasis on sacrifice. But whose sacrifice? Of which macaque, the Twelfth or the Thirteenth? The Betrayer or the Saviour? And who would be the traitor, Guido? Guido in the skin of a gray Hanuman languor, named for the monkey god of the Ramayana; and who would be the redeemer, Simon-Jona? Simon in the skin of the uncatchable "wild liontailed macaque with a tufted tail and a bushy mane," who is finally killed with a shot from the carbine of the character symbolizing Envy, who is in the service of Death?[15] "The biblical nuances are obvious," said Charlotte," but from the Text- the Screen—they appear to be of a blasphemous and desacralizing nature."

She then turned to the subject of hedonism and attempted a definition. According to her, it is a subtle vice that insinuates itself with tacit fraud. In art its purpose is practical rather than aesthetic. Nor does it even aim at creating an artistically valid work, consequently it instrumentalizes the product, shaping it and utilizing it to achieve some alien purpose—and in the case of

---

[15] Simon Dona's middlename was Gionata, or Jonathan, son of Saul and friend of David (in the Old Testament,) but some of his colleagues, perhaps to annoy him, called him Simon-Jona. This was an obvious reference to Jonah who, as the Old Testament tells us, uplived for three days in the wale's belly and who decided to accomplish his assigned mission only after he is vomited onto the beach. But they also called him *Corvo di Salaparuta* because of his fondness for that Sicilian wine which he had sent to him from Italy, in small cases.

this precise film, a purpose that can be defined as impure, sacrilegious! It fondles and stimulates that area of light and shade lying between spirit and sense.

"Both Simon-Jona and Andrew," Charlotte added, as she rustled the sheets in a masturbatory motion, "by parodying the mores and customs of academic society wanted to derive something romantic and adventurous from a schematic plot, by recourse to sexual and startling ingredients in order to titillate the senses. They have made a film of content, based on a rich series of orgies and various erotic performances, embroidering with a subtle perfidy the biblical idea underlying the subject: namely, Lesbianism as Rebirth. The hidden thesis of this film suggests, in a porno-theological form, that love is inexorably linked to our personal crucifixion. Eve, like Guido, will betray us in the very act in which she approaches us to plant a kiss on our lips. Life and resurrection are indissolubly linked to death. Nevertheless our only hope of salvation and, therefore, of redemption, lies in acceptance of the cross, not as sacrifice or martyrdom but as the price for having left the Regime, and for having betrayed it. Without Eve, life is naught else but a cruel game played by children tumbling down staircases. Love is self-love because betrayal exists, and life is life because death exists. Hardly a great revelation!"

"I would add," interjected Zinghelli from the floor, "that God is God because Satan exists, and Jesus is Jesus because Judas exists."

"I'm really sorry," retorted Charlotte.

6.

And now everybody is at the party, even Charlotte. She continues to discuss the film from her feminist viewpoint, at first with
Anacleto Zinghelli, the fiercest critic of the Administration which,
benignly, has never retaliated, and then with Barth Bellicapelli, an
authority on the Mafia,[1] whose major interest is to gather and

---

[1] Barth Bellicapelli has won a reputation of sorts with his analysis of Italian/
Americans from the viewpoint of a scientific police investigation, in an attempt
to discredit the myth of the Mafia as the exclusive organization of a particular
ethnic group, namely the Italian. His thesis is as follows:

THE MAFIA MYSTIQUE

The word "Mafia" first cropped up in America in 1891. This was the year of
the New Orleans Massacre. Thirteen Italian immigrants, two of whom were still
Italian citizens, were lynched by a mob in the "Parish Prison" of New Orleans
after they had been absolved by the court. The Massacre was sparked by the
murder of the police chief, Hennessy, which was attributed to members of an
Italian criminal society. Actually Hennessy was involved with one of the two
Italian "families" who were trying to control the waterfront. According to the
documents Hennessy, as he lay dying on the front doorstep of his mother's
house, had accused "them" — the Italians. When he was specifically asked to state
who had fired at him, he shook his head as if to say 'I don't know'. Nevertheless
the authorities channeled popular feelings along zenophobic lines, directed
against Italians in this instance: the police had found some old sawed-off
shotguns of Sicilian make.

The Massacre made headlines in all the world's newspapers, but the New
York newspapers blazoned the word "Mafia" on their front pages, a code word
for an underground criminal organization. The Italian government protested
vehemently, the United States government finally apologized and committed
itself to make reparations.

At times the word "Mafia" was conveniently used by the Bureau of
Immigrants and Naturalization to restrict the flow of immigrants from Southern
Europe. And at other times the anti-narcotics bureau played on the word for its
own purposes. When, subsequently, and conveniently, the term "Cosa Nostra"
was added to "Mafia", the Justice Department used it to print the tons of
documents lying in its files. It is interesting to note that the word Mafia did not

redistribute (after his personal revision) intelligence data on the academic regime. A motto dear to Alphonse Bertillon hangs on the door of his office: "One can see only what one observes, and one observes only the things already in his mind."

Charlotte had once made a stylistic study of Barth's novels, which were quite well known in the film world and in CIA circles. She defined them as "exercises in hedonistic literature to be ranked between the psychologism of James and the abnormal and decadent predilections of the esoteric Huysmans."[2] At this point

---

crop up in the 20's and 30's when gangsters drove up and down Michigan Avenue, machine-gunning each other down. There are criminals, to be sure, but where is the Mafia? The word "Mafia" is a convenient label used by law enforcement agencies to cover their own deficiencies. The Mafia mystique has come into being, but nobody knows just where the Mafia is.

[2] Feminism and anti-sexuality often go arm in *arm*. Although lust is equally strong in man and woman with the result that both sexes are preoccupied with sex, sexual freedom is not sufficient to neutralize woman's power in sexual transactions. A whole ancient and contemporary ritual, drawn from the vast literature on human sexuality, documents that among all peoples it is generally the man who courts, proposes, seduces, uses gifts in exchange for sex, and avails himself of the service of prostitutes.

It is generally understood that sex is something that women have and that men want. It constitutes a service or a favor that women grant, or deny, to man in general. And these are services or favors for which man has to pay. The love-economy in the world is a series of transactions between male and female in which the male exchanges proofs of "commitment" to the woman in order to obtain sexual access to her. In the last analysis, sexual access to a woman is a commodity that she can offer or withhold in order to maximize its value. In heterosexual interactions woman retains the power *for* access to sexual pleasure, hence it is understandable that Charlotte should condemn hedonism as a masculine form to obtain access to that power, its use of woman as object and its transformation of her into one. This transformation would reduce woman to nonbeing and this was clearly perceived by the English suffragette Pankhurst who coined the slogan, "Vote for woman and the chastity of man." This protest against machismo and against sex as such presaged man's hatred of feminism and vice versa. The suffragettes, of whom Charlotte was a representative, began to believe that man, on a lower plane, is an "undeveloped woman" and that "Life is feminine", perceiving deep signification in the fact that in the absence of the male testosterone hormone, the mammalian embryo develops a feminine morphology.

Charlotte draws Barth's attention to the fact that "this film is a product *of* the will to power in sexually impotent authors." "Oh, no, not at all!" Barth replies, laughing. "It's just a game being played by two guys who want to free themselves of their respective wives."

G.O. is also at the party. Charlotte contends that he imitates Gustave Moreau and draws phallic flowers in the manner of Josephin Peladan. G.O. is his usual gentle and subtle self, he chastely kisses Vera on the forehead, and kisses Simon square on the mouth, tonguing him lightly.

"What am I to call this," I protest in utter disbelief, "the kiss of Guido?" Nevertheless we all laugh, but Phedra shakes her head, looking worried.

Morris Elliot is also present. He is a man with tiny very blue eyes, with curly hair, with a crooked nose like that of the Duke of Urbino, and his thin lips easily expand into a smile suspended somewhere between irony and fear. He dresses like the generic executive type, and when he shows up at gatherings he never greets anyone in particular, sits down anywhere and suddenly begins to speak in fits and starts, usually about a trivial happening, after which he just as unceremoniously takes his leave for an ever unknown destination. He screws Anna in his office while the students are stretched out in the corridor, in front of the door, waiting for it to be opened and for him to appear at the door, his chin looking more withered than ever after his coital exertions, a

---

The thesis of scholars such as Blau, Malinowski, Siskind and Symonds demonstrate that although modem feminism does not appear to be anti-sexual, contemporary feminist writings on female sexuality emphasize masturbation and, frequently, lesbianism which in a certain sense are political equivalents of anti-sexuality.

Charlotte and her group saw in "hedonistic" literature an action on the part of males that simultaneously reveals and restricts female supremacy in sexual transactions.

sign that he is ready to resume his interminable seminar on the Black Hole of the universe.[3]

In addition to Matthias and Dionigi and Carmen with their wives, to Jack and Bob, also present were Roland and Kate DeeCee with King Priapus who makes love with Kate in his sauna with Roland's permission. Larry and Williamina Fourdays are also there. Larry weaves in and out among the couples, patting female asses. He starts his patting procedure with Vera, moves on to Blanche, Dionigi's wife, to Williamina who is trying to interest Roland in her belly, no longer tautly adolescent, and finally to Anna who has just made her entry and stretches herself out on the divan in front of the fireplace, resting her little curled head like a puff on my slumbering cock. The voices that are heard here and there are commenting on Charlotte's critique, remembering now that the death of the Master had left a void, but one which nobody really felt anymore.

WILLIAMINA: No, he was not a real humanist. He didn't give a damn about people.

---

[3] Anna Madison's heterosexual and sophisticated oddities were of such a kind and quantity that some of them had leaked out to the male world. Simon Dona, in his talks to the selected, trusted few, often compared the sexual prowess of this woman with her Mangaian or Polynesian model-counterpart. Anna subjected her partners to an intensive sexual investigation, testing their virility and masculinity, their gift-giving and courtship practices, before they were granted access to the moist charms of her inner sanctum. On one occasion Anna, following the example of a girl on Cook's island, did not wash her intimate parts for several days after which she asked Morris, at that time a candidate for loverhood, to practice cunnilingus on her before entry of a more conventional and more intimate character.

Another of the virility tests administered by Anna and her Polynesian model, challenged the new lover to engage in normal copulation, touching no other part of the body except the genitalia. Punks, her husband, was not annoyed by her kinkiness but he was decidedly weary of it and already giving some thought to changing career and mate alike. Indeed he transmitted this weariness to Simon, even though the latter had always believed himself strongly attracted by Anna's aberrations. Perhaps there was more truth than wit in Barth's remark: "It's just a game being played by two guys who want to free themselves of their respective wives."

ROLAND: Not for man as he has existed up to now, but for man in the making.

LARRY: But he opposed his own influence. He considered literature to be bourgeois, and repeated, "I write. It's my vice, but it doesn't feed hungry children." He said that political commitment was all, and asked to be forgiven for writing.

BLANCHE: If I were to reduce his thesis to a single sentence, I would say that "the subconscious is structured like a language." And who knows what it means? It is linked to the new religiosity, antirational, anti-scientific, anti-positivist. "Try to be impossible," are among its slogans.

WILLIAMINA: Yes, we are making a return to a tolerance of different points of view, which we thought had been lost forever. Yes, there's really been a clean break.

All the guests leave except for Simon and Vera (and by chance Zinghelli, curled up on the floor in a dark corner.) The lights go out, and a slight grudge against everything somehow clings to us, but we choose to defer for the time being. The smoke has been an hallucinatory effect on all our minds, but the effect seems also to be boredom. In fact, Anna observes: "Boredom is heat."

"This film is the beginning of the end," I reply.

"Of Academe or of us?"

"Of us, of you, of them, what do I know?"

"We'll also keep on going, along separate paths," Anna says.

The feeling of dullness comes from the dullness of the hour, from the cold of the uncurtained window panes that let in the night, from the heat that warms the central part of my body, from the weight of this tiny head that is obscurely arousing the worm lying in ambush. She rubs her face against it, then she reaches out a hand to grab mine, which is inert, and transfers it from her tit to her twot which is flat and throb-less but I also know that naked it is crude, wild, and fruitless.

Poor Simon-Jona, you've met only arid women, soft and flattering women, and absolutely and sovereignly liberty.

Suddenly I become aware of Vera's absence. But I don't make a move. I try to survey the surveyable corners of the room from a corner of my eye. Vera is in a corner with Andrew, chair against chair, leg against leg, face against face like two porcelain statues hanging on a wall. Vera is smiling like a doltish Gioconda, and there's a glint of slyness in Andrew's gleaming eye. Then I hear them get up like two feathers, descend the stairs and enter the room below.

"You stay here," Anna murmurs, grabbing me. Minutes later, when the only sound in the semi-darkness comes from the fire, she un-zippers me, touches my penis, now poised upright, and greedily sinks her head into it.

"You know that's a stupid thing to be doing," I murmur. "Yet, it's happening."

"What's happening?"

"Punks and I are swapping wives!"

"It's not your doing or his. It's the wives who want it that way."

When she's finished, I get up, fix my tie, and pull up my zipper. I feel benumbed and dissatisfied. And I begin to think that there is nothing more pathetic than an unjustified sense of guilt. Nevertheless I feel guilty. And I, too, descend the stairs, hesitantly because I am about to trespass on someone else's turf. The moment I see her, I bark out the order:

"Let's go home, right away!"

"No! Why?" she protests.

They are stretched out on the waterbed, excited and resentful of my intrusion. Anna, too, has appeared in the doorway; she had followed me down the stairs. "How about the four of us trying that waterbed?" she suggests. Without further ado she begins to strip off her clothes throwing her dress and bra to one side, and her panties in my face.

"No, no, Simon," Punks protests. "Three's fine, but four's out..." He tries to get on his feet, but he slips and falls back on the mattress.

"The fourth, Andrew, couldn't come because he's ill at home," I say, with a sardonic inflection. "That's how the *Timaeus* begins. The threesome relation is always preferred."

To Vera I simply announce: "I'll wait for you in the car." She follows me carrying her shoes.

Anacleto is huddled up on the back-seat of the car like a ball.

"What are you doing here?"

"I'm holding my belly. You have all poisoned me, tonight."

On the way back the countryside looked smoothly flowing and luminous. The thinking floats, it's muddy.

"Do you like Punks?"

"Very much."

"Would you make it together with him?"

"I've got a date with him tomorrow in the afternoon, in a motel..."

"Which one?"

"The *Tom Sawyer.*"

"Will you go?"

"I told him no. And you, will you go with Anna ?"

"Anna is too capricious. I need something else..."

"You need to be less exclusive." And she adds: "For the time being you don't have to worry about it. I'll let you know when I'm about to betray you."

"Jesus! What then?" exclaims Anacleto.

Vera is startled and scared out of her wits. She sees Zinghelli and begins to cry. She really would like to slap his face.

"But what are you doing here? You've heard everything... "

7.

"The first one of us that becomes a God will die, mortified by the solitude," wrote Andrew to Simon.

It was a warning, and I knew it.

Just as I knew something else, namely that "freedom is not free." Surrounded by lawyers and gossip-mongers nobody is free. And it's even worse if a state employee is involved.

The dominant idea: *"Why not make a bonfire of the whole business and take off on the motorcycle?"*

Sure, of course. But where? Every inch of the earth is under surveillance. And if you should happen to stop for the night in a hotel with a gas pump on the highway and there's a Gabby Maple eager for a change of scene and willing to run off to France or to Alaska with you to study art and fish for salmon, inevitably a Bogart will pop up from somewhere and hold you at gun point from the stage.[4]

Anna and Andrew separated one month later. She took the initiative.

---

[4] This is an accidental reference to Robert Sherwood's play, *The Petrified Forrest*, starring Leslie Howard and Humphrey Bogart on Broadway (1936) and later made into a film by Archie Mayo. Alan Squier (Leslie Howard) is a disenchanted writer on a vagabond tour of America in search of a reason for existence, a utopian life far from the reality of a world that no longer offers space to dreamers. But he plunges headlong into another dream, Gabby Maple, (Bette Davis), daughter of the owner of the restaurant with a gas pump on the highway on the edge of the forest. Out of the blue Duke Mantee (Bogart), erupts into their world. He is a desperado, an escaped convict, embodying brute force, the ultimate evil.

The reference may serve to stress that, on the one hand, Simon still harbors illusions and, on the other, that he is also conscious of the inevitability failure and of his own cynicism.

"Why?" I ask Vera.

"Punk is exclusive."

"Exclusive? In what sense?"

"Like yourself. Whereas Anna is generous."

"Generous? In what sense?"

It was irritating and sarcastic: my irony, her patience. Then she recites a fable: "There was once a Young Husband and a Young Wife who before becoming man and wife had lived together for two years, loving each other intensely and loving intensely whoever they had decided to love: together or separately. They got involved with different persons at the same time that they loved each other, because they wanted to explore all the secrets of sex and of human nature before the nuptial veil and the civil profession. But Punks continued to have friends even afterwards, and Anna did likewise. One fine day Punks brought home one of his laboratory colleagues, Barbara. Do you remember her? The relation became trine. He wanted it so, and the two women submitted. Anna, however, never got over the shock. From that moment on she sought out other men and other women. And she began to go to the shrink..."

"The moral of your fable," I interject, "seems to be that the Trinity is dangerous!"

Several months later a similar episode happened to us. And the so fatal Number 3 was called Roseanne Spiram. During the lectures I jokingly called her Miss Spiro, Miss Spirito, Miss Soffio, Miss Anemos, Miss Spiramen, Miss Spirito santo, and so forth and so forth. Embarrassment and annoyance drove the girl to following me around at conferences, in the library, in the cafeteria and in my office where for some time, even during my absence, she would spend hours seated in a corner, reading my books, doing her homework, oblivious to the coming and going of students and even Vera's. One day she sarcastically asked her if she had been promoted as my assistant or guardian angel.

On another occasion I asked her:

"Just what is it that you're looking for, Roseanne?"

"Me? Nothing."

"You are like my soul, my bad conscience."

"I want to become a nun."

"Why not find yourself a nice boy, instead."

"I had one. He was Sinbad the sailor. But then he died on Prudhoe Bay, hunting whales."

"Did they discover oil there?"

"Yes, of course. But he was hunting whales."

Hunting whales?

Some years before I had journeyed to the Arctic Polar Circle. From Greenland I moved on to Alaska, visiting Barrow, Prudhoe Bay, Kotzebue and Nome in bush pilot planes. And often my dreams were peopled with Eskimos, huskies, bears and caribous. I, too, as a boy had seen myself as a kind of Sinbad. And now, through her voice, Alaska was coming back to me.

"I would have liked to live in Alaska, but then I would have been sad, very sad," I said.

Without lifting her eyes from the book, she replied:

"I was born in Ketchikan, but they took me away. "

Now her people were living in Utica where they owned a small dairy factory and a farm with goats and cows, on the Mohawk River. When she returned from her week-end visits home sometimes she brought back special fresh cheese for her friends. One day she brought back a whole wheel of cheese for me too. And Vera ate almost all of it.

I advised her to read lung and to see horror movies, to stop bringing me cheese from home and to study in her own room, or in the library. She replied that lung was difficult and that horror movies turned her off. But she stopped coming to the office, to Vera's relief and to that of my malevolent colleagues. One day, however, I found a tiny handmade totem pole on my desk, and an envelope that contained a poem she had written. I suddenly realized that the girl had taken a shine to me and demanded a retribution.[5]

It became clear when she stopped coming to my lectures, leaving me to suspect that she had given up the course. I phoned her at the dormitory. She answered that she had not given up the course, but that she was sick.

When teachers become overly protective they express themselves as follows:

"Sick? What's the matter? And why didn't you let me know?"

"It's no physical ailment, I'm just homesick for Ketchikan."

"Ah !"

"Is the totem that you left in the office *from* Ketchikan?"

Surprised, she said:

"It's Chief Johnson's pole, don't you recognize it?"

Why must an anthropologist know everything? One of my earliest passions had indeed been to study the connection between Christian mythology and the supernatural, as expressed in the to-

---

[5] Simon's papers contain a special folder with many love letters from girls. One of them, by Roseanne Spiram, has the above-mentioned poem, entitled *"Our Silence."* Apparently it was written in Simon's office, at school, because it was signed from that room.

The first few stanzas read:

You *sit in your "professor seat" behind your desk.*
I sit, in my "student seat" opposite you:
  your desk is the connecting link between us.

We carry on a conversation no *one else can see or hear,*
because we don't use words,
  because we don't need them to communicate.

During our conversations no *one else can intrude,*
because no *outside reality exists,*
save that which we create in the silence.

There are three other stanzas, eliminated here, because they seem to be variants of the preceding ones.

temic figurations of the various Indian peoples of the Pacific such as Haida, the Nootka, the Nass, the Tsimsyan and the Tlingit. If, on the one hand, totem poles are primarily heraldic monuments in which a family, generally the family of a chief, symbolize the myths that attest its nobility by tracing its history and genealogy, on the other, the myths contain elements that are more supernatural than divine in character. Some poles were carved by christianized artists and others, like the myth of the Martyr-Bear that recurs among the Indians of British Columbia, were used by Missionaries to explain the history and the spirit of Christianity in terms of Indian concepts. In fact the Pacific Coast Indians have legends which in addition to Christian elements we come upon personages and myths with a Mediterranean flavor reminiscent of Orpheus, Prometheus, Samson and Hercules. These myths predate the coming of the white man and their similarities with Mediterranean myths suggest the existence of a human world myth (lung's "collective unconscious,") or of "personifications" of needs common to people of all races. But in contrast to the Hebraic-Christian religions according to which man was created in one single day and as being different and superior to the animal, and unlike certain Hinduistic religions which hold that man is equal to the animal, in Indian mythology man is inferior to the animal because the animal is also a spirit. The animal eludes man with magical arts and at times, as does the bear, it offers itself to the martyrdom of the hunt for the good and welfare of the people under its protection. The bear transforms itself into man at will, whereas among men only the hero can successfully transmute himself into an animal.

The myth of the Bear-Martyr in particular shares similarities with Christianity. The American Indians, as well as the Ural-Altaic peoples of Siberia, call the bear "the grandfather," the "beloved uncle," "the lord," "the godfather." And before the hunt they utter the prayer: "Permit us to kill thee." The Thompson

River Indians address the bear with the petition: "Be not angry with the hunter, defend not thyself." And the Lamutes of Siberia say: "Frighten us not, please. Die of thy own free will."

According to the Canadian anthropologist Marius Barbous the Bear myth is perhaps the most universal one among the Indians because it includes all the elementary essentials:

1) the union between a supernatural being and a human being for the procreation of progeny who will share both the human and the supernatural attributes of the parents;

2) the agony to which the supernatural being voluntarily subject himself to, for the good of the clan or of the entire community;

3) the ceremony derived from the myth in which those protected by the self-immolation of the supernatural being eat his sacred flesh as a special form of respect;

4) the function of intermediary between humanity and divinity that is assumed by the supernatural being.

Thus the legend of the Bear-Martyr has elements that approach the life, the death and the divinity of Jesus.

On the other hand, in the tradition of the Tlingit Indians, living in the small area of south-east Alaska, there are many that make the Raven a human hero and a divine being. The transformation of the characteristics of the myth were carved on the pole as if to fix the aspects of the supernatural.

The Raven created man, brought light, fixed rivers and lakes in their particular place, and had a predilection for wanton adventures. But if often changed aspects, according to need, as it voyaged through the world, often it appears as man, concealing its supernatural identity from others. And for the purpose of achieving other desired aims, it has often transformed itself into a woman, into a child born of the daughter of a tribal chief, or even into a pine needle. It has swam under oceans, it has lived in the belly of a whale, and it has ascended to the heavens just because it felt like doing so.

But I knew almost nothing about the Tlingit Indians who still live in Ketchikan, Alaska.

I answered: "There's an eagle at the top that must symbolize the emblem of the clan, the heraldic genealogy. Besides, there is the usual Raven seated atop the head of the Pisces Woman."

"That Raven," she said with a sigh, "is my father. And that woman is my mother."

Likewise sighing, I asked, "And you carved your mother and your father for me? The colors are still fresh, my princess."

"Don't you like them?"

"Of course, I like them! Very much!" And with a shudder I immediately bethrought myself of my age: me, the Corvo of Salaparuta, her father, and Vera, the Pisces Woman, her mother! An incestuous situation! But incest is as much abhorred among the Tlingit Indians as it is among Christians.

I learned later that the Tlingit trace their descent through the maternal line, hence the crests of the totemic poles are not a family insignia but belong to the whole clan or to the line of genealogical descent. Every Tlingit belongs to one or the other of the two subdivisions, or phratries, named after the Raven or the Wolf. Often the Wolves are called Eagles by some Tlingit tribes. All the Ravens are kindred and this also holds true for the Wolves (or Eagles.) Among these phratries there are smaller groups, or clans, whose members enjoy close bonds. The clans are subdivided into further groups or genealogical lines. Babies born into the group take on the mother's name and thus they become not only members of her clan but also of the phratry. Since marriages between members of the same phratria are prohibited, the man and his bride always belong to opposite phratries: one or the other, accordingly, must descend either from the phratry of the Raven or from the phratry of the Wolf, or Eagle.

In the old days every Tlingit belonged to a hereditary class within which he was born and from which it was very difficult for him to escape. It was generally a class with an advantageous social tradition and one that was well-off economically. They also owned slaves, either captured during forays against neighboring peoples or bought from other slave-owners.

Later Roseanne told me that her parents abandoned their smoked salmon factory in Ketchikan when, after the end of World War II, they began to lose money and business as the result of the installation of modern fish-drying plants, and competition from foreign concerns. Their flight could not be to neighboring towns, it had to be definitive as a form of total forgetfulness. The State of New York, through a competition of war veterans, seeded several acres of uncultivated land near the Mohawk River to her father for transformation into a dairy farm.

After the lengthy phone conversation, as pleasant as it was constructive, reverting to my usual irony, I said to her:

"You know, the Holy Spirit is missing in class. Why don't you come back?"

"I don't understand why you call me by that name, and by the others as well."

"But you do understand the meaning of the figures on that totem, right?"

"It's the history of my family."

"Then you should also be able to understand lung."

Roseanne did return to class. Now she looked like a real red Indian to me. She had accentuated her origins with her broad, red lips and with her elongated eyes behind a veil of mascara and her smooth, almost oily and self-cut raven black hair. Over her jeans she wore a white cotton T-shirt featuring the Ketchikan totem pole, painted in harsh and violent colors. The large blue wings of an eagle, or a falcon, atop the pole stood out protectively on her bosom.

"Would you like to explain it to the class," I asked her.

"Must I really?" she smiled, looking uncertainly at her classmates.

The students, fifteen in all, immediately expressed their approval, urging her to take my place. Finally I sat in her seat and she sat in mine, looking as tall as the pole that identified her.

"As a premise," she began, "I would like to state that this totem is still situated in the exact place in which it was erected, between Mission and Stedman Streets in Ketchikan, Alaska. It belongs to the House of Kadjuk of the Raven clan. It was carved and installed in its present location by the head of the clan, known as Chief Johnson, in 1901. My father, a member of the clan, was born in that year."

I shuddered. My father was also born in that year, but in Selimo, on the Adriatic Appennine Mountain Chain overlooking the beautiful and beloved Italian shores. And Roseanne herself was born in 1953, the same year in which my first book was published, which I called "son." While the real son, Sandro, (the first of three) was born three years later. My father also had three children, as also did Roseanne's father.

I jotted down these notes. And she continued: "Before Ketchikan was built, the members of the Kadjuk House and others from subordinated house, owned the land at the source of the stream now called Ketchikan Creek. They had a summer encampment here and smoke houses where the salmon, caught on the spot, were laid out to dry for the winter."

She spoke slowly and tonelessly as if she were reading.

"The legendary bird called Kadjuk can be seen at the top of the pole. It is as large as a blue falcon, which it resembles, and it lives very high in the mountain, never descending to the lower peaks. Some say that its color is brown though the tips of its wings and of its tail are black, while others contend that the bird is white. It has not been seen for many years, but I believe that I once saw it when I was a child. The bird is the crest, or the emblem, of the administrative head of the Kadjuk House and nobody can use it without the chief's express permission. Chief Johnson, who had the pole erected, was the administrative head of the Kadjuk House in 1901, the year in which my father was born, a member of the same clan, namely that of the Raven."

Here she paused and emitted a prolonged sigh after which she resumed her recital: "The long smooth and undecorated space that separates Kadjuk from the other figures, symbolizes the bird's elevated habitation and the great respect in which the crest, the heraldic sign, is held. The two bird figures, side by side, under Kadjuk are Gitsanuk and Gitsaqueq, slaves of the Raven who stands below them. The Raven's breast, as you can see (here Roseanne pointed to her stomach) actually forms the hair-do of his wife below him, and his wings extend to both sides of her head. On her lower lip the woman is wearing one of the big plugs that indicate a woman of rank among the Tlingit people. In her hands she is holding two salmon, the first in the world, which she created. The two faces at the top of the tails of the salmon re-present wealth in the form of two slaves carved higher up on the pole, and in addition the wealth of fish that people now enjoy. She is called the Fog Woman. The Indians identify her with the in-between seasons when the fog hanging low over the source of the creek coincides with the mad salmon run to the sea. It was the Fog Woman" Roseanne concluded, "who created all the varieties of salmon and put them in the streams."

"But do these figures suggest many stories or legends?" asked a student.

"No. All the figures on the pole, with the exception of Kadjuk, symbolize a unique story that stands out among the Raven's adventures."

"It would be of great interest to know the story," said another student.

"It's time to go," I interjected as I noticed students of another class impatiently pressing on the door to the lecture hall. As we filed out and walked towards the office I, unwittingly, grasped the hand of the girl who claimed to be the daughter of the Raven and of the Fog Woman.[6]

---

[6] Among Dona's papers there was a translation, probably made by Roseanne, of the ancient Indian legend of the Raven and of the Fog-Woman. It contained many corrections and different words in the language of the Tlingit people. There was also a brief footnote in red ink, in Simon's handwriting. "So, even Indian women divorce! Fate is ever the same: love or die."

I reproduce the text:

A long time ago Raven and his slaves, Gitfanuk and Gitmqueq, built a camp at the source of a creek and set out to fish for their winter food supply. But Raven managed only to catch bullheads so they decided to return to the camp. As they were rowing campward, a fog descended on the bay; so thick was the fog that they could no longer see their route to the shore. They were lost. Suddenly a woman, seating herself in the middle of the canoe, appeared to them. Neither Raven nor his slaves could figure out how she had arrived there. She asked for the hat that Raven was wearing, made of spruce-root. Then she placed it at her left side. The fog poured into the hat to the last drop of vapor, the sun shone again and in consequence they were able to return to the camp safely.

Several days later Raven devised another method for making a big catch of fish. He left his wife, Fog-Woman, in the camp with Gitsanuk, taking only Gitsaqueq along with him. During their absence, Fog-Woman and Gitsaqueq got hungry so she ordered the slave to fill a bucket with water from the creek and bring it to her. She dipped a finger into the water. Then she commanded the slave to empty the water bucket toward the sea. He did as directed and immediately he sighted a large sockeye salmon splashing around in the spot where he had poured out the water. She ordered him to strike the salmon with a club and to cook it before Raven's return. After the dinner she ordered him to thoroughly clean the particles of meat that had remained stuck between his teeth so that Raven would not notice that they had had something to eat. She also ordered him not to say a word about the catch, under any circumstances.

When Raven landed, Gitsanuk ran to greet him, exultant with joy. Raven, who was very shrewed, immediately became suspicious. He was also skillful in wresting secrets from others. Noticing a meat particle clinging to Gitsanuks teeth, he asked: "What's that between your teeth?" "Oh, nothing" replied the slave. "That's only flesh of bullheads." Raven insisted, waxing angrier by the minute until, finally, Gitsanuk blurted out the story of the sockeye.

Raven sent for his wife and asked her how she had managed to find the salmon. Fog-Woman loved her husband, so she confided the secret to him. She asked him, to bring his hat and to fill it with water, just as she had previously commanded the slave. Raven was

8.

Roseanne took the initiative to phone me a few days later. She wanted a book by Jung that had been recommended as supple-

---

so famished that he quickly ran to fetch the water, pouring it into his hat and setting it down in front of her. She dipper her fingers into the water after which she ordered him to spill it out on the ground, which he did. Instantly, four blue salmon were squirming helplessly on the ground.

They cooked the fish and enjoyed a festive repast.

After eating Raven asked Fog- woman to produce more fish. She told him to build a smoke-house first. When it was finished, she asked Raven to bring her a bucket of water. Then she ordered Raven to bring the water bucket to the spring from which he had taken fish and set them to dry in the smoke-house. They filled it with salmon and there were still many left over for the smoke-house.

Raven was so mad with joy that he began to speak rudely to his wife, forgetting that she was the one who had wrought the miracle of the salmon. They quarreled and Raven struck her. She threatened to return to her father's house, but Raven continued to insult her. Fog-Woman then began to comb her hair. A sound similar to a violent gust of wind came from the smoke-house. She left the house and walked towards the water, and the wind flew louder and stronger. Raven, realizing that she was really leaving, tried to stop her but his hands slid over her as if she were made of fog or water.

Since Fog-Woman was walking towards the sea, all the salmon began to follow her, even those on the rocks and those already dried and wrapped in bundles wriggled after her. Raven commanded the slaves to salvage as many of the fish as possible, but their efforts came to naught because Fog-Woman had by now vanished from sight and with her all the salmon.

When I read for the third time and started annotating these Diaries, August 3, 1980, I was also able to consult *The Wolf and the Raven Totem Poles of Southeastern Alaska* by Viola E. Garfield and Linn A. Forrest (Seattle and London: University of Washington Press, 1948.)There have been different editions of this book and the copy that "Princess Cruises" of Los Angeles presented me with, on the occasion of a trip of mine to Alaska (June 2O-July II, 1980, during which I visited ports such as Ketchikan, Juneau, Skagway and Sitka,) is the fourth edition of 1968.

Apparently both Roseanne and Simon knew of the book, Simon, at any rate, because he finds echoes of the anthropological prose of Viola Garfield in Roseanne's "lecture." I was able to base the authenticity of Roseanne's original translation on the legend of the Raven and of the Fog-Woman on Garfield and Forrest.

mentary reading for the course, and that was not available in the library. I didn't have the car because Vera had taken it for her trip to New Canaan. It was raining and I had no desire to deliver the book by motorcycle. But since I didn't live far from the campus, she decided to brave the rain and come on foot.

I took the book down from the shelf and handed it to her.

"But it's in German!"

Simon, laughing, intones: "The Holy Spirit manifests himself in all languages." Then he kisses her, and is kissed in return. Her lips are red and big, like plums. "The Holy Spirit manifested himself to the apostles in the form of a little flame. You have that flame in your mouth..."

She disengages herself without really breaking away. They sit down on the rug, cross-legged, and the book falls between them. Carl G. Jung: *Symbolik des Geistes*.

"Why do you always pronounce that name? Even in class it makes me feel ashamed. It strikes me as obscene."

"True," Simon murmurs, "obscenity is part and parcel of the sacred, my princess."

"What have I got to do with that name?"

Simon picks up the book and opens it. "You are called Spiram, and not Spearam. Nevertheless it's pronounced like spear."

"Like Shake-speare...?" she laughs.

Since the encounter was becoming something like a seduction —lecture, and since it was raining outside, and since Vera was away, I dropped Jung and took the dictionary down from the shelf, not without a twinge of self-consciousness in connection with the trick that I was about to play.

"Open it to the word Spir, please."

She obeys: "It's not here!"

"How about the word that follows?"

"The following word is Spirit."

"Read it, please."

"Spirit: soul. God is pure spirit. We were with thee in spirit. Spirit of the time. Objective spirit. *Spiritus vegetativus*. The cold blasts of spirits. And of course these phenomena are really the work of spirits, etc."

"And this is also your name," I observe. "Spiram means Spirit, and it must be the Christian translation of your Indian name; Spiram is the truncated form of Spiramen which in Latin means breath; but also means soul because the soul is essentially breath."

She lays the dictionary down, and he picks up Jung.

"Jung explains the matter more or less as follows. It's true that the breath is, in the first place, an activity of the body. But, viewed independently, it is a substance next to the body. If this concept is applied to the formula of the Trinity one quite properly could say Father, Son and Life, that is, Holy Spirit who proceeds from the Father and from the Son, and is lived by both of them."

"Now you're losing me."

"The Father is the universal One, the Son is the Other of the Father, the Holy Spirit is the Third in that he has emanated from both, that is to say he is in common between Father and Son and points to an abolition of the duality."

"Why do you speak of duality between father and son?"

"Because both form an antithesis. The Father tries to maintain his being in oneness and aloneness, while the Son strives to be another vis-à-vis the One. The father does not want to release the son because he would lose his character, and the son detaches himself from the father in order to exist. There is an antithetic tension between them. And as everyone knows, every tension of this kind drives towards an outlet, from which the Third derives, resolving the tension in the process. The Third is knowledge, vital breath. Jung says that the Triad is a development of the one in cognizability."[7]

---

[7] Among the notes on the study course of that academic year (1972-73) entitled *Social Anthropology: An Introduction* (which included Behavior and Culture,

"Then you would be the Father...," she murmurs after a reflective pause.

Simon, mentally recalling the totemic pole, laughingly asserts:

"In fact, they call me Raven..."

"Your wife would be the Daughter..."

"She is the Pisces Woman, in fact..."

"And I would be the Spirit breathed by the two of you... It's fantastic and obscene."

"My God, I'm not suggesting a *menage a trios*... that would be terrible!"

"Why terrible?"

Simon reaches for one of Vera's lipstick tubes lying in a nearby ashtray, picks up a sheet of paper from the desk on which he traces the scheme as drawn below:

PATER
FILIUS DIABOLUS

Linguistics and Phonology, Ethnology and Folklore,) Simon had left some quotations from Jung. They are very thick and it would be worthwhile to consult the *Symbolik des Geistes*. It was published in Italian by Einaudi in 1959 in a translation by Olga Bovero Caporali with the title, *La simbolica dello spirito – Studi sulla fenomenologia psichica.*

On the basis of this edition I cite some passages that Dona underlined in red:

"... In the *Liber Spiritu* of the late Middle Ages a psychic interpretation of the Trinity was attempted, starting out from the premise that one can arrive at a knowledge of God through self-knowledge. The *mens rationalis,* i.e. the thinking intellect is, in the highest degree, similar to God, since it is *excellenter et proprie ad similitudinem illius facta.* If it recognizes its own likeness to God, all the more easily will it recognize its creator. Thus begins the knowledge of the Trinity: in fact the mind sees how wisdom (sa.*pientia*) comes from itself and how it may love it. Hence love *(amor)* proceeds from it and from wisdom and thus the three appear in one: the mind, wisdom and love. Wisdom proceeds from the mind, and love from both. Now, God is the origin of all wisdom. Hence He corresponds to the mind; wisdom, generated by the mind, corresponds to the Son; but love, to the Spirit that bloweth between Father and Son. The *sapientia Dei* was often identified with the cosmogonic *Logos,* and therefore with Christ. The medieval spirit naturally derives the structure of the psyche from the Trinity whereas the modern point of view reverses the relation."

"Because we would be reducing ourselves to this," he says, as he rushes to the bathroom. He sticks his head under the faucet and soaks himself like a pullet. His head is in a tangle, confused and bombarded from all sides. Nothing much is required, he muses, prattle about mystery and these girls literally fall into your arms. It's unsportsmanlike. It's to nobody's advantage to study the Trinity.

Upon emerging from the bathroom, brusquely, he says: "Let's go now. I'll take you back to the dormitory."

The rain is still coming down hard, but they are wearing yellow raincoats and motorcycle helmets. They pierce the rain through the headlights of the motorcycle, an inebriating experience. The idea of sex and spirituality drowns in the anxious concern to avoid a fatal accident on the highway.

Simon, of course, continues to meet Roseanne by day or night, but secretly, and he takes her driving through the woods on his motorcycle. They make love on the haystacks and in roadside ditches, they eat in anonymous diners frequented by truck drivers, they join other groups of motorcyclists, they bathe in the nude in lakes under the moon, but Vera's image often comes between them, and in order not to chase it away (because they both love her) they resume talking about the symbology of the One and of the Three.

> Trine. Triad.
> Trinidad — an island in the Little Antilles.
> Trinidad — city in Cuba, on the Jayoba River. Trinidad — city in Uruguay, department of Flores. Trinidad — city in Colorado, *USA*, on the Purgatoire River.
> Trinity River — in Texas.
> The Order of the Trinity — medieval monks of love, 1198.
> Elsa Triolet — French woman writer.

Church of the Trinity—in Rome.

Bridge of the Holy Trinity—in Florence. Trinitapoli—in Puglie, Italy.

Troy—city in Asia Minor, near Hellespont, sung by Homer.

Troia—city in the Puglie, Italy.

Troy—city in the State of New York.

Triolism—*menage a trois.*

Troika—Russian carriage drawn by three horses. Troilus—Priam's youngest son, killed by Achilles.

Terza Rima—see Dante.

Trinitrololuene—a high explosive.

But now Simon is assailed by terrible guilt complexes. He would like to break off the strange relationship with Roseanne, he now wishes that nothing had come between them. Instead, she continues to sit beside him during his lectures. One day Vera and Anna pass by and stop to peep in the window, their eyes go from Simon, who is talking to the class, to Roseanne, who is sitting beside him.

"She'll take him away from you," Anna murmurs to Vera.

Vera reports Anna's warning to Simon who, irritatedly, replies: "So what if it should really turn out so?"

"If it should really turn out so, 1'd be free!" she replies, in a burst of laughter.

There is also the day when Vera sets out for New York, but she gets a flat tire en route. She decides to return with the flattened tire and leave the job of changing it to Simon. Simon is in the small room with Roseanne. Both are naked and at ease, drinking coca-cola. And when Vera suddenly appears at the door Roseanne smiles at her. Simon, instead, hides his head under the pillow and tosses about like one obsessed.

"Spy, you did it deliberately!" he shouts.

Vera runs off, she phones Anna and Anna phones Charlotte. Charlotte recommends that Vera consult Susie Spring, the analyst, or Margie Lower, the divorce lawyer.

"A scandal of this kind can get Simon kicked out," Charlotte says.

"Simon can be kicked out only if they abolish his department, an impossible task," observes Anna.

"We can bring that about, too. It's enough to want it to happen," threatens Charlotte. Anna is now frightened, she tells Simon about the conversation, and Simon telephones Matthias, the Vice President, who has already been fully informed.

"I feel sorry for Vera," he says.

"I'd like to punch a hole in Charlotte's belly."

"I'm handing in my resignation from this University next year," adds Matthias. "There's altogether too much feminist politics on the one hand, and altogether too much worldly-minded activity, on the other. We're all losing our tempers, all of us... Do you really want to stay on here?"

Simon knows that his days are numbered, and cheers up. The scholastic year is coming to a close. He gets on his knees and begs Vera to forgive all his infidelities. Vera pretends to believe him. She even invites Roseanne to dinner. They talk about the difference between sex and love, between anima and animus according to Jung, of the concept of the cave according to Plato, and of the concept of the cave according to Jung. Finally Vera declares that she is madly in love with Simon, and Roseanne declares that she too loves Simon but not so madly.

"And whom do you love, Simon?" the two women ask.

"Charlotte!" Simon shouts, in exasperation.

Several days later Roseanne leaves, she has been granted her degree. Her greatest aspiration is to become an airline stewardess, and even to obtain a pilot's license.

But soon after her departure, Vera observes: "You're sad and sulky, love. Why don't you phone her? Why don't you invite her to spend a weekend with us?"

"A weekend? All three of us?"

"Why not? After all I like Roseanne and you like her, and we two ladies like you. Simple."

"Ridiculous. What do you want me to do with two women in the same bed?"

"What do you know about what two women can do to you in the same bed?"

Finally it's Vera who makes the phone call. Roseanne makes some excuses. Simon picks up the phone to persuade her. She expresses the opinion that a separation is in the making between Simon and Vera and she would not want to be its cause.

"No, not at all," Simon reassures her. "We merely want a threesome."

Roseanne finally arrives for a three-day stay. The triadic relation in fact lasts only three days, at the end of which an exasperated Vera collapses. She orders Roseanne out of the house, and threatens to kill her if she ever shows up again.

Vera is hysterical. She has many good reasons to be in such a state, and her only ideal now is to destroy Simon's scaffoldings one by one. She, too, following Anna and Charlotte's advice, ends up visiting a shrink. The analyst is Susie Spring, Charlotte's secret bride. Vera has become an extremely tenuous threads of nerves. Vera has become a blinding streak of light. Simon truly loves her, but he knows very well that Vera will leave him. In fact its a matter of days, perhaps months.

And Simon, now seeing himself being turned *out of* doors, invites little satan Shait and his wife, with ever greater frequency to his house. G.O. has a soporific power over Vera, he knows how to talk to her in a simple, vague kind of voice about his infinite solitude as husband, about his absolute lack of ambition, and about his deep desire for a pure, disinterested loving relationship. Vera swallows everything, and wildly records her physical and psychic experiences in the *Diary*. Often she leaves the notebook on the table, open, so that Simon may read it. And he does. He also reads about an afternoon when Susie Spring receives Vera in a nightgown, invites her into the bedroom where on the bed she sees Anna nude, smoking her fortieth cigarette of the day.

"Are we to repeat the threesome?" Vera exclaims, in mocking unbelief.

"There's an important difference," says Susie the analyst, "there are no men!"

Vera, stunned, returns home. But she no longer protests, she sobs for days on end, grips Simon like a desperate woman, continually beseeching to be raped, to the point of total desperation, to the point of death itself.

"This is what death is," she murmurs, "life ceases to hurt."

9.

The mail has been lying on the table since this morning, since Vera left. I open a letter from Italy and read:

"Here we live waiting, Italy is knee-deep in scandals, the ruling class is more shameless than ever. Only the uninvolved save themselves, the obtuse. But, personally, I am very much concerned. After all it could also be described as a source of amusement and in reality I find it amusing. It's a farce Italian-style, with a pinch of Neapolitan pantomime. The past few days have revealed that everybody has been stealing in the thirty years since the war. Presidents of the Republic, ministers, party leaders, errand boys, clients, favorites (male and female,) priests, colonels, ambassadors, generals, cardinals, perhaps even the Pope. This entire establishment makes one laugh. Allow me to amuse myself, Palazzeschi used to say, and now I understand him, only it is not just a question of personal amusement. There is a fear of the aftermath, when the party is over. The party, in short, can be interrupted and transform itself into a tragedy. Terrorism has come upon the stage... And what are you doing in America?"

It's from Ugo, the gentlest homosexual I have ever encountered in the world. He lives in Rome as in a rose, wandering from a job in some ministry to one in the editorial room of some newspaper.

What am I doing in America?

I'm twiddling my thumbs, as I'm doing on this very day as my wife has left for New York City!

She takes the Greyhoud in Anaconda and gets off at the Port Authority in New York around eleven in the morning. Then she walks down to Saks Fifth Avenue, slips into the lady's room and sees her mother sitting there, reading *Cosmopolitan*. Her mother takes the train in New Canaan, she gets off at the Grand Central in New York, walks down to Saks Fifth Avenue, slips into the lady's room and sees her daughter sitting there, reading Spenser.

Whoever arrives first, waits.

They go have breakfast, they go shopping. Then the mother goes to meet her lover whom she first met thirty-five years ago. He has children and grandchildren now, and over a vodka-martini they discuss business, fashion and talk about remembrances. They no longer screw, they are good friends, and she buys him gold cuff- links each time he goes on a vacation.

He's the one who replaced the Genoese officer whom she met during one of her vacations on the old stately liner Rex, seeing him regularly thereafter each time the Rex docked in New York. They made love passionately, and then the Rex no longer docked in New York because it was sunk during the Second World War. She became pregnant through him although she had a husband in New Canaan, a French teacher. But they did not love each other, it had been an arranged marriage, childless, and now she wanted a daughter from the Italian. The Italian died and all that has remained of him is this creature, Vera, a daughter of the waves like Venus, thin-lipped and with a deep pubis. She raised her like a marmot, very jealously, button by button, hat by hat. They slept together in the same bed, they wore the same dresses and when they were on vacation the fast-living baboons called them sisters.

Vera slept alone for the first time in college, and the first time that she let a hunter possess her was in New York, in the summer of 1960. And the hunter was Simon Dona, scientist and satyr.

Now Vera is either in Rizzoli's book store on Fifth Avenue or at a movie, waiting for the dinner hour with her mother, waiting to take the bus back to Anaconda. But at times, like today, she sleeps in the city, alone or with her mother, or with G.O. Nobody really knows.

Simon remains alone at home, but he is not really alone. When a union is based on trust, the risk of betrayal is a real possibility with which one has to live continually. Therefore, it is part of the trust just as doubt is part of the living faith.

Simon remains alone at home, but he is not really alone. Since today is pay-day, the professorial pay-check goes directly to the bank. He has no economic problems up to now unless his school should go bankrupt, which is a probability, in which case he will have to end up as a jungle anthropologist for the Smithsonian Institute in Washington, D.C.

Or shoot himself.

But up to now no serious drama is in the immediate offing, except for a few little problems linked to his illness.

Illness is useful when we realize that it is no longer possible to expel it. Everything takes another course, we slip into the groove. And to register the fall signifies to descend into the Avernus, among the Furies. But one adjusts even to this state of affairs. See, what an optimist I am!

It's not true that only the sun and light are warming. Night is also tender. One can sleep. Indeed it's necessary to sleep for the morrow, for a moment or for a day that are still in the making. Hence I am alone but not really alone.

This house is vast and narrow, it seems to be made of furniture, of objects. But when she's here it seems to be an extension of her self, and even time is no longer with me, she makes me act. But time is a vague cognition; the writer finds it by isolating himself, the lover by exhibiting himself, by talking, by caressing. The best time is always that spent with another person, the worst is with a blank sheet of paper staring at you and the memory that fills it. It is a time-frame as narrow and vast as this house. Yet everything is going well and is still going well. I loaf about, I put on a record, I take a shot of gin, I go out to the garden; the tomatoes are red and big on the stalks, as are the enormous rosebushes in which one can mangle oneself. The squirrels scamper down from the trees and like electric presences they sniff about and run off. I go back to my desk and look outside on the patch of woods, I feel her absence and desire her presence, I get drunk and I get mixed up. The phone rings now and then, and finally all that remains is the blank sheet staring me in the face. Remembrance is the only presence, along with sleep. I sleep more than ever when she's not here, weariness accumulates and sleep shakes it off. I gently indulge in ironic self-reflection, observing my face in profile.

It's not true that I want to rid myself of my wife. But there is the illness, the physical illness and the illness of the feelings.

What's the illness all about?

Let's see.

Facial symptology.

Symptoms: fierce pains in the ocular globe (internal) like stiletto thrusts. The eye contracts and closes, sometimes it tears intensely. At other times it is dry and sandy. The nose begins to drip. A feeling of intense anxiety. A void in the stomach. Precipitate arrhythmia. Difficult breathing. A feeling of total depletion, as if all the blood had flown out (probably fall of pressure.) At times intestinal disturbances (diarrhea). The whole organism feels as though it's been shaken by a cyclone.

The crisis always occurs, upon awakening, in the morning. Sometimes it comes on during sleep and triggers the sudden awakening.

The first crisis occurred at the age of 17, when I was a prisoner of the Nazis in Villafranca, Verona. Diagnosed (badly) as neuralgia of the trigeminal nerve, it was never properly treated except with analgesics at the moment of crisis. In time the crisis increased in frequency and in intensity. They became intolerable during the marriage with Billie, the Roman wife, whom I later divorced in Mexico and subsequently in Italy. The mother promoted the divorces more than did the daughter. She was an aristocratic Hungarian who had been raised in Turkey where she married a Neapolitan colonel of the carabinieri. Doctor friends continued to talk about the trigeminal nerve, but sometimes the crisis occurred in the left eye, sometimes in the right eye whereas always comes from one side. Nobody had ever given that a thought!

Finally, a neurology professor made a correct diagnosis. His name was Shen, and he struck me as a character in James Joyce's *Dublin*. He tried some treatments without results. The illness had now become chronic because too much time has passed and there's nothing more to be done: more than twenty years have gone by! Relief could come only from a continual displacement from city to city or from continent to continent. The crises are provoked by meteorological phenomena, by changes in the atmospheric pressure, storms, excessive heat and excessive cold, etc.

From the age of 20 to today (I am now 49) I have dressed in the clothes of the unfortunate Leopardian Icelander and I have traveled throughout the world looking for the right climate, the right displacement. And this search has brought me to France, Lapland, Brazil, Amazonia, Egypt, Israel, Turkey, India, Labrador, on the Churchill Bay, California, Mexico, Morocco, Sicily, Senegal, Louisiana, the Caspian Sea (Kirkenes), British Columbia, Alaska, writing diaries and hefty anthropological works, shooting films, taking photographs, often surviving on Jewish bagels which I baked myself. I went to these places without knowing why I went there, nor why I wanted to go there, but I wanted to feel better.

I lived all one summer in the woods of the Yukon, counting trees and fleeing from the bloodthirsty fury of the bears native to the region. I have crossed the United States from Seattle to Washington, D.C. in freight cars with drug addicts and pop musicians, recognizing and appeasing the criminal when he stuck a knife against my back. I have flown tin plate planes, First World War rejects, in the storms of the Canadian arctic in order to retrieve frost-bitten geologists looking for uranium, and adventurers looking for traps belonging to others and furred animals. They called me Jesus. And all this because I wanted to feel better. In the tundra women invited me to sleep on the white warmth of their thighs.

Yet, according to the neurologist Shen, the triggering cause of the crisis was certainly psychosomatic.

At the age of 35 I met Vera Jones in a Yale University classroom. I was now in Academe, a kind of Arcadia peopled by little men with red pencils and disarming smiles, but who were always in heat, like my dog, and always complaining of headaches.

My eye feels better now. It reads, teaches, and learns. And for several years, despite the difficulty of my relations with Vera, the crises have almost disappeared. The relation with her was always a capricious one, often because of her mother who was oversexed and hostile to professors. Vera was also at fault because she missed Daniel, our son, who her mother, Dress, took away from us with the excuse that the child could not be subjected to our continual exploratory journeys to Tanzania or on the Orinoco, during which we often ate white worms for breakfast.

As a result of the deterioration of the relation with Vera, the crises have reappeared of late, increasing in frequency and intensity. I have become Job. Most of the time the crisis is resolved by keeping the eye closed and contracted, almost strabic. The eye then opens and normalizes itself with the passage of time.

My ophthalmologist in Anaconda, the apostle Peter, diagnoses it as glaucoma, a veritable social illness because of its frequency (it affects more than 2% of the world population over 40) which is characterized by an increase of ocular pressure which determines a gradual loss of sight. I learn that Milton became blind as a consequence of glaucoma, and the same is true of Homer. But I am neither Milton nor the blind Homer, to be sure, but only a man frightened of the darkness.

At the present time, however, the crisis are only rarely very acute. I continue to treat them with analgesic's (two tablets of Nisidina) the moment they start. Then I stay in bed and try to read. During the acute crisis I get some relief by eating something, bagels usually, or even bits of cement which I scratch off the walls of my home.

A violent quarrel can also serve as a safety valve and make me feel better.

What am I doing in America?

I'm twiddling my thumbs, as I'm doing this very day as my wife has left for New York.[8]

---

[8] Simon included this piece also in his autobiography, *Selimo Selimo,* published in Selimo, Italy, on behalf of the regional Administration in June of 1978. After his divorce from Vera in 1975, he resumed his travels through Italy and Africa, and in Selimo especially he believed that he had *found* his identity and his *roots.* The book was born of this impact, the effects of which continued for another two years during which he worked on it. The stir that was occasioned by the publication of *Selimo Selimo* was accompanied by an immediate displeasure that filtered into Simon's soul after having seen Three Fates in the city of Tomola where Elio had organized the "homecoming." Save for his heart, Simon no longer had anything in that town that he could call his own. Nevertheless, with a touch of Machiavellian irony, he toyed with the idea of establishing new roots. But he quickly realized that it was better to pack up and leave. And so he did, but tactfully.

He wrote, however, a rather indulgent and mysteriosophic letter to Elio which several months later produced a reply *from* him. After receipt of this letter Simon leaped onto his motorcycle for the last time.

It should be pointed out that Simon's spiritual cronies were in the city of Is, in upper Selimo. It was the only city in Selimo that preserve a sense of history and of human, universal culture, whereas in Tomola traditional political practices and fashionable social were the rule. Simon, however, was from Lower Selimo and *from* his childhood he had always breathed in the scent of the sea and of escape that came to him from Tomola, imagining Is as his only miracle-producing base, a mirage for his creativity during his peregrinations.

Elio therefore became his carnal friend, whereas those of Is, like Giambattista and Sebastiano were the friends of his mind.

Simon believed in the divine. He also believed in the stars and, consequently, in the seasons and in death that recurs in life. He believed that he had lived three lives, all in a total form in as much as they included life and death. The first stretched *from* five years after his birth to his twentieth birthday.

Fundamental things had come to pass in those 15 years: the town school, more boorish than ignorant, the higher school in the Seminary, very learned but not to be permanently embraced, after which came the civil war, the horror of which mortally burned him, body and soul. The second phase, which also lasted 15 years, was in the realm of writer and traveler, somewhat in the manner of Stendhal, his favorite author. He willingly committed suicide for that life, adducing as a reason his congenital incapacity to enter into diving apparatus, and survive amid a hail of blows and a hurricane of laughter. He laughed too loudly at the hurricanes that, finally, the storm that he himself provoked drowned him. He began a third life allover again in America, which lasted another 15 years, along a path that he had always liked best, wholly dedicated to his ancestral passion, anthropology. But here too, as the *Diary* suggests, after fifteen years in a university chair he arrived at his third death.

Now only Selimo could still give him something, a fourth and perhaps last life. But this did not come to pass.

The letter reproduced here is less explicit than his *Diary*, but it sheds a different light on a personality so complex that no one will ever know how to obstruct it and reduce it to an ultimate, definitive death.

This is the text:

My dear Elio, I owe you a letter, especially because it's not necessary. This moment is not necessary, indeed it is useless. I am taking advantage of it for this reason. Useless moments are all that remain to me, and I want to utilize them. This happens because the real has become water to me, and water always signifies travel. Water is the only thing that I have sought when I have decided on a story.

So I write you about nothing in particular from Sabbioneta, Italy, after a brief flight to Israel.

I spent three days in Jaffa — I made love with the woman who was waiting for me in Rome from the United States. I saw three persons and flew back. I found my-self alone in Milan. I wrote postcards to my wife, who is now re-married, and to an Indian girl who pilots small bush planes in Alaska. But in Mantua I met an old acquaintance; she was very young and so was I, but now she is married and saddled with children, unhappy and unfit. We banded together so as not to avoid the pangs of regrets after this new encounter.

* * *

What do you do when you meet the arcane and you talk to it?

I've never been afraid of death, but this was death in person. She had the face of infancy, of daisies in a meadow, of her Army officer father, of the kitchen range, of the uneducated shopper. In sum she was a tiny wandering star, a town girl at bottom.

I, however, woke my own reckonings, and carefully, each time something grabs me. Generally I left myself be grabbed because I am pure and curious, but also because I alone know where the location of the real exit door is.

She tells me that she saw me studying lotus flowers on the banks of the Mincio, years and years ago. And it's true, because years and years ago I did study lotus flowers on the bank of the Mincio. She would watch me from a screened window. I answered yes: years ago I studied the synthetic lotus at the suggestion of the Mantuan Piero Dallarana who, she tells me, is her uncle. To which I reply that in that year, at least for me, Piero Dallarana was a kind of Mantegna, the painter.

There is a bar on the public square to which she leads me. So this woman of other times who nevertheless dresses in the elegant fripperies of Fiorucci, tells me sixteenth century tales when the local lords kept a man, half-dead and half-alive, in a cage on the square, exhibited to the public. These were the cruel times of the Renaissance, she explains, when a man half-dead and half-alive exhibited in a cage on the public square in fact and symbol proclaimed the seigneurial power.

It was also the time in which my favorite artists signed contracts with the Tyrant. But today the Tyrant is dead, I say, and the Artist is still alive. But she, disinterestedly, observes that artists of that caliber no longer exist on the earth, precisely because all the tyrants are dead. Artists today are quite ordinary people.

I reply that today the tyrants have different face and consequently the artists are also different. Then I tell her about a town of a marine character, where love makes love with lilies of the valley, which have an abbey-like scent about them and where funerals are still festive occasions, where the olive tree still sturdily.I talk about my people and about their modesty. I talk about my people and about their pragmatism. I speak with a nervous voice but my hands are motionless because I do not want to create a familiar stage setting.

How stupid this death!

I typewrite what I've seen in the old city, in Tel Aviv, eating slices of **eggplants**, *fried in the holy oil of the Messiah. Oaken trunks, arranged in piles during the night, bum on the streets of the ghetto creating pillars of smoke. The black Jews who helped elect Begin now want to dump him. The apartments built for them cost more than they earn, so that they are occupied by those who have more money than one earns. Life costs so much here that one gets the impression that life counts for naught.*

This world, I realize, is so wicked, so stupid. There is noting mystical about Israel. It's inhabited by a tough people, a people that have endured much. It is a people that knows how to write and govern. It is a people that knows how to mourn its dead. It is a people, however, that does nothing else but revenge itself.

I see the collateral strata, the Arabs, camouflaged through the ghetto. They are so determined and so violent that they lose themselves because of an uncontrolled sexuality. It is a people destined to be massacred. It is a people that aspires to massacre. They do not have much wisdom, nor temperance. They always want to burn what they do not know.

It is forbidden to walk on the dunes.

My Jewish-American girlfriend, with whom I ate the eggplant slices in the Jaffa ghetto watching the fires from the balcony, has decided to go to Jerusalem in order to enter a competition to which she will submit a **proposal**: *Fir the reconstruction of Noah's Ark.*

It is to be set up in a zoo.

In fact, she invited me here to help her to sell the project. The special feature about the Ark would be its intact re-birth on the basis of its dimensions as described in Genesis.

According to her calculations the Ark should be 300 coudees long, 50 high and 30 in width. The "coudee" corresponds to the length of a man's forearm, more or less around 50 centimeters. Therefore, the Ark should measure about 150 meters in length. It will contain a biblical restaurant, biblical animals and be set in a location between the Mediterranean and the Dead Sea, the exact site of the Jerusalem zoo. It will cost 400,000 dollars, part of which will be paid by an American sponsor: the competition, and the rest by the city of Jerusalem.

***

I flew back to take another look at Milan. Love walks with me, but we never cut ourselves off from the ship canal. We go into a bar, we come out of a bookstore, walk along the canal, and glance at the vanishing wine in the bottle. Boredom has the taste of silence and sultry bedsheets and when a spot, which is a drop of her sweat, falls on the hand, I cautiously gather it up with the thin blade of my fingernails and out of modesty, I let it dry in the air.

I sleep without let-up and always dream. She never sleeps and torments me. She doesn't know me, we do not know each other, nevertheless she kisses my body as though it were water, and I kiss her back and her body feels like marble. She often drives away in her Alfa-Sud, staying away for hours at a time, but she always comes back with a different dress and with a bag of apples. She has a hamper-like purse in which she carries apples and she eats only these apples, even when we dine.

She often talks to me about her husband and her daughter, and of the two boys she has chosen to be her lovers. The one she seduced, during a French lesson, is now 18 but at that time he was 15. She went biking with her husband and she went to the movies with him. Eventually the husband found out, as did the boy's mother. Nothing really happened save that the husband put all the property in his name, except for this villa which belongs to her. The boy now works as a mechanic in Mantua where her husband is the head physician in the hospital. The other boy is 23, very handsome according to her, and he is studying and living in Milan. But she truly loves the 18-year old who, in turn, loves her 10-year old daughter.

I now find myself in the middle of this knotty situation, but it seems that she quintessentializes me in all her men, having found them again in one person. She, however, is the only one to perceive my mystery, which is that which always takes me away from emotions. To her love seems simple, but for me love is something that wears out. I tell her that love is something that is squandered, as we are doing now, and that love is that which is not or that which will blossom soon. For love is never what you have: otherwise we would not be talking about it, so much as we are doing now while walking along the canal in shorts. She says that she always makes love, and she likes to insult her partner and moan in order to get over the eternal threshold of the orgasm, and achieve it in one final gasp. It's been a struggle that she has been waging for years, and she still doesn't know how much it might be worth.

Now with me there, no voice comes over the radio or from the television set, nor is there any J&B. But when the play begins, always in the heat of the afternoon, it comes to a close only when the moon rises above the pinetrees overlooking the canal.

It's always so simple, it 's always without a word, but I always voyage through a whole life. And once again I see things that I had set aside: the nail clippers ,for example, lost in India; the white dunes of thistle on Cape Cod over which I flew with a small plane; the impatient kiss I placed on the lips of the girl I loved after stopping the car at the roadside ditch in Georgia, as the result of which the car irretrievable sank in the thicket of the marshes, and we were set back on the road by a crane belonging to a group of KKK witch-hunters. And in my mind's eye I also recalled that tragic turn in Vermont, where a high tension wire split in two and fell in front of my speeding motorcycle, and I missed decapitation by a millimeter. I see many things again, and it is always summer, even if certain things transpired in the snow.

Then she becomes increasingly more whorish and she wants my wrist watch, my ball pen, the address of a friend, a piece of my right calf which she tried to cut out with a razor blade. Finally she shaved off the hairs of that calf and made a tiny pile of them on a sheet of cigarette paper which she folded and smoked, scorching the tip of her nose. Now she has placed a bandaid on it and she has taken my underwear and my stockings and gone down to the canal to wash them, beating the wash on the stone of the graveled bank.

I am reading **The Best of Sholem Aleichen** which I bought in Israel. And I come upon the pure Hebrew of the psalm, **Hamadvil beyn Koydesh l'kho** which means that some make the chaff while others work.

I begin to pack my things, she is outside. I walk on the bank of the canal, but I feel the presence of the dead or dying man in the cage of the Gonzagas. My invisible companion insists on taking my suitcase and I stubbornly refuse to give it to him. He's not breathing hard but he's walking fast albeit in fits and starts without, however, passing me. He smokes and smokes, and he even takes a pill. At one time he was a pharmacist, but he never carried aspirin with him. He asks me if there's a relation between my trip to Nicaragua and my trip to Israel. I say no. I don't concern myself with politics. But he thinks I work, like Kajka, for a luminous and mysterious system. I reply brusquely that I tour here and there with the sole ambition of wanting to die. Nano stops musing and finally he says:

"You are an exceptional man, really. The more I look at you, the younger you seem."

"By necessity," I reply. "I was born in the time of Pliny. It's also as if the ashes had not touched me at all."

It is described in a letter of Pliny the Younger to Tacitus:

"He was in Misen where he commanded the fleet. Toward the seventh hour of August 24 my mother pointed out to him a cloud uncommon for its form and size. He had just been sunbathing, followed by a shower after which he stretched out eating something and reading. He asks for his sandals and goes up to a site from which he could obtain a better view of that mysterious thing. A cloud was rising (and to anyone watching it, it was uncertain to determine the mountain of origin — only later did it become known that it was Vesuvius) and no other tree than a Mediterranean pine would have better suggested its form, with an extremely long trunk rising skyward and spreading in various branches because, I believe, it was being raised by afresh wind and later. when the wind dropped, or when it was overcome by its own weight, it dissolved at the same time as it widened its spread, at times white, at times dirty and spotted, depending on whether it was carrying earth or ashes. ..

10.

The pep-pills are finished.

I stop writing and put the radio on. An anxious and distant voice, that of a commercial, shouts: Mrs. Jones, oh Mrs. Jones.

Next time use Mop and Glo. No, no more Mop and Glo, Mrs. Jones. This house is up for sale.

And now it's late, it's late. There's not a voice to be heard in the woods, not a light to be seen. The last bus from New York will arrive at one in the morning. Maybe she'll be on it, she'll take a

---

The old man went to take a look, going as far as the shore where he fell asleep. Thus did the ashes preserve him for us.

The man walking at my side finally admits to being tired and stretches himself out in an urn of water. He is thoroughly composed, the expression on his face is serious but not troubled and I look at him absent-mindedly, as it were, because I am being drawn by the din of what sounds like a discotheque. It turns out to be coming, instead, from the Town Hall that rises on the canal where a festival with speeches is in progress, and three ladies are selling a box of curious items to arriving patrons, each one of which tells something about the man by whom it was crafted. They flit about, taking and offering. They are wearing heavy cufflings around their short necks, constantly and obsequiously followed by a tall man who looks like an athletic or a nightbird type. They are chasing after a gentleman dressed in white who enters and exits from mysterious offices equipped with machines and microphones, wires and tapes. Finally they stop him in the middle of the wires, and the woman with the fish around her neck displays a pair of scissors, a well-known and advertised brand. The man dressed in white knows that she wants to cut his life, and he immobilizes her with the flash of his "miniscule Argus" which he always carries with him. The man dressed in white is the inventor of the box, but the three women sell it as if it were their property.

Finally, when he's outside, the man finds himself on the bank of the canal again. Now two women are talking to him through the urn of water containing the dead man. They are dressed like twins, sport a pinkish color in their hair and the custom jewelry they are wearing is as light as their young years. They are talking about that Mediterranean pine which is a cloud, at times white and at times spotted, depending on whether it is carrying earth or ashes.

There's the smell of water-lilies on the canal, soon the dawn of another life will break. I perceive the meaning of it and I bid farewell to the companion who is lying still. Pliny, too, had no inkling of his predestined misfortune.

taxi, or maybe she'll call and ask me to pick her up... It has been a torrid day.

Tomorrow night I'll be having dinner in the home of Norina and Franz, young French professors from California, who are going to stay. She's a lesbian, he's a gay. They will be getting married in September.

The 23rd and the 24th will be registration days in the Gym, students coming and going, professors coming and going, chaos, gossipings, new books, old colleagues, new colleagues, routine, boredom. Lectures will begin on Monday, the 26th, Academic Year of 1974-75. Everything comes to an end and everything starts all over again.

I'm thinking of Peru.

PART TWO

VERA'S DIARY

The fire I started in the mountains,
the tough straw I lit on the peak,
will be flaming,
will be flaming.
Oh, see if the mountain still is in flames! And if there is fire, go to it,
child!
With your innocent tears
put out the fire;
cry over the blaze
and turn it to ash with your innocent tears.

Mark Strand, 18 *Poems from the Quechua*

According to the hermetic tradition, Mercury is polyhedral, changeable, *varius ille Mercurius,* says Dorneus; another author calls him versipellis (one who changes faces, one who is clever.) Generally he is considered as being of dual nature (duplex.) Of him it is said that he courses across the earth, equally enjoying the company of good and bad people. He is the "two dragons," he is the "twin" *(geminus)* formed of two natures or "substances." He is the *gigas geminae substantiae,* a qualification commented on by the text in Matthew, XXVI, wherein is discussed the institution of the Eucharist, whereby the analogy with Christ is made clear.

Carl G. Jung, *Symbolik des Geistes*

11.

(April 24, 1973)

Today we made love in the afternoon. It is Tuesday.

It was on a Tuesday afternoon that I came upon them together, him and Roseanne. The memory of the scene is so alive that today, while we were making love, I got to thinking that he was comparing me to her.

How does Roseanne make love?[1]

---

[1] Only after much reflection, without arriving at any liberative solution, roughly 73 days after the job of re-reading for the third time and annotating Simon's diary. I did set about doing the same with Vera's diary.

Today is April 21, 1981, a Tuesday, and the calendar lists two illustrious birthdays: Pierre Abelard, 1079, and Charlotte Bronte, 1816. To start anew today, for the fourth time, augurs well.

The reader has already noted that Vera's *Diary* precedes Simon's by one year, nevertheless I have placed hers after his. Actually Vera records and recounts events and episodes of their co- existence that preceded Simon's narrative which, among other things, also refers to these same events and episodes. I note, however, that the chronological leap between the two *Diaries* places the book in a different perspective. Vera's *Diary* suggests that the book is something in the making whereas Simon's *Diary* comes across as an already finished product. The two narratives intertwine as a totality reciprocally complementing each other, or so it seems, even though they remain technically autonomous. The labyrinth consists in determining who has managed to make his or her way out of it. Or are they all still caught in its mazes while I, with my notes, try my hand at cartography by mapping it out?

The main reason for the time delay before devoting myself to Vera's labour is, perhaps, due to the fact that I pursued Simon's remembrances much more than I did Vera's. Physically she attracted me very much but I was honor-bound to respect Simon's friendship and the traditions that he cultivated. So I always repressed my sensuality in her presence even though we both played perilously with our respective sensualities. Truth to tell I was attracted more to him than to her so that she soon realized that there were other copulations, all of them stupendous but seasonal. In short I could not fully believe that Simon was dead. One is dead when funeral services are held. Simon, instead, had simply vanished into the thin air. Hence I was convinced that Simon was alive in some country of this world, maybe even with a different identity and profession. For the death of a love also signifies dying of that love.

But Simon was a sorcerer more or less like his friend Elio.

I was suddenly and piercingly struck by an idea: Alaska! So I set out on June 20, 1980 with the pretext of going on a cruise whereas it was really an exploration. I liked the idea of impersonating H.M. Stanley who, after many vicissitudes, found his Livingstone. I was certain that he had hidden himself away in Ketchikan with Roseanne.

Oh, Ketchikan!

It was drizzling there when I prowled through it like a looter, inquiring of everybody about a certain Miss Spiram. And it certainly must be drizzling there today. It drizzles every day in Ketchikan, so much so that whoever goes there by boat or hydroplane looking for lumber and fish, minerals and fresh air soon realizes that the city's greatest resource is a liquid sunshine, and that which weather forecasts call precipitations, rainfall, showers. One gets soaked to the skin imperceptibly, absorbing one inch of water daily, 18 inches monthly and 22 feet yearly.

I also inquired of people in the countryside about Miss Spiram. They use the rain for their wells and cisterns, for augmenting the constant flow of brooks and streams where the salmon sprout, and as nourishment for lumber. The people wear wide-brimmed hats, and rubber jackets and trousers. Here rubber boots are perfectly in order with formal attire at evening dances and picnics.

Oh to see Simon and Roseanne in formal evening attire wearing rubber boots!

There are no Eskimos, no igloos, no polar bears nor icebergs. The marine climate is redolent of mud and fish, of humidity and fog. The City extends as far as the front docks of the port and covering it involves a walk of roughly three miles and in three hours everything comes to light under the liquid sunshine. Even Simon, I hope.

Fishing smacks and ferry boats, laden with lumber, and tankers mass on the Tongass Narrows, the channel that brings the ships from Pacific ports to Ketchikan. Even the few streets are piled up on the water line, bearing generic names: Front, Main, Water, Dock. Here is where unfolds the maritime life as well as that of the few remaining miners and gold seekers and of hurried visitors looking for wrought ivory and ounces of gold in the gift shops, or a glass of brandy at the Frontier Saloon or a bed at the Hilltop Lounge, or a bunch of flowers at Helen's, a slice of salmon at Angela's or at the Little Dipper. I went often to the Little Dipper.

Do you know a girl named Roseanne, Roseanne Spiram?

But it is the special smell of resin and oysters, of musk and of rotting bridges that swathes houses and streets that is instantly alarming. And it is sex. A sedentary traveler like myself has had visions. Couples walk as if fused in the liquid sunshine, following that mysterious, sexual stream which is in the air like invisible pollen, which is on door-knobs, on the old, chipped walls, on the big piles of lumber, on the smooth stones of the brooks where the salmon runs, as if broken-hearted, going upriver again in order to arrive at the source, deposit the eggs and then die.

On several occasions I halted couples, crying: Simon?

I was there just at the end of the season of sacrifice, the musky fog that tinges the environing Deer Mountain with phantasms, of the moist campers' tents in the forest filled with voices, footprints and flights of the eagle, of the brown bear, of the mink, of the cormorants and herons. I knocked on the tents of the camping sites, but I found only forget-me-nots in the forest paths. So thick was the forest that I could not see the rain through the trees. And I got to thinking that if I had been in love with love, if I had been Simon and she Roseanne, I would have come, or returned, here to Ketchikan. For, in fact,

We made love in the little room on the battered mattress which we had used during the first years of our marriage. It had become flaccid and lumpy with the passage of time and uncomfortable nights, one of us always atop the other with the innumerable couplings and uncouplings between brief, occasional dreams. No matter how much I beat it in the garden and spray it with special detergents it still smells of urine and sperm and the effect is suffocating. It's like dried-out leather and horse manure in stables. Once I passed my tongue over it first, especially during the afternoons of desire and dizziness, but he was away at school. I licked the dry roses of sperm, which today are rusty like decalcomanias and thus gave vent to my venery. But today, after Roseanne, it no longer attracts me.

He bought it at a sale in Scarsdale, Westchester County, N.Y., when Dress, my mother, bought us our first house in 1963. I didn't sleep much in it because at that time I was pregnant with Daniel and I spent a great deal of my time in New Canaan where my mother insisted I should give birth.

---

one comes to Ketchikan in order to make love with love, that is to say, in order to vanish from the face of the earth.

I didn't find them. But on Creek Street someone who was visiting the house run by Dolly, the prostitute of the "gold-fever" said, "Try Yellowknife. All lovers end up at Yellowknife." I recollected that Simon had been in the Yukon years before, Yellowknife was in the Northwestern Territories, in Canada. I became suspicious even if in that moment I shelved the idea. No, it's not so easy to play H.M. Stanley in search of David Livingstone.

Ah, Livingstone! Through an association of ideas I thought of the Livingstons of Anaconda, politically related to the Shaits, in consequence of which I returned to this slimy city of New York State with the intention of seeking the truth by interviewing G.O. Shait, Vera's present husband, over and over again. Why this idea? I was suddenly struck by the idea that G.O. had been the one who had disposed of my friend Simon also physically. But upon realizing, soon thereafter, that such ideas were foolish, I decided no longer to have ideas, not even that of meeting with G.O. Instead I promised myself to go ahead with the reading of the *Diaries* and to seek only in them for the key to the labyrinth.

With Daniel's birth, which coincided with Simon's first clamorous break with my mother, Dress evicted him from that house.[2]

And she at the same time insisted that I should divorce him, reminding me that she had two savings bank books for me: the first, containing a modest sum was for my studies; the second, containing lots of money ($175,000!) was for my adulthood when I would have found the man that she, too, would have approved as a groom, that is to say when she would have made the choice for me. But since I had made an insane choice by marrying Simon, she now wanted me to divorce him. She adduced two reasons: (1) she was afraid of Simon's intelligence and independence considered as important as her own intelligence and independence; (2) I and the baby, by living with her in the same house would serve as a shield against the flaccid presence of her husband, whose wretched existence had been reduced to correcting homework assignments in elementary French and to walking the dog in the garden.

She had never taught me to call him dad.

Like everybody else, in fact, I called him Prick, which was his name, a diminutive for Patrick. And he said nothing, never a word; he was totally aware of and offended by his situation but he could not escape, he had never wanted to escape. I believe that Dress, jealous and displeased, must have been wracked for many nights and days by the crazy notion that the stranger Simon was

---

[2] The reasons for that eviction are to be sought in the irrational component that resides in human reason. Connecticut has a hospital law that guarantees to the father, and to the father alone if he is findable within reach, the first visit to the woman in child-birth and to the new-born infant. Ms. Dress, relying on the strength of her purse, contended that she and she alone should be the first to visit her daughter and the new-born babe. When Simon arrived from Stamford, after risking his life on the icy highway, Ms. Dress violently attacked him in the ante-room and there she decided that her daughter would remain with her in New Canaan and that he had two days to vacate the house in Scarsdale.

Simon had often referred to this episode in the past in order to underline the difficulties of his relationships with his mother- in-law, the woman who had always looked at him with a lover's eye.

none other than her Italian lover who had died at sea at the outbreak of World War II. And that now, transformed, he had come back to her in the guise of Simon in order to retrieve his daughter by marrying her and thus relegate Dress to an unsmiling old age and to her wierdish widowhood.[3]

Desperate, my mother had even attempted to have him arrested in connection with the disappearance of some jewelry from the house in New Canaan, one Sunday when Simon had remained alone at home while we had gone to a wedding.

Simon told the police that he had spent his time on the porch, reading. And he declared that he had never set foot in the house, not even to fetch himself a glass of water. My mother had hidden the jewels in some drawer, but I don't believe that she had done so purposely. In fact she found them years later when to her resigned eyes we began to appear as a well-matched, compatible couple.

When she evicted him from Scarsdale, Simon realized that he had his back to the wall. The world continued to be against him. He had always said that the world was against him. But he did not want to be saved. He did not want to end up like Prick, the man who would have been so happy if I had called him "dad" even if only once and for all time. So Simon sold everything he had bought for our house, keeping only his books and his mattress. He rented a U-Haul and dragged that mattress back to his old studio in New York City, on East 94th Street.

I didn't want to divorce him but in this situation it was not even possible to live together especially because of the hemorrhages that afflicted me after the baby's birth. They were of great

---

[3] Capricious Ms. Dress believes in reincarnation. Her favorite book, as attested by Simon, was *The Edgar Cayce Story of Reincarnation* by Gina Cerminara, published in 1950. Among Simon's notes I found these sentences: "Have read in New Canaan, *Many Mansions* by Gina Cerminara, a gift from my mother-in-law. The sentences Dress drew to my attention are the following: *Love does not possess! Love is. Marriage usually begins in the illusion of love as possession. Its vicissitudes and sorrows are intended only that we shall learn the truth of love as being.*

help to my mother in her plan to super-protect me and keep me for herself. I had already recovered, I wanted and desired him so I went to New York once a week—even though Dress's approval contained a tacit reproach—and I became his weekend prostitute.

I carefully checked that mattress for signs of other occupants but all I could detect were the cat's prints. But I could not reproach him because he waited for me and I for him, in consequence of which we made love like two desperate persons. I really wanted to stay with him and start all over again with him so I urged him to take me away but now, as quickly as possible because I, too, wanted to escape from my mother's overbearingness. He understood and made a further sacrifice, giving up his teaching career at Yale. He accepted a teaching job with the University of British Columbia in Vancouver, Canada, which paid less but which, at least, had a fine supply of monkeys. And I didn't even know where Vancouver was!

"Punningly I call it Vaffancu, and it is located on the northern Pacific Coast. But it is beautiful, hygienic. Our son will grow up there and become a fisherman," he said. That was fine. But I had already decided to leave Daniel with my mother since I had no desire to play the mother role and she would be pleased to learn how to be a grandmother. But he insisted that I should return to fetch him once we were settled down. I agreed and we loaded all our belongings on the Imperial 63, the automobile which my mother had given us as a gift. And the mattress, of course.

From the East we set out for the Northwest, using the mattress in the orchards, on the edges of roads in the South, on the beaches of California, and in the woods of Oregon. We would stop and he would pull it out of the car. Once on the ground that mattress was already home, the encampment, copulation, canned foods, laughter, and our future.

We called the mattress Byron and Milly Bloom, Molly's Daughter.

One morning, as we were making love on that mattress, in our house in Vaffancu, an earthquake tremor paralyzed us. Crouched, he remained inside me, especially when the TV set fell from the stool accompanied by the noise of shattered window panes. Shuddering he said, "I've impaled you, I can't pull it out." I panicked, forgetting all about the earthquake. I had read about cases of priapism in medical pocket books and about how it required medical intervention. But if, on the one hand, I did not want the doctor or the ambulance to take us to the hospital fastened to each other, on the other, I wanted to get out of the house.

It had been a light quake. In order to calm me down, he said, "You'll see, there'll be no further quakes. We should phone First Aid."

We lived in a two-story house on the edge of the campus, and the telephone was on the lower floor. He lifted me up by my bottom and I suddenly realized that I was soaking wet, and it was blood. I figured that my menstrual period had begun one week in advance of schedule precisely because of my panic fear. I dripped as he carried me in that peculiar position across the room and down the stairs up to the kitchen where the phone was located, and I was dripping still all over his legs.

"There's only one way to do it," he said, laughing. "Origen's cut!"

Upon finally reaching the room below, Simon freed himself with a sudden backward thrust and set me down on the couch in a sitting posture. In between brief and nervous outbursts of laughter, licking the blood off his legs, I wept silently.

"Why did you want to scare me?"

"So as to make you forget the real scare, the earthquake."

And, in fact, I had already forgotten everything. The scattered pieces of the shattered TV set were all that remained of the earthquake's arrival, and a puddle of blood on the mattress was all that remained of Simon's priapism. He gathered up the splinters of glass, while I washed the mattress with a duster. And as I was engaged in cleaning up the mess, desire seized me again because the unfinished business remained inside me like a tug of anxiety. And this time the fucking lasted all day and it was different from every other time because we felt like people who had miraculously escaped disaster.

On the following day he paid homage to me by presenting me with one of his poems, a rare courtesy. It was titled "New Life", but I didn't understand what it should mean, save for that blood on the stairs.[4]

---

[4] *Since I found the poem among Simon's papers, I am reproducing it here. It is very strange and written in the style of Ted Hughes, the English poet who was the husband of the American poet Sylvia Plath, who committed suicide. It contains a remembrance of blood and even a distinct lugubrious air that is akin to Plath's imagination. I assume that in this poem, born of a grotesque incident that occurred in the first years of the Sixties, there is a suicidal germ of which, perhaps, the author was aware:*

> *Deafness is a leaping roundness at my knees*
> *Can you utter life from the dead bees*
> *Can you open the dead shutters*
> *Can you move in the dark around*
> *Can you fright the cold within*
>
> *I am not talking of autumn leaves*
> *Her mouth was rusty and blurred*
> *Her eyes had a sugarlumps glare*
> *The little blood left from the night*
> *Was a greenmint river on the stairs*
>
> *I tried to lick my bony elbow today*
> *Carved as an eel round my neck*
> *Children were playing on the railing*
> *Jet while that little blood was running on the deck*
> *She remained crushed on her own back*
>
> *There is a fight that starts from the day*
> *There is a door that opens only on the alley*
> *There is a whisper that thrives the lies*
> *But at night I'm only mortal, ma'am:*
> *A mountain in a mountain within spikes*

I wanted to free myself of that mattress. I wanted a king-size but he feigned deafness. And for awhile I did not insist. I knew that he was fond of that mattress because it symbolized home, family. To change mattresses for him signified a breaking-up of the home, like wife-swapping. And Italians with a tradition like his, stemming from immigrated peasants, change mattresses only when one of the spouses dies. Even divorce, or carnal separation, is like death for them.

His mother was born in Montreal, Canada. And his mother's father had been born in New Orleans, Louisiana, of Italian parents in the second half of the 19th century. Simon always contended that his maternal great grandfather, Rodolfo, fought in the confederate army during the American civil war. This Rodolfo became a Justice of the Peace in the Reconstruction period, while his son Tony became one of the white pioneers of jazz. But he betook himself to Montreal in 1891 when some Italians were lynched in a jail of New Orleans by a mob that had been incited to a murderous fury by the local media and authorities.[5]

As an old man he decided to leave Canada as well because of the cold and he settled down in Selimo, the Italian region from which his father had taken leave years before Garibaldi arrived there to unite it with the kingdom of Italy. Along with him he took his daughter, Concetta Immacolata, who was still a child at that time, and built a big house in Napelitte, the center of the village called Kalena, where he died. Concetta Immacolata married a town dandy and gave birth to three children. But she had always entertained that idea of returning to America. Fascism prevented its actualization, and she had to wait for more than twenty years. Immediately World War II came to a close, Concetta Immacolata was one of the very first to board an America-bound ship with her

---

[5] Apart from Bartolomeo Bellicapelli, a colleague of Simon, who traces the Mafia mystique back to that episode in 1891, Simon also has discussed it in his autobiographical memoir, *Selimo Selimo*, already cited.

husband and her two youngest children. Simon stayed behind because at that time he was studying in Paris. One of the books written when Simon was a young man, published in Milan in 1958, begins with the following sentences: "My mother returned to her country along the route of the immigrants. She returned there bringing with her the mattress, all her dishes and glasses, and a portrait of her dead father. Six thousand miles of sea!"

His face contorted when I told him that I was fed up with life in Vaffancu and that he should find a new teaching job in the States. "For me America is where I am well off," he said. Later, nevertheless, he accepted an offer from the University of California, so we transferred to Los Angeles with the mattress duly loaded in our Imperial 63.

We set up home in Malibu in a house on the water from which we could fish while seated on the terrace. Daniel continued to remain with his grandmother in New Canaan because I felt no particular affection for him whereas he was a consolation for my mother, poor woman. Simon protested, but I told him quite clearly: "If you insist you will have neither me nor Daniel, because I'll divorce you."

It was like a slap in the face, but in the end he resignedly bowed to my threat. We made many trips together but he always avoided going to New Canaan to meet his son. He was thinking of his mother-in-law, not of his son. And when in 1967 I told him that I was also fed up with California and that I wanted to return to New York City he almost hit me. "According to your lights," he said, "am I always to begin all over again from scratch? Leave a job and find another one the moment we're acclimatized to it?" He stormed out of the house in a fury and went fishing on the Grand River in the Rocky Mountains. When he came back, he was in a totally different state of mind. He said that he had met a doctor and a chemist from Anaconda, New York, and that they had suggested that he transfer and go to work with them.

Even this move turned out to be easy.

In Anaconda we bought a house and other furniture and, at long last, also a king-sized bed. But we had also brought the old mattress along with us, and it has now found its proper place in the small room. I had the presentiment that the transfer of that mattress signified not only a slight alienation from him, but also from ourselves. Such turned out to be the case, in fact. When Simon's parents came for a visit they slept on that mattress in the small room. When Daniel came from New Canaan he slept on that mattress. And when his sons came from Italy or when his friends came for a visit they also slept on that couch. It had become a place of arrival for everybody, but no longer for us. And one day Simon was to bring also Roseanne onto that mattress.

Today he brought me there too, a Tuesday afternoon.

12.

We have made love in the afternoon so many times. The reason for this is that we did not have daily office hours or fixed days of rest for extravagances. A professor is always free, even when he is working, for whether he be in the office or at home, he is always working. Sex is the logical sublimation of this continuous work.

On the other hand, today's American academic life encourages constant production and not so much specialized research work that requires years; it does not wait for the masterpiece of the historian, of the philosopher or of the man of letters, the great books. Rather, it demands specific works, something quickly put together, like text-books. Simon is aware of this so, with a monotonous regularity, he produces studies and monographs with which he himself, often, is not content but which permit him to remain on the uppermost rung of the ladder. In the university ambience publications and research studies have only the frame of the ancient humanistic passion. One publishes only in order to arrive at political positions within the administration, or in order to be promoted, or in order to obtain lifetime tenure. But given the economic restrictions that ever weigh on private and state universities alike and which are the underlying causes for dismembering departments, for firings which lead to court suites and litigation lasting for years, indeed department heads often must turn to private persons for funds and donations which allow some programs to be kept alive. Simon himself is almost always involved in campaigns for the collection of hundreds of thousands of dollars so as to assure the survival of his monkeys and of his experiments. And in order to do so he not only immerses himself in conferences and embarks on trips of all kinds but also produces, together with Andrew, a series of scientific films with a sexual base inasmuch as he is of the opinion that sex should be taught in schools at all levels since it lies at the base of every human and social activity.[6]

After the laboratory and the seminars he comes back home if he so wishes, and he often brings friends and students along: they talk, write, study labyrinthine maps, or they just listen to music. With Simon one is always in the classroom. He writes, paints, plays the organ, rides a motorcycle, works in the garden, cooks, visits his monkeys. He knows a little of everything (in gloomy moments he is won to repeat, "I was born dead because I belong to the times of Leon Battista Alberti, and those times have gone forever!"), but above all he is a consummate conversationalist.

Often we give parties which he does not deduct from his income tax as professional expenses, despite my insistence. They

---

[6] True.

There were colleagues, however, not wholly convinced of his efforts to draw money and prestige into his studies channel.

Professor J.J. De Pepperoy, a former chairperson of Simon's Department, sharply and bitterly criticized Simon's undertakings. On the occasion of a Symposium which officially inaugurated a CENTER FOR SUBJECTIVE ANTHROPOLOGY in Anaconda, Professor De Pepperoy sent the following sarcastic mini memo to administrators and colleagues:

A month has passed since the Dona Symposium was held, and so we are able now to analyze its meaning from a little distance. Our main conclusion has to be that Professor Dona has done nothing to dispel the inescapable judgment that the Center and the Symposium are just alternative names for his own illustrious person. The Center and the Symposium have never existed as objective entities, either en el parto *or* antes del parto, *and especially those entities continue not to exist* despues del parto, *even if Professor Dona has had ample time to regularize the situation, if he had ever wanted to do so, which does not seem to be the case. Great efforts have been made to convince us that Professor Dona, his Center and his Symposium are a holy trinity, three individual entities united by one purpose, but the only god—or the only idol—we can see is the ubiquitous Mr. Dona himself: the sole owner and manager of the whole show. When we are told that the Center has been officially inaugurated we must realize that since there is no organization that may be called the Center, what has been inaugurated is the person of Mr. Dona. Let us congratulate our colleague for having succeeded in this unprecedented feat: the official inauguration of a self-glorified individual. He ought to send a note on this rare event to the Guinness Book of Records in order to have it registered for immortality.*

involve cultural activities linked to his professional work, but he prefers to deduct his trips having to do with his professional researches rather than fiscally exploit his social encounters and friendships which often are the prime impulse and the financial backing for his journeys on behalf of his scholarly pursuits. We have a lot of friends but Cara and Bart, Peter and Punks are the ones closest to us, and it is only rarely that we get a visit from Matthias and his wife, Sue, with whom I have had ties of friendship for many years. Nevertheless we enjoy a perfect harmony with them.

We are never in agreement on everything with Simon, instinctively realizing that each one of us would have done exactly what he or she planned to do, sharing the woe or the weal ensuing from the action. But in the matter of love we have always been in agreement and, like him, I prefer it in the afternoon, the siesta hours in which I melt away and swoon. In the Spring, desire suddenly comes over me in the car or in the library or watching the bulge in the pants of someone walking alongside me. I never raise my eyes when I walk, but I do keep them half-raised, thereby checking the point of my sandals and that which appears to me at medium level, that is, legs, bodies, then the face and then the trunk, the legs and, again, the point of my sandals. At home, however, I complain if he is not there. I vent my feelings by getting down to work on my Ph.D. thesis which, given the market, is worth nothing. *And I am no scholar!* Yet, recently, I have not made love in the afternoon for several weeks. And it is only for this reason that I suspected that he was comparing me to Roseanne.

The little three-quarter bed, the mattress of our first years of marriage and now of his affair with Roseanne, was a premeditated choice on his part.

"This is the bed of sex," he told me once, "whereas the other, the king-size is the bed of love."

I understood what he meant, but now I also know that I am very jealous of this mattress in the small room. Is love jealous? I had seen myself as brought up in a system that views jealousy as a crime against the independent person, and I was mistaken. Instead, jealousy gnaws away at me and, at times, it makes me see things through dark, tragic, movie-like tones.

I see that everything is crumbling and I'm afraid of dying under the ruins. So now while he was caressing me, I was thinking of Roseanne, then of Roseanne with us two, she in my skin and in his, I with her and with him and she with me and with him. I became so ecstatic over these thoughts that as a result of persistently pursuing them further I came, suddenly, but my whole body was suffused by a supreme, sinking feeling of utter sweetness. Alas, it was too soon because he was still pulsating inside me and this time—strangely—like a miner: seeking, whirling around, beating, caressing, biting, riveting me, slavering. I came again and this time the Van Goghian suns re-appeared to my eyes, those I had seen as an adolescent with Matthias.[7]

They were in my eyes and on my face, I was tattooed with sun-flowers. But soon the mind resumed dominion over the senses and the torturing analyses. Did Roseanne ever enjoy a moment like this? Did she ever have an orgasm? Did she ever take his member in her mouth? Had she ever taken a shower together with him? Did she ever have anal sex with him?

I reasoned in this way, being now sexually passive because actually Roseanne was not with us and I was not she even if for a certain period of time I had not given myself to him but to her in the anxiety of a stupid emulation which after all was wholly in my mind. But my pleasure had been succeeded by the anxiety that he

---

[7] In 1954, when Vera was 14, vacationing in a summer cottage in New England, she had her first sexual experience with a married man, Matthias, Sue's husband. But it was not until 1962 that Vera wrote about that episode and of other episodes before that. She wrote about them in New York City at Simon's request. Those *Diaries* also form pan of Simon's behest.

may love her more than me, and this gave the afternoon a touch of sadness. Also because I wanted to believe that my thoughts were inconsistent as, after all, Simon did love me well and very effectively in the extended, oriental manner marked by rapid and sinuous movements inside and outside my flesh. My second orgasm was devastated by the way he brought it to a conclusion in an absolutely new way. He withdrew and came on my breasts which was exceedingly strange since I was taking the pill.

"Why did you do that?" I asked him, flabbergasted. I looked at his warm sperm on my nipples.

"You can eat it, if you like."

I gathered it up with a finger and I ate it. I suddenly felt most unwell. Now I was certain that he had been thinking about her while making love to me since coming outside was his contraceptive method. He was against abortion in principle. But he quickly drew me to himself again, adjusted his body to mine and said, "Let's sleep now. It was very beautiful!"

He slept like a baby, sucking a nipple while I caressed his hair. I didn't know whether I loved him. But he had give me comfort, he had given me pleasure. Nevertheless, perhaps stupidly, I asked, "Has Roseanne ever had an orgasm?"

He gave a start.

"Why do you bring her up?" he asked.

"I would have liked her to have been with us this afternoon."

"It's a thing of the past, over and done with. Does it still bother you?"

"Not any more. But I would like to be her friend."

"It's dangerous. Are you looking for trouble?" he said, smiling.

I took his hand and placed it on my cunt. I wanted to be masturbated. He understood and did it with a delicacy that made me come. It was a different kind of orgasm, and it gave me a sudden yen to eat cheese. And in fact we ate some together, in a big hurry, suddenly realizing that we both had to get back to school. As we were getting into the car curiosity overcame me again and I asked: "What kind of orgasms does Roseanne have? Clitoral?"

He did not answer, looking suddenly sad. We parted company in the parking lot, he walking toward his office, I toward the library. It seemed like a real separation. In fact both of us forgot to make the customary appointment to meet later so that we could go back home in the only car we had. But that had happened many times before and we always waited for each other in the parking lot.

Determined to continue my work on the *Amoretti,* I went to my cubicle in the library. A message scotch-taped on the door made me change my mind. "If you'd like a coffee, you'll find me at Ratt's." It was from Slingerlink, my thesis adviser, who was an affable and distinguished Spenserian scholar. I went. By a strange coincidence Matthias was having a cup of coffee with him. Both of them looked at me guessing that I had just been making love. I half-shut my eyes and again felt normal.[8]

---

[8] In the preceding footnote I referred to other diaries written by Vera at Simon's suggestion in New York in 1962 when the two lived together as lovers. They deal with her mother, her father. New England and, above all, with a personage called Matthias Freedman, who at that time was Dean of a University in Maine. The Simon-Roseanne relationship which at this point seems so greatly to disturb Vera, had been experienced by Vera herself when, unwittingly, she played a role even more intimate than that which Roseanne had played with Simon.

In the light of this document it can be assumed that Vera was, ab initio, an unwitting provocateur of sexual reactions from adults and, significantly, from married men one of whom, Simon, divorced his first wife in order to take up with her and the other, Matthias, was deeply hurt by it.

The style of the pages that follow is more direct and unconstrained than the recent diaries, but in no way less valid. At 14 Vera was already a clever expert in matters of subterfuge, lying, self-flagellation and self-sublimation. Although she suffered from no economic necessity, her flight to Bath, Maine, to work as a summer nursery-maid in Matthias' house also reveals another aspect of her personality: to escape her mother's super- protection and to seek self-liberation in the world on her own. This is the text:

Despite the idealistic nature of my relationship with Matthias, who played the dual role of lover and father, there were two grave defects in the curious course of my existence during that summer. The game involved infinite subtleties and I, in my unconsciousness and innocence, probably played the roles of nursery-maid, of friend to

Matthias' wife and that of being only a fortuitous friend to Matthias, with much more ease than I could conscientiously display today. In my situation of that time I was ignorant of what I was doing to myself, to Matthias, to Sue. At that age I knew only that I loved what was unforeseeable and bright in life, and I loved to weave lively colors together, the reds counterpoised to the violets. I nourished my imagination with intrigues and uncertainties, uncaring of the effects that they could have on others.

It is a surprising experience to re-examine the past with different eyes. It is a little like looking into a kaleidoscope in which the tiny pieces of glass have been systematized into a regular, perfect scheme. Later when we again look into the kaleidoscope we note the irregularities and the imperfections in what had first seemed an ideal situation. The red and violet colors now contain tiny black chips.

All that I knew about myself at that time was that I was bored by my life and by people in general. I was fed up with being a child, so I ventured forth into the adult world that was waiting for me, but which I found within easy reach. Matthias in fact was waiting for me. He wanted to be distracted from his life and I from mine. It was normal therefore that together we should take a brief, magnificent flight, now inexplicable. It is something that still makes him blush a little today, but which suggests to me a friendly and maternal smile as regards him. He revealed his defects to me with a stubborn simplicity, in the manner of a child who shows his moth- eaten toy to a stranger.

Matthias, among other things, had no strength of will to resist the temptations of any woman or girl who to his view possessed a minimum of femininity. As if in a strange dance we hypnotized each other and like swollen and flexible reeds we reciprocally bent to our desires. What a magic that summer! The fragrance of the woods, the lapping of the water on our legs, and the light but wild rubbing of the pine needles against the sides of the house where we lived. The suggestions were too strong for us and like two small, lower suns of Van Gogh, we revolved with ever greater velocity in that motion of our attraction until we united. He was the First Man and I was the First Woman in our world of that time, and that which surrounded us, objects and persons, were only shadows and superficial imprints in our absolute.

What folly drove me to live with Sue, to be her friend by day and her betrayer by night? And what induced her to tolerate my presence?

Matthias and I both knew that she was aware of what was happening. But she continued to smile at me and to confide in me notwithstanding. We were apparently open and honest in regard to ourselves, but underneath that honesty lay a disastrous silence. Sue wasn't stupid. She understood, and I liked her for this reason. She, too, had had an experience similar to mine once when Matthias had been away from home. The "trapped wife" had felt terribly alone one New Year's eve so she had accepted an invitation to a party for distraction's sake. There she met a young doctor, the same one who attended to her children when they were ill. Sue is a methodical and sensible woman, but that night she forgot to be herself. The doctor accompanied her home after the party, and she invited him into her bedroom.

It was such a stupid thing that when Matthias returned she told him all about it to his face, asking him to help her. But Matthias made no attempt whatsoever to understand her, and poor Sue, desperate, accused him of having been a poor husband. She ended up by seeing a shrink but Matthias refused to accompany her. He said that she alone was responsible for her actions, and that what was done could not be undone. Matthias left her to her own devices, inflicting terrible punishments on her.

In the meanwhile the doctor's wife had also learned about the happening. In a big city something of this kind would have passed unobserved, nobody would have paid it any attention and nobody would have cared. But in Bath the doctor's wife decided to make her story known to the whole town and to make of Sue a modern Esther Prynne. Instead a war broke out. At a cocktail party, attended by the town's elite, the doctor's wife seated herself on a divan already occupied by Sue and at a certain moment she emptied a glass of scotch into her face. It was at this point, I believe, that Matthias realized how alone his wife was, and how much he had forsaken her at the moment when she needed him most.

These events took place in the summer before the summer I spent with Mathias and Sue. Matthias was still debating with himself as to whether or not he should see a shrink because he felt at once confused and outraged. But he was afraid to sit in front of a stranger and unload his troubles. And, among other things, there were many elements in his own character which he did not fully understand and with which he had never managed to engage in disputation.

I met him when he was at such a point of exhaustion that all his defenses had fallen and everything in him was vulnerable. He lived like a robot, trying not to think so as not to magnify his problems. He tried to forget his wife's betrayal and his shame in front of the townspeople, assuming an indifferent and detached air as if he no longer cared about what she did, with whom she went to bed. Truth to tell, his laugh was hallow and raucous and when he smiled his mouth formed a grimace. Matthias was a dead shell, and I was consumed with a desire to restore life and faith to him. I had his souls in my hands at one of the most memorable moments in his life.

At first he watched me only with one eye, diffident like an animal caught in a trap. Then he realized that I was completely harmless, and he let himself go.

* * *

Our nightly appointments had taken the form of flights into the darkness.

Sue would go to bed early and I would sit in the living room of the ground floor reading or listening to the insects madly beating wings against the window-panes. Waiting until Matthias contrived the reasons for the nightflight became an essential part of my relationship with him. Each meeting was characterized by a prelude of bogus "good nights" that I managed to pick up from the place where I was seated while my heart began to throb in my ears and I was suddenly overcome by a sensation of hollowness that contrasted strangely with a desire of an excruciating, indefinite character. I remember once that I was on the verge of screaming and fainting since this feeling of unhappiness that suddenly swept over me had become intolerable. The sight of Matthias descending the stairs wearing a dark blue sweater and a pair of kakhi shorts so excited me that I wanted to rush at him in order to touch him, kiss him and let him bite me. I wanted to become a vital part of him and to force him to become a vital part of me. I wanted to walk inside of him, read his thoughts, feel what he was feeling, know the things that he knows and hate the things that he hated. For I knew that Matthias was crushed under the weight of his many hatreds. But this was belied by his casual, indifferent air as he came down the stairs a complete body separated from me, as I was with my feet glued to the floor, my leaden, fingers automatically clutching the arms of the chair as in one of Picasso's cubist figures.

"Well, are we ready for a swim?"

Usually the night was cold when we set out for the rocks. On the beach there was a shack used as a sauna, and sometimes Matthias would light a fire in the ancient pot-bellied stove. Then he would put stones on the stove and when they were sufficiently hot he poured water over them in order to change the heat into steam. I always manage to see him when he silently goes about his work in the tiny shack. And when enough steam was generated we took off our clothes and sat on the benches waiting for the vapors to make us sweat and suffer. The sauna is a real agony, especially when the heat penetrates the skin, burning it to the point where it becomes red. When the heat became intolerable we would run out together to the lake, diving into the cold water.

Shivering with cold, laughing at ourselves, naked like miniscule white fish, we let the water, smooth and hard as cold marble, caress our bodies and then he began to talk about the Italian Renaissance, hedonism, about Walter Pater's interest in Botticelli, Michelangelo and Leonardo whereas his real interest revolved only around the realization that no fixed principles, religious or moral, exist that can be considered certain and that. in consequence. the only thing worth living for is the momentary joy because the soul dissolves to death within elements fated nevermore to be reunited.

Once I read the conclusion of Pater's famous book, Studies in the History of the Italian Renaissance *(1873) which left me perplexed.*

"We have an interval and then our place knows us no more. Some spend this interval in listlessness, some in high passions, the wisest in art and song. For our one chance is in expanding that interval, in getting as many pulsations as possible into the given time. High passions give one this quickened sense of life, ecstasy and sorrow of love, political or religious enthusiasm, or the 'enthusiasm of humanity'."

Only one must be sure that it if a passion that begets a quickened, multiplied consciousness. Matthias was the first man who ever spoke to me of consciousness. And the sauna, probably, was *the viaduct for this strange consciousness. For us now it had the significance of a purification rite educated to the superstition. And once we were purified in the sauna we sat down like Greek statues on enormous white towels laid out on the water's edge. But often, after the sauna, we repaired to an old abandoned house which smelt of freshly cut pine. There Matthias stretched himself out on the enormous bed with brass railings and I would massage his back, pulling his hair and biting his lips in order to excite him. The game of pursuit started immediately and when he caught me he buried me underneath him with his legs over mine while his hands nailed my arms to the mattress. This lay was followed by a long silence, interrupted only by our long breathing and the noise made by our mouths that moved rapidly, drinking the blood of life from each other like vampires. I now knew every part of his body and nevertheless refused that which he passionately wanted from me. I would excite him to a maximum pitch but then I would leave him alone, too frightened to continue. But he was very nice about it and realized that I was afraid of the pain of defloration. My limited imagination also feared that if I let myself be penetrated by Matthias I would become a whore and that he would be disgusted with me. At that time I was not yet aware of the strength that women have and of the completely different effect that complete carnal possession can have in stimulating and deepening a relationship.*

I vividly remember Matthias' agony the first time we went into the pine-scented little house! As we lay in the bed, he whispered into my ear, "It would be nice for you and for me. It would be very nice!" But I moved to one side when he began to crawl over me, panting, twisting and writhing. I watched him, looking vulnerable and almost ridiculous, when in the throes of orgasm he began to tremble and bounce up and down on my body. In my fear I almost laughed at his strange, repellent actions, utterly alien to me. His hand sought mine in a blind fury so that I should help him in the final liberating touch. Instead, I saw an absolutely comic side in all those junctions, but then I was suddenly saddened at the sight of his pathetic twistings and turnings, and by his lamentations. In wonderment I discovered that those movements which at first seemed to me to be those of a puppet that mimes an act to elicit public compassion were, instead, the anxieties of a man overcome by excitement, swept away to sea by the sprawling and mobile waves of desire. I adapted myself to the rhythm of his body and I gave him my hand so that he could teach me how to free himself from that obsession. "Take it! Hold it tight!" His hand moved frenetically over mine wrapped around his member which at that moment was in a state of complete erection. "Take it in your mouth. Now, now!" He tried to force my head downwards towards his groin, but his brusque and raucous voice had placed me on the defensive. I gave him a shove, pushing him on his side and I left him there lying on the bed alone and with himself, letting him come by himself and on his own. When it was all over, with the sperm spots lying in a glacial puddle he took my head between his hands and pressed it against his chest. "Did I frighten you, Bes? Forgive me!" After which he fell asleep like a child.

We woke up many times during that first night together. And each time he wanted to start all over again. Finally, when the sun began to color the sky with a blue subtly matched by the darker blue of the lake, Matthias, smiling, said: "The problem with you is that you excite me and then you get scared and you don't want to finish what you yourself had started. If you didn't mean anything to me, I would have already had you, believe me. I would have already taken you at least a dozen times. Now you must know that you can't play around with a man the way you play, especially if you lie naked with him, and on your back". Matthias became a strict teacher and taught me how to defend myself against any man in lustful heat. Hit him on the balls! "Even if you happen to be the man?" I asked. "No, no," he replied. "It's so painful that murder might be the response. And I wouldn't kill you. "

"Bes, listen. I've got to go now. I must be home before Sue wake sup. I'll see you tonight when I get back from work. o.k."?

I suddenly became conscious of the cold.

"Matty!"

"Whats it you want now?"

"...oh, nothing. I'll see you tonight, o.k.?"

He leaned over the side of the bed almost touching my head. "Bes, before I go, tell me clearly I LOVE you. "

"I can't. And you Matty?" I called him Matty the way he called me Bes.

He remained silent, and then he took off without saying a word, slipping away among the trees. He slid into nothingness. And I remained on the bed, exhausted, except for a great feeling of languor and that sudden sense of solitude that makes a woman dependent in love. I got up to call out to him, but I was calling out into the void. Then I began to cry until I fell asleep.

* * *

Matthias was honest with me, at least in admitting that for him our relationship represented an escape from routine, from the house, from his children, whom he adored. His love for me was fashioned of dismantled stones and I soon realized that even our moon, the trees and the lake in which we bathed in the nude were made of paper-mache. I was growing up. During one of our nocturnal trysts Matthias had a crisis of conscience and voiced his guilt feelings. It was hard for him. He told me how much he loved his wife, Sue, and how much he had made her suffer. But he considered her to be the guilty party and could not bring himself to forgive her.

So I said to him, "Why do you want to revenge yourself with me?"

He was at a loss for words, flabbergasted. He looked at me in a different way now, not as an enemy but as if I represented one more worry to be added to his worries over his wife. He stood aloof from me for a moment just as Sue had stood aloof for him and for me: let the world come tumbling down! Nevertheless she got used to a husband who eyed me for long stretches of time, and she got used to inventing excuses for helping me in the kitchen or when I took the children out swimming on the lake because like Matthias she, too, wanted to remain attached to me in a relation that should not become a total estrangement from him.

Then came the night when she knew that there could be no lingering doubts as to my relationship with Matthias. And this was also the most embarrassing night of my life. Matthias would come into my room, barefooted, around 1 a.m. and remain there for an hour or two. He would enter very cautiously and quietly without waking me up until he had slipped between the sheets and began to cover me with kisses. I would wake up to find his body on top of mine as his hands were already clasping me in a frenetic embrace. And we would remain that way, hot and sweaty as we hugged each other in the sultry darkness. He would come over on me, after which he would leave wordlessly and return to the room he shared with Sue. But on that particular night one of the babies began to cry. Matthias jumped out of my bed, he very much loved his children and was an excellent father. But at the very moment that he left my room Sue was already in the hallway.

"Matty, what were you doing in Bes's room?"

"Oh, we were just talking. After all you have your shrink and all I have is Bes. "

This utterance was sarcastic, but nevertheless it seemed to be laden with affection for her. Then there was silence, then the quiet rubbing of bare feet on the floor, the baby's cry in his sleep, and then a new silence that enveloped the house. In the morning I would have preferred to die rather than sit down at the table around which the whole family was gathered for breakfast.

"Good morning, Bes."

"Good morning, Matty... Good morning, Sue."

Sue faced that morning with a seeming unconcern, but with utmost skill. Her cordiality underwent no change, but I knew that she wanted to show Matthias that his nightly escapades with me did not bother her at all. Several days later I heard from Matthias that Sue had asked him whether he had ever kissed me. And he had answered, "Yes, once or twice." She smiled at him, and never again raised the subject.

Often, when she lay alone in bed, Sue must have heard the squeak of the metal canoe being lowered in the water, or the splash of the swimmer and/or my happy burst of laughter. But she must have also realized that, sexually, she was no longer compatible with him. It was also obvious, to her not to me, that Matthias was becoming aware of his

13.

You came to look for me in the library to my utter surprise, and you smiled at me and caressingly rested a hand. I find that very strange, you know.

What of me and you remains with you and me is not this particular minute but yesterday afternoon. The night following the afternoon, which we also spent together in the usual room and in the usual bed, has been so cancelled out now that you are beside me that I cannot manage even to recall the many other nights of our life spent together in a state of remorse or weariness. If you were to ask me, as you always do, to write down what we did last night, even what we ate, the phone calls received, I could write down nothing because I have no memory of last night. And now you come and you ask, "Are you feeling better?" with your strange smile.

When you noticed my diary open on the table I understood your curiosity and without the slightest hesitation I said, "You can read it, if you wish." But as I was telling you to read it, you had already done so because I saw you flip through the pages at a rate

---

age, he was afraid of growing old so that it was also a plausible notion that he should play with new toys like me who would eventually leave him along again with her, Sue.

That summer was full of double lives, of secrets and of hypocrisy. On several occasions Sue invited to dinner a very handsome and distinguished man whom Matthias called Walter. Walter Pater, sarcastically. And she made Matthias and me understand that she wanted to be alone with him. It was a wound returned in the mad joy of a polite revenge. But, in reality, we were all children making faces at each other, engaged in a silent and subtle war hidden under the masks of smiles and happy faces.

The children knew nothing of all this. And they saw no difference between me and their mother when, nude, we swam together with their father, also in the nude.

of 500 words per minute thanks to your speed-reading skills. This horrifies me. Usually you read a book in a half hour, and you annotate it in two hours after a re-reading. You read 30/40 books a week while I require three days, five for a James novel, and spend two weeks in re-reading it and making notes. What horrifies me is your racing around in a thousand directions which disorients me and leaves me behind.

Now, however, I feel stronger after yesterday afternoon.

You said: "I've the impression that you have invented 90% of your feelings by committing them to writing, and now that they are down on paper they serve you as an alibi every time you feel like accusing me of something."

"It's only my point of view of the situation," I reported. Then you picked up the diary and said, "I'll now write my point of view right above this, o.k.?" You went out and came back in 15 minutes. "It's all here. Now I'm going back to my office. As for tonight... if you'd like, come pick me up and we'll go home together."

I paid no attention to what he had said, but I began to read what he had written:

It began this way, Vera, a few minutes ago in your cubicle where, full of love, I dropped for a visit. You wanted to ask me why I had a strange smile on my face, but you did not do so. You sat back in your seat in order the better to determine whether a relationship between you and me still existed. Your diary is more intelligent than accurate and now you are using it to erect walls. Instead of making true revelations in the diary you begin to hide things and to hide yourself in it. The diary of your life in New England, that I asked you to write at the beginning of our relationship in New York, had a greater "purity".

I compare you? I didn't even remember that yesterday was Tuesday. And the other Tuesday, the one you cite involving Roseanne, had been cancelled from my memory for a long time. I simply don't understand why you should insist upon bringing it up. Actually, I know why: that Tuesday serves your purposes more than mine. This is so because you want to run away, you are at a turn in the road and are looking for a big excuse. I compare you? Roseanne wasn't at all in my consciousness yesterday afternoon when I was making love with you. But now, after some reflection or perhaps because your diary suggests it to me, I must admit that Roseanne s image at a certain moment came between you and me. It was when you arched your back, raising your pelvis higher so that you could receive me more snugly inside yourself. It was something that you had never done before.

Roseanne is built differently from you. She has a round, high arse, a distant, hidden pubis, almost attached to her back and it is difficult to reach in a perfectly horizontal position. Roseanne becomes a pallium and an offertory. In order to effect entry I had to lift her legs onto my shoulders and bend her over by 90 degrees, a position that introduces and guarantees a certain amount of balance in the pleasure procured but this also entails a certain amount of pain. With you, instead, the Franciscan position is beautiful because your pubis is very exposed, it is a frontal star. It is nearer to the navel than to the back. You have a pear-shaped arse, whereas hers has the form of an orange. Now, here s the comparison you seemingly wanted: entry with you is easy as is remaining there, I being the bucket and you the well. And yesterday, as many, many times before, it was beautiful to make love to you. Would you like to know what two professors of mathematics were saying today as they were eating the sandwiches prepared for them by their wives the night before? "Do you fuck regularly?" They confessed to each other that it was no longer regular, perhaps once a month. And one of them admitted with an appalling metaphor, "We are like two blocks of marble in the graveyard of our bed."

Oh, Vera, if our love dies it will not be because of Roseanne. It's convenient to play the injured party, now. The difficult thing to learn, if we want to continue to be together, is merely to re-discover ourselves with absolute probity.

Shall we try it?

I bend over these pages and I feel the hollowness of my life. Try it? I would like to, but I am more disenchanted than ever. One gets used to love the way one gets used to the suffering of love. Why not try it? In fact the sufferance of love is something that could be overcome by other commitments, indeed by other loves. But what I don't want now is to be left alone with myself. I want to be "me" and no longer me with "you" or in terms of you. My confessions began from the moment that you asked them of me, Father Confessor. So that you could nourish yourself on me. Now I'm going to throw everything topsy-turvy and all alone with myself I shall set out towards that great experience because what in reality urges me on beckoningly, at age 33, is precisely the great experience. And at this point I avail myself of your beloved lung. He writes: "The *One* does not wish to choose the *Other* because he is afraid of losing his character, and the *Other* breaks off from the *One* in order to exist."

I am the *Other*, Simon![9]

---

[9] The defect of a diary is the excruciating monotony of the hours spent in writing it and, so it seems, exclusively for the purpose of sublimating absolutely personal matters without which neither this type of personalities or this type of sublimations would exist. The positive thing about a diary is that it is an education in the style of feelings. Feelings that dredge the grave. The diary itself is a form of death. The energy that flows to write it fills the whole day, and then it draws near night. But there is a zest also in dying because, actually, every confession is a defeat. Only this dying is always a re-dying, a ritual sacrifice that conserves energy and religiosity in itself.

One gets the impression that Simon and Vera, suspected of sin since the beginning of their relationship, managed to stay together through the years thanks to the confessions contained in the diaries but which the passing years themselves have distorted as regards moods, style and creativeness.

It seems strange that Vera herself should write about herself and Matthias, yet a strain of constant paranoia courses through her diaries, from those written in New York to those of most recent date, detectable in the exuberant description of emotion as well as in its classification, now consisting of sexual cerebralism above all.

Since it is Simon himself who reminds his wife of her earlier diaries, described as containing a greater "purity" than the later ones, and since it is Vera who finally resolves to throw everything to the winds which appear almost to have been "extorted" from her by the Father Confessor, i.e. Simon, I deem it necessary to reproduce some fragments from the earlier diaries. Like the pages on Matty, they are reminiscences written in New York City in 1962 when she would stop over for the night or for the week-end in Simon's studio on East 94th Street. At that time Simon lived with his Roman wife and his two children, Sandro and Dino, plus an Italian governess, in an apartment on Riverside Drive near Columbia University. And when he would leave her to return to his family, Vera killed the time by writing about herself knowing that he would read her notes on the following day. It was a form of continuing co-existence even during temporary separations, and a way of making a clean breast of things and saying, "This is my present and this is my past: now do with me whatever you please!"

The history of the affair with Matthias re-emerges from the following fragments. It seems to have been a traumatic experience in Vera's life and along with it there emerges a bitter-sweet tale about a contemporary of hers called Clair. For the first time Vera voices a certain affection in regard to her father, Patrick, even though at that time she already knew that she was the illegitimate daughter of an Italian sailor.

Other elements come to light even though certain data are not stressed. On the basis of some researches that I have conducted recently it turned out that New Canaan is, in fact, the town in Connecticut where Vera was born and where her mother was born. Her mother still owns a clothing shop, a kind of Army & Navy store, in New Canaan while Patrick, who taught French in the local high school, recently died of cancer. Patrick hailed from Bath, Maine, where he had a house in which Vera spent her childhood and adolescence, where she felt the constrictions of the New England atmosphere deeply within her, so much so that she hankered to escape.

These remembrances, so suffused with the New England atmosphere, once more reveal Vera's passionate nature and the ways, now direct and now vague and undefined, with which she sought her very first and lucid experiences.

(New York, June 12, 1962)

You have just left and I am looking out on the empty street below, pressing my nose against the window pane, trying to still get a glimpse of you as you hurry homeward where your children and supper await you. But I never manage to see you, and that strikes me as symbolic: you stay with me for a certain time in this room full of whisperings and in which drums and trumpets are played in muffled tones amid the hum of the air conditioner, and then you disappear without a trace into the savage din of the city. All that remains to me is the contact of your lips on mine, the song of your raucous laughter, akin to that of a bear, and which echoes in my head. I feel something warm and marvelous towards you which I can express only with a ready-made expression: "I love you." But it is so void of sense for me right now because I have repeated it so many times before during my dolorous and awkward adolescent flirtations and even later, when I became a Lolita. Thinking over these times, I see now that I was talking to the air, to a languid and laden shadow, to a mask in space, to a sneering mask. I take a step backward in time and see myself again at the window leaning out over the sidewalk; I see nothing but my mind instead sees a Faulkner-like figure, consumed by desire and by the all too many repressed words, tense under pressure of an anxiety of being ignorant of her future and desirous of knowing it. I see in this figure only tears, and later I feel them in your embrace when, upon embracing me, you make me feel like a fish in a net. I also feel the sadness of this city, the brevity of the time we spend together, the loss of time that we suffered and the void that I already envisage once I'm back home again among stony faces. My mother keeps me, but she is not my family. The family that I would like to create is made up of those whom I have loved, of you whom I love, and of those whom I will love. I feel a little bit like the ancient mariner... I am strewn and sprinkled with tiny shreds of remembrances, fashioned of love and hate. I already know everything, but most of all I'm sad.

Your face is now a collage that glides through my thoughts like a clear yet transparent face of a Braque pasted on forms of wood and cloth, and tenuous sounds of music.

* * *

It will seem strange if I tell you that I will not let myself go so far as to love you totally, and for the following reason. If I were to allow myself to love you with all my capacity to love, then I would no longer allow you to return to your wife. And since you would go back, I would be intolerably mortified. This does not mean that I do not love you. I'm merely telling you that our love is being strangulated by your social position, and by the brevity of your meetings. The more I let my life for you intensify, the more I feel that I would never want to be separated from you. This makes me extremely unhappy. And to avoid this I retire into my corner, loving you with some reservation but never excluding a deep feeling for you from this reserve of love.

Many are the things that make you dear to me: your bear's voice and your laughter that reverberates in me as if I had just heard a dirty joke. Perhaps I should identify you with a sexual roar. I don't know. But after your voice I love your mouth, the curve of the upper lip and your smile. If I were to meet you in the years to come I think my first impulse would be to bite you softly on the lips. But there are also secondary things I like about you. The more I know you the more I realize that we have much in common. Both of us are fed by the same fire that blazes skyward. God, how alone I'm going to feel when I'm home again, thinking about what I've left behind in New York! Because you have been structured by this city also. And for me you are inseparable from this city, even if you have left shreds of life in so many cities which I do not know, in which you have lived and I have not.

At the beginning, I didn't trust you, nor did I trust myself I didn't trust anybody. But you changed me and now I feel better, in fact I can bring myself to write. All this is the ideal side of love, the beautiful part that I see when the city fades away in its warm obscurity, or when it lies under the heat of the afternoon which drapes people and us in a sparkling sweat. Ironically, this side of love makes me melancholy because it makes the hours of separation so long. And it is during this long interval that at times I think of when it will be all over, when I will again be alone with the strange shriek of the seagulls enveloped in the fog and the incessant rippling of the waves on the rocks. I know from experience that then I will regret not having told you many of the things that I must tell you.

* * *

Like it or not, I'm a daughter of New England. My real roots are in Bath, Maine, the city of many shaded streets where I learned to love and to hate. I escape from that city by attiring myself in the clothes (if another city, New Canaan, or in those of other cities of my imagination. But I know that I run without arriving anywhere. I run away from New England and from its superstition, but I wrench my soul while running because I know that I am tied only to what I know, the true essence of New England, the sweet smell of apples rotting in autumn, the smell of leaves at springtime, and the smell of those dry and dusty places, symbolized by its narrow streets and by the people living inside the houses lining them. New England has always appeared to me as a world in which little persons of upright character live in little wooden houses along the arid streets. Their hearts are as narrow and dry as the streets, hardened by long winters and by the scarcity of money.

Although my mother is a strong and adventurous woman, steeped in the traditions of a southern clime, she too has succumbed to the influence of New England. The winter has dried up her heart and has caused her to crackle like a dry, split log, before her time. So I grew up between Bath and New Canaan, in contact only with the coarse and worn out facade of my parents. As a child I learned that people are to be feared. For us people were empty gourds inside which rumbled the dead seeds of autumn. So I, too, learned to be harsh, not to look people in the eye, and to pay no attention to their words. I soon understood that these people had nothing to say and I myself soon learned not to say anything, living attached to the earth like a stupid animal.

There is no need of words between the stone statue of New England. Words do not exist, only the monosyllables required of the farmer who sells corn and vegetables on the edge of the street. And I must remember all this if I want to live because this if all I have, New England's cold and silent stones.

* * *

In my opinion what represents New England more than anything else are the small white and poor wooden churches with their croaking ministers and wooden pews. Only two years ago I refused to go to church, thinking that God is not love. Or, at least, God is not the love of Sunday. Yet God wordlessly granted me his Sundays, and in these Sundays a boy, Clair,

My first true love was a boy called Clair, like the light of the moon because he and I used to walk under the moon near the ocean. It was an untouchable love and pervading love since it was compounded of hours and hours of mute looking into each other s eyes. Our eyes were almost exactly at the same level and I always had the impression of looking at myself in a mirror when I looked into his eyes, dark, deep-set and endlessly deep. But he was too fragile with his inert lips and his supplicant hands, always revolving in a void. We covered the dusty streets of Maine with a raiment of black velvet which was my Fairy god-mother cloak and stretched ourselves on it, listening to the tum-tum of our hearts. But he would remain in that position for all too long a time with closed eyes and a girlish smile on his face. He was selfishly wrapped up in his own ecstasy, slow and timid as he reached out a hand to touch me out for fear of frightening me. He did not at all sense that I was impatiently waiting for him to place his hand on my breasts, and for his leg to press strongly against mine. He did not want to make the first move, so I did and it elicited his disapproval.

"Clair, I love you very much," I told him one night. "But tell me if you love me because if you don't I can't go any further with you. Here I'm waiting for you, whereas it should be the other way around."

He tensed and explained that he did not yet know the meaning of love.

We remained seated together all night on the edge of a dusty street until the moon waned and dawn broke, he enveloped in silence and me impatiently waiting for some final decision. Finally, he took my hand, rubbed it with extreme gentleness and said in a soft, slow voice, "Yes, I do love you!" But he sounded like a robot. And I was too young and too happy then to understand that those words marked the end of a relationship. After that night we still dated each other for a month, yet that month was marvelous.

Knowing all I know now, remembering it, I feel only bitterness.

* * *

That summer had the taste of salt spume, of rotting sea ropes and of the wild smell of the earth battered by the wind, almost uncontaminated, almost perfect.

In the following year, when I was in college, I received strange and distant letters from Clair. I began to see him as if he belonged to a different world than mine, and very different, very different from the world of New England with its roses and ocean spume. Clair had let himself be tamed by the world. His shoulders were bent, his eyes were constantly fixed on his shoes, observing the cleavages of the terrain as he walked up and down Harvard's famous. He believed that what he was thinking at that time were important thoughts, and perhaps they were. But I understood that I had lost his identity with the mist of the sea. He sank to the level of normalcy, already adult and distant while I, standing behind him, screamed at him and scratched him, now that I was determined to liberate him with the offering of my body. But he did not understand my sacrifice, indeed it aroused his disgust.

Many times I still think of awaiting his return so that he can seduce me with his very beautiful eyes, court me and then be proud of his conquest... But since he is still a boy, Clair would be ashamed to see me naked at his side, open for him, upon waking up in our bed the morning after.

* * *

It is strange to place this love before the one that I had when I was not yet seventeen because, actually, I was only 14 when I met Matthias. That love was also more ripe for two reasons: he was already a mature adult, a high level academic administrator, and I felt proud and very self-assured.

We spent a summer avid for each other, nevertheless I was reluctant, even frightened, because he wanted total love. Matthias was the first link in the chain of my liberation from puritanism. For my present relation and the one with Clair suffered from frustration precisely because of puritanism, because each time that passion flared it was always one of us who said no to something that was very beautiful.

I vividly recall a time when Clair and I were walking in the rain. We sought shelter in a boat shed and waited for the rain to stop. The shed was humid and some rotting boats were soared rolled over on their sides. Clair began to kiss me but he suddenly pulled away from me after ten minutes. He explained that he was embarrassed because of the strange effects that my kisses had on him. I felt as though he had slapped my face. He had almost been on the verge of throwing me into one of those boats and taking me, but he had suddenly felt ashamed of his impulse like a child that wets its pants.

After estranging myself from Clair, I had other petty and insignificant relationships with different boys. One of them studied at Yale and thought me beautiful. He came to Vassar to show off his mannerism with me. We smoked a lot and we did a lot of racing together in order to avoid having to talk. He often asked me to go to bed with him and once he almost raped me but I delivered a punch to his testicles and sent him back to Yale. But his place was taken by other boys like him. insipid, sweaty palmed, always uncertain as to what to do in order to take me to a motel. But I knew that if any of them had been more sure of himself and quicker he would have succeeded. Unfortunately they pawed and handled me as if I were a cheap trinket. Only one day, a boy whom I had never seen before actually moved with swiftness and directness one dark and rainy night. Before I realized what was happening to me, he had slipped his hand into my vagina, moving his fingers quickly in order to excite me. Then, relaxed, he sat himself down to observe my reactions. He said that he would come only after seeing how he made me come. I suspected that he was impotent and that his penis was not bigger than an inch. I slapped his face with all my strength, leaving him in a dull stupor, oscillating back and forth, a wooden idol.

After these few not too interesting experiences with typically handsome men, I instinctively sought for relationships with strange people. Today faces with perfect lineaments bore me. I need a person who would take me violently, like an animal, one who should hurt me, wound me, who would suffocate me to the point of death because I need a new violent form of Love in order to excite myself. I need someone who is different from others, who would manage to involve all my capacities, who would test me, taste me and who need not necessarily love me. Often I think of going to Europe, after I finish college, and work full time in a brothel.

I'm so full of resentments. This world, swarms with fat and ole filthy persons who pollute the world and render it sterile with their sweaty and pending pricks. They rub against you in buses and subways in search of a last flash of flesh, but they leave a stink behind when they get off at stops leading nowhere. College boys and dirty old men are equal as regards the disgust they provoke in me. Oh, how I hate the weak and flabby flesh, surmounted by a carpet of thick, coarse hairs!

* * *

I am waiting for dawn in order to begin my day with sleep, and to find some relief from the questions as to who I am and why I am here.

I manage to Love New York as I have never loved any other city because there is a strangulating passion in its streets and in its steel-glass towers. And it is only here that I experience things that I have never experienced in my life. Life streams and swells, perhaps it speedily projects itself towards death on the rocks, but it is passionate and mystically veiled and still it manifests itself like the burning sun at high noon.

I have told the story of my loves yet I consider them a nullity in the presence of this city. After all its easier to love cities than persons, still I love this city above all because of my love for those who live there, because without their love New York would be only a cold pit in my mind.

The perfect way to become alcoholized in a city Like New York is that of Listening to jazz by yourself during the night. I begin to think of the days when, at the age of ten, I already had boyfriends, and of that time when I told a twelve-year old boy that a girl becomes a woman at the onset of menstruation. He laughed, made fun of me, and I was so furious that sometime later I showed him my blood to confirm to him that what I said was true. He was so affected that he asked me to become his lover on Sundays, after mass. From that time on we spent our Sunday afternoons in an old abandoned house, but I would tell him scoffingly that he was too young to get a hard on. He would bite me all over my body as we lay on a dirty mattress among this mute, dead walls. He had a delicate and impotent body, and I already had long and slender curves like a Modigliani nude. Together we learned to laugh over everything as a joke, and to draw nude figures in grotesque poses.

* * *

I am a daughter of New England but slowly and inexorably I have detached myself from that earth, unsmiling and soundless, save for the cackling of some hen. I am learning to talk, to thrust the earth from my mouth, and to welcome the day. My childhood is full of gossipy neighbors who prescribed Epsom Salts for every ailment, ranging from a lost love to broken legs. I played the violin for five years and at least for two of those years when I was eleven or twelve and already menstruating—the persons— around me, Prick and my mother usually and some neighbors, were forced to endure the squeaking of the strings. I subjected myself to that practice and to the lessons like a child doomed to martyrdom. But slowly, little by little, I began to love the shiny, well-chiseled wood of the instrument, the humid smell of the red velvet of the inside of its cracked and worn case that had belonged to my grandfather. I also began to love the dry and bitter smell of the resin that I smeared on the bow. It is strange to recall and to realize that at that time, after the first two years of lessons, I began to appreciate the violin as a person, as a companion to whom to turn when I was sad and angry. It was more or less at that time that my body began to become thick and taut and to vibrate spasmodically when I held theviolin under my chin. I could distinctly feel the vibrations of its strings through my body. It was as if I and it, the violin,were fused in the same flesh. I would mistreat it, wresting deep sounds from it. And on one of these occasions, I remember; Prick stood there listening. He hardly ever spoke and was not used to paying compliments. But this time he looked at me in such a way that I could feel his eyes pierce my flesh. I immediately stopped playing and the spell was broken, the violin slid down my shoulder as if his reproachful eyes had split it in two.

* * *

The first time that Matthias and I were alone we never exchanged even a word. We sat down our eyes fixed on the lake outside the window that sparkled in the afternoon sun. So many things have happened to me near the water that it has become an integral part of my existence. I was conceived on the water, during one of my mother's escapades.

I already knew what would happen. Matthias and I would have a very intimate relationship, both bound by a strange spell composed of trysts and constant little tricks to effect escape from our routines. In that first summer fl our acquaintance he taught me many things, including a lesson on how to extricate myself from difficult situations. And I acquired a feeling of compassion for him, and often was surprised to hear my voice giving him advice on how to solve his various problems.

It was not because of his wife but she certainly set the bait when one evening she suggested that he and I go for a canoe ride on the lake. It was cold on the lake and I curled myself up in a blanket on the bottom of the boat while Matthias related to me stories of his growing up poor, of his father being killed in a car accident, of his grandparents killed by the Nazi in a concentration camp, during the war.

"It's cold," he said suddenly, and I noticed that he began to tremble, his face drawn in a strange expression.

The silence of the night and the rustle of the water against the sides of the canoe enveloped us in a momentary embrace. I was won by his inability to help himself and by his naked humanity. Still sadly embraced, but languid and by now intimate with each other, we got up and he drew my head to his knees. For the first time I took a man's penis in my mouth.

It was a strange thing, totally unreal. But I was too young then and I didn't know men's habits. I could have hated him. Afterwards, instead, a total silence ensued, we remained for a long time cuddled in the canoe. Now he was bent over me, fixing his gaze on my face while I, leaning backward and recline my head with my throat arched, looked back into his eyes. I felt that I no longer had a body. My hands and legs had evaporated in the mist. I was only an enormous round head in which there beat the low and rapid rhythm of a drum.

I saw him on the following day, and the days that followed fused into a single, continuous day.

Matthias came and went, and each night my heart died a little. I faded away from languor when I heard his car enter the driveway with the children running out to greet him, I could always see five blond, curly-haired heads jumping up and down like corks on the sea when he lilted them up in the air one by one. Sue would follow the children outside, slowly and surely like a cow when she knows that the owner is waiting for her at the gate. Matthias would turn his attention to her, kiss her demurely, after which the whole family entered the house where I usually sat seated on the sofa, reading.

14.

(April 30, 1973)

Another crisis.

Now all the lies with which we have lived no longer function, and illusions are inter-communicable. Being one and the same thing, they are necessary to one who advances in life with an appearance of well-being. But when one arrives at seeing the light, this life appears to us as a state of boredom and mental distress. Such a life lacks permanence.

Often, I find myself surprisingly thinking about the man of the Middle Ages. He knew little more than fear, sickness and death. Yet he was ensconced in the comforting faith that the universe had a purpose because it had been created by God's sapient hand. And even though this man was naught else but a grain of dust in the life of nature, he was still part of the design of God who was absolute and therefore permanent. Now we all need permanence. This, too, signifies an ignorance of the nature of things. But at the base of today's experience there is the agonizing awareness that everything is unstable, everything is in flux, everything is just words, i.e. lies.

The most beautiful lies are to be found in the *Our Father* (56 words), in the *Gettysburg Address* (266 words), in the *Ten Commandments* (297 words), in the *Declaration of Independence* (297 words), and in a *Federal Ordinance* (26, 911 words) that establishes the price of cabbages for the year.

I know very well that we create these lies for ourselves in order to preserve our attachment to the illusion of permanence. The lie is the capital of storekeeperism. Only it's different for me, now. I had attached myself so firmly to our reciprocal lie of permanence in love that now that it has surfaced I am upset and feel lost, I'm the fish out of water gasping for breath. I needed this illusion. I always wanted something to which to attach myself, I'm a believer. And what I have always wanted, in order to sustain myself in life, is what Roseanne and you have taken away from me.

I've once again thought of committing suicide. Do you think it's something to laugh about?

This time in order to punish myself for what I have seen. I don't want to tear my eyes out only because these eyes have seen, but I do want to tear myself radically away from you, Simon, from the life that you represent for me.

This idea of suicide is subtle and perfidious, yet it is so absolute that it resembles certain of our afternoon fucking sessions, when I feel as though I can't breathe and that I am dying, suffocated by abundance. It usually happens to me when I ask you for what's forbidden, that you tie my wrists behind my back with a nylon string from your guitar and that you blindfold me with one of your coloured kerchiefs. It is I who wants to be tied, it is I who wants to be gagged. I admit it, so don't protest. For this is my game of love and death, even if you satisfy it reluctantly, thinking I'm a sick chick. Well, I am sick. But this is how I've discovered the peak pleasure of coming. And once this fantasy is removed, the other idea crops up: to slash the veins on my wrists and then let them be sewed up in time, because otherwise boredom supervenes.

From the first time this idea occurred to me, when we were lovers in Manhattan, and I believed that I had lost you because you had gone back home to live with your wife, this idea has never been totally cancelled in my mind; it remains dozing and almost lost in the folds of my mind, it beats like a heart, at times it rises like a wing and I observe it. It is timid, very timid and bewildered at the beginning, it is small and bloodless but I watch over it, I breathe under it, I make it live. It is a black wing and everything around it is darksome, yet I see it. And now here it is pulsating anew. It usually happens to me in the evening when I think of you being outside with Roseanne after your last class. This wing whirls around my head, it whirls around the peak point of my fragility becoming as whirlwind, then a mirage. I see Virginia Woolf in her white dress who walks in the waters of the river following the mirage. And then, in a twinkling, she is no more. Little bubbles linger at the point where she has stopped walking. But only briefly. The river has not left its course for a moment. And it happens to me in the evening. And one evening I survived and when you returned I said, "Don't you think, Simon, that suicide is the sincerest form of self-criticism?"

You laughed, most embarrassedly. In the last few days you had been working on an essay on Pavese, welded together around the theme of suicide. The books you used as bibliographical sources are still around the house: Durkheim, Frazer, A. Alvarez, and Morselli. And in a footnote to your *curriculum vitae* you have written that you yourself at the age of seventeen, had attempted to commit suicide. You wanted to kill yourself because you had been disappointed by something, perhaps by the seminary, perhaps by your half-Jewish origin. But just now you laughed, embarrassed; you managed to assume a swaggering tone, and replied, "As we grow older, becoming gnomish, suicide strikes us as ever more improbable because there's so much less to kill."

"But you're driving me to suicide," I answered. "No, no. You're a coward. You'll never make another attempt to do away with yourself."

"I've never tried."

"Have you forgotten April 18, 1962? In a telephone booth next to the New York Public Library? Have you forgotten?"

"It was a farce."

"I know that, you wanted me to feel sorry for you. You delicately cut your wrists with my razor. Then you phoned me and asked me to rush you to the hospital. There, with your wrists in bandages, the moment I entered your room, you said, 'I want to make love'. And we did so with the door wide open. A nurse also saw us, she was young and cute, but she turned her back without a word, covering her face. And then I went to Mexico to get my divorce, and later, in our state of euphoria, we conceived a child in Provincetown, Cape Cod. Then we had ourselves married by a Justice of the Peace, by trade a mechanic, in Vermont, without a soul knowing about it. Your attempted suicide of that time, precisely because it was a farce, has brought us to these outrageous days..."

"I was afraid that you'd go back to your wife in Italy."

"I should have done so! During my separation from you, I used to lay Elena, the girl from Milan."

"And Nancy, too, my old Vassar roommate."

"No. She had already left for Spain. And you, meanwhile, what were you doing with Worth?"

"It was a silly, stupid thing, I'm almost sorry it ever happened."

"You mean it was a small fuck, of no great importance?"

"Precisely."

"But you didn't understand that Roseanne was the same thing for me?"

"It's different now, because we're different."

"And you want to commit suicide because we are different?"

"I'm taking formal note of the end of the lie."

Both of us were in a pathetic state. You bent over to kiss me, Simon, but we were also laughing like a tubercular patient spitting blood. For a moment I thought that you were the real suicide. Instead you merely wanted to play around again and get me back. Some pages of my thesis, stained with whiskey and tears, were spread out on the rug. And, looking at them, you said maliciously, "No, my dear. Suicides are a thing of the past. Once they were the aristocrats of death, God's neo-graduates. Instead of writing their thesis, they wanted to impersonate them, thus proving how limited the alternatives that God has granted to himself and to his creatures, are. The show they put on became a magnificent literary criticism: Hart Crane, Randal Jarrell, Hemingway, Mark Rothko, Cesare Pavese, Yukio Mishima. These were people who still wanted to offer something. But by growing older, a suicide fails. There's almost nothing more to kill. And you are old, Vera, and a born whore."

Then you went into the kitchen to make yourself a tuna-fish sandwich, and you were whistling without letup. I got up, made my way to the garage quietly, started the car, pulled out of the driveway and drove along the highway at a crazy speed, looking for an accident. Or just to let off steam. You see, Simon, after I came upon you with Roseanne, you rebelled against my reactions of rage and real pain, accusing me of treating you like a piece of property. You told me that you were my bank, my fur coat, my house, my studies, my friends. The false sense of stability that comes to me from the fact of having a husband or a house or a bank account, which is your bank account, the false sense comes to me from you because my trust consisted in my attachment to you. The real pain came to me from the breakdown of my only true illusion: the lie that somehow guaranteed stability and a certain permanence in my life. My illusion was the trust that our love was different from my loves and your loves that had preceded ours. I believed that your love would be permanent. Now I realize that all unions are condemned, mine and yours as well as Roseanne's with you. In our stupid search for a long-lasting union, we have suddenly ended up alone. It's not only a matter of your loneliness and mine, but also of Roseanne's. It is a cosmic loneliness because the sacred lie is no more, that lie which, often, wreathes absolute loneliness in a smile.

So now I shall have to learn the harsh lesson of living without a lie, of living in the present without further need for drugs or karma. Once trust is no more all that remains is the naked reality, which is disconsolate, upset, and in which we move and have our being like two strangers. I have loved Mercury, this fantastic elf, this youthful, this elderly seducer who suffused me with animation. Now the animation has flown away, and I've become a rag.[10]

---

[10] An alchemical reference to the rites of Mercury often recurs in Simon's *Diaries*. At times Mercury is viewed as possessing chthonic, profane qualities, at other times, he is viewed as a divine being, a "fantastic elf" as Vera precisely describes him. He is, perhaps, also hermaphroditic, at times darksome, at times lucent, which in the alchemist tradition comes to assume the aspects of so many things and, above all, he is pointed to as *vital principle* and *anima mundi*.

In his *Symbolik des Geistes* lung dissertates at length on Mercury as soul and spirit, as unity and trinity, as arcane substance and as two-fold nature. This fundamental text underlines the ambiguous structure of both diaries, Simon's and Vera's.

15.

How did the new crisis arise?

That night Simon was dining out with some other members of the faculty, together with a candidate for the position of Assistant Professor in his department. In the last few weeks there have been many interviews, many conferences, and also many dinners. There was a constant coming and going by new graduates, or graduate students in the process of completing their Ph.D. thesis. Charlotte, feeling outraged by the male world, from her observation post in the Inner Circle persistently pointed out to various deans and vice- presidents the necessity of re-evaluating the position and the status of women in civil service jobs, particularly if they were academics. Both she and Matthias insisted on publications and research as a basic qualification prior to any appointments and promotions. Although men were not much better prepared than women, reality indicated that they had more experience, including job experience, behind them. Though they were excellent as researchers, women continued to receive unfavorable reports from their male colleagues either because their publications were scarce or of a quality inferior to those of male aspirants. Charlotte herself had published very little and, in the opinion of male judges, second and third hand in terms of quality. A memorandum to the President, signed by a group of males with alleged high qualifications, stated that Charlotte's "publications are, in our view, much below the academic standard."[1] Charlotte,

---

[1] In another footnote of Vera's diary discarded here, we read that "academics are jealous and vindictive, authoritarians, capricious, full of arrogance, rarely

notwithstanding, undaunted, held her head higher than ever, perhaps ignorant of the stake at which she will be burnt alive one day, continued to flourish her sword.[2] Simon had mixed feelings in regard to her: he admired her and felt sorry for her. But, at times, when he was enraged, he called her a plagiarist.

So that night it was again a matter of bringing a male to dinner. I had been invited, but I refused, taking Charlotte's side. I, too, began to be annoyed by these bronzed and virile males, bearded, with the science of lofty scorn in their words and in their idol-like movements. Oh, Simon! You tried to estrange me during this winter of discontent. True, you were working very hard at all hours and, in addition, you had to cope with some troubles that had arisen in your department. You were frustrated, deprived of

---

intelligent." All this is a matter of opinion. It is nevertheless true that the "internal" war often did not involve only women. In the case of one thesis rejected by the Committee, its director (J.J. De Pepperoy) registered a protest in the press, seemingly for reasons of selfdefense. He charged (I) that one of the judges, age 66, had never published or written a scientific book, but knew how to condemn a thesis; (2) another of the judges did not have a doctorate degree, but knew how to condemn a thesis; (3) a third judge (a woman) had received her doctorate without ever having written a thesis in her own hand; (4) none of the three judges speaks the language of the author studied by the candidate, with the exception of the candidate himself, author of the rejected thesis, and his advisor, Professor De Pepperoy. "These three Professors," the article concluded, "have used the weight of their authority to destroy not only a poor devil of a candidate but also his academic advisor."

[2] Here Vera is referring to the Joan of Arc airs that Charlotte had assumed as a kind of identifying feature of her person. Voltaire had tried to ridicule the female warrior, burned at the stake in Rouen, May 30, 1431, with his famous pseudo-heroic poem La Pucelle D' Orleans (1755). The academics had tried to ridicule Charlotte by calling her at times, "our Harlot" and, at other times, "our Pucelle D'A" (A meaning anus). It was known to many of them that when Sylvia Pankhurst was released from Hollowat prison, the procession of suffragettes was led by a woman dressed as Joan of Arc, in full armor. Charlotte had the innocence to recall the episode in one of her readings of the women warriors of the Renaissance (i.e. those of the various epochs of the Renaissance, such as Clorinda, Angelica, Bradamante etc.), heaping high praise on these women for their amazonian spirit but, at the same time, deploring their erotic surrender to the superiority of the male warrior. But not Joan, the virgin disguised as a man who ate very little and didn't menstruate at all.

the normal passage of day and night, you ate badly, your eyes hurt you, your stomach hurt you, and for some strange reason you wanted to be alone to meditate, but I knew that you were unhappy with our life. You often said that you couldn't take the regularity with which it proceeded, we were always together, you complained, at home, in the bathroom, in school, at the movies, in the supermarket. And I would reply: "It's because of the cold, it will pass." Yet that cold had paralyzed our emotions. I refused your invitation to dinner in order to leave you free, so I accepted an invitation to go to the movies with Anna and her new friend from the philosophy department, Allen Murdock. I shouldn't have done it, because you detested Anna, she knew too much about our affairs. And Anna, in fact, does know everything. She is the friend to whom I turned on the evening of that terrible Tuesday when I discovered the both of you at home, in the small room. After the recriminations, the shock and the sense of loss occasioned by that encounter, you brought Roseanne, who herself was in a state of shock and bewilderment, back to the dormitory, saying, "Don't wait for me, I've got some people to see." And by that you meant to say that you'd be back later or, perhaps, that you wouldn't come back at all. But that night I wanted you to come back no matter what, and only for the purpose of continuing the clash we had had in the afternoon. I had a great advantage over you, and I wanted to exploit it. But you're a salamander, you cover yourself with ashes when you're in the fire.[3]

---

[3] Jung, *op.cit.*: "Mercury, the revelatory light of nature, is also the infernal fire which, strangely, is none other than a composition or system of that which is above, i.e. of the celestial, spiritual virtues, below, in the chathonic sphere, hence in this material world, which already at the time of St. Paul was considered itself to be dominated by the devil. The infernal fire, the energy proper to evil, appears here as a clear antithesis to that which is above, spiritual and good and in a certain way essentially identical as substance. Since Mercury himself is of the nature of fire, fire has no harmful effect on him, he remains in it in all his substance: and this is important in regard to the *symbolism of the salamander*."

My fragility lies in my inability to be alone. The house appeared like a trap to me. I bit my hand, my eyes were puffed. I phoned Anna and she came immediately, concerned, affectionate, to take me to her apartment on State Street, where she plied me with Scotch and supportive attention.

"So, Vera... you've been through it, too." She sat down next to me on the sofa, ready to listen to everything even though she already knew everything.

Anna was now living her exclusive moment, free of Punks' surveillance, like a spider in possession of the whole web. I let myself be pitied, half drunk as I was with Scotch and tears, her hands in mine, like two sisters, I empathizing with her nakedness and she with mine. She advised me to see Susie Spring: I suddenly felt ashamed of myself, I was becoming your enemy. And even if I had not gone to see her personally, Anna would have attended to this matter on her own and Susie, in turn, would have informed Charlotte, and Charlotte, Matthias. Soon the State Street feminists would be embracing a new sister, and a divorce to boot. Everything suddenly took shape in my mind: the future. Matthias' position was a fragile one. Charlotte probably knew of my old relationship with him and, at this point, Charlotte would have blackmailed him. To your harm. I know Matthias. He always makes others pay the toll. And now it would be your turn. Revenge would be mine. Again, I was deeply ashamed of myself. But shame is nothing when it alleviates an offense. Anna, however, was understanding and tactful and you hated her for this. She had become a shield between us. And this is why when she and Allen came to pick me up, you quipped perversely.

According to certain of Simon's footnotes, Vera used books not because she was culturally drawn to them but, like Jorge Luis Borges who seeks for the key of the universe in an immense labyrinthine library, she sought in them the key that would open to her the *sanctum* of the mysteries that adumbrated her growth. Reading Jung must have served her to acquire a better understanding of Simon and of his relationship with Roseanne.

"Verily, verily I say unto ye... I would like to stay at home and make love with my wife instead of going to this dinner... Now... enjoy yourselves, I beseech ye, because I'll be doing the same."

This phrase of yours whirled around my head all night, and I realized, with displeasure, that I was still jealous of you, that I was still tied to you. I tried to dismiss the thought, I even thought about Sonny Morebugs: what pleasure could there be in letting him screw you? Often disappointed and drunken wives would ring his bell and let themselves be laid in the sauna. Later they would confess to him that they had done it only to revenge themselves on their husbands.

"It doesn't matter," Sonny would reply. "If that's the cure you want, it's alright with me too, thanks."

So I, too, thought of him. But your phrase was stronger. After the movie, when I was again alone in the house, I thought I was going crazy. To be sure, you were with the Ph.D. candidate. But what if you were with Roseanne, instead? No, Roseanne was still in Florida for the Easter vacation. But Evelyn was in town...

Yes, I tormented myself. All this torment because I no longer had any trust. I then remembered a conversation I had in the library with Gee Jay. His affair with Pauline, the wife of that poor wretch, Professor J.J. De Pepperoy, had ruined his marriage with Virginia. And although they still lived together, just as you and I still do, Virginia's problem with Gee had become identical with my problem with you.

"When you love," Gee had said, "you are dealing with one person. When something happens that breaks that oneness you are compelled to deal with two persons."

I cited this utterance of Gee to you and you pronounced it important, indeed "very important", but with the cutting edge of your irony. But you quickly found refuge in the language of ideas which you employ when it suits your convenience as well as for the purpose of better embarrassing your conversational partner, of making him suspicious, of provoking him and then leaving him in a corner like an old rag. So you spoke about Pythagoras, saying that Gee's wife, poor girl, cannot grasp the concept that oneness is the first numerical entity from which all the other numbers derive, and in which all the opposite properties of numbers, the unequal and the equal, are also reunited. You explained that two was the first *equal* number whereas three is the first *unequal* number and as such perfect. (How I hate professors!) And you further explained that the beginning, the middle and the end exist in number three. You spoke of three as if it were God's cipher book! And, instead, all you wanted to say was that Virginia, the betrayed wife, should have accepted Pauline as a necessity, just as I should accept Roseanne: a middle that continues to tie you to me but which, at the same time, forms an equilateral triangle, or am I mistaken?

I waited for you in my overcoat, with the bottle of Scotch and the cigarettes beside me. I was watching the TV, but I saw nothing. Yet I needed its hum in the void, people came and went on the screen, talked, and I felt as if I were wrapped in a blanket. But after one o'clock, when the transmissions end (at least on the channels we have,) what would I have done still wearing the overcoat? Would I have begun to phone people far away?

Suddenly you came back before one 0' clock, tanked up and merry but upon seeing me in the overcoat and looking upset alongside the bottle of Scotch and the cigarettes, your facial expression sobered.

"Have you been with Evelyn?"

"No such luck! But what's bugging you?"

"I'm going to find myself a lover, do you know that?"

This remark made you explode and you threw your glasses against the TV just as you had done with your typewriter on that other night of crisis (so many crisis in only a few days !), wanting to destroy precisely those things that were vital to you, i.e. your real, true self. But I didn't want this. I tried to stop you, I picked up your glasses, I took you in my arms, but you were stubborn and desired no contacts. You tried to extricate yourself from my grasp and by so doing your elbow hit my nose which immediately began to bleed. Then you locked yourself up in the bathroom. When I came into the bathroom to fetch a towel in the mirror I saw a tear-stained, bloody, sad and ugly face, and I saw you, sitting on the toilet seat, looking very distressed, no longer knowing what to do with yourself. I felt a deep sadness for the two of us. And I waited for you. I tried to embrace you in bed, I needed comfort, I needed love. You paid me back in a fogged and vindictive manner. It had been different at other times, it had been natural. I hadn't liked it at first, then I allowed you to do it. But now it struck me as a sadistic act of violence, frigid in the extreme, because you turned me around with a rude impatience so as to sodomize me, and when I rebelled you rejected me with such force that I fell off on the other side of the bed.

Oh, Simon, its so sad not to love one another any more.

16.

Today is Sunday, and yesterday we spent a pleasant Saturday evening together: you, me and the Holy Spirit. Did I say pleasing? No, unusual. In fact I no longer know what is normal and what is abnormal. Nor do I care, I'm caught up in the wave and I'm swimming with difficulty and I'm only trying to keep my head above water. Our quarrels are repeated with an ever greater frequency, and if a day goes by smoothly it seems that I'm almost missing something. We had quarreled again Friday night because of now uncontrollable jealousy. Finally, in order to get away from me, you said, "I'm going to work at the office." Perhaps it was true, but to me it sounded like a new excuse to meet Roseanne. I replied, "If that's really the case, let's go together, I'll study in the library."

"Are you thinking about Roseanne?" you replied.

"I don't care about her anymore," I lied. "In fact, you could even invite her to the Snack Bar. Won't you offer me a coffee?"

"Now what are you lotting? Why do you want to invite Roseanne?"

"I'd like to get to know her better, talk with her... "

You shook your head. Then, still mistrustful, you wrote her number on a piece of paper. "If that's the way it is, call her up yourself, tell her 'welcome back, darling, would it displease you to make love with me and my husband, tonight'?" Impulsively, I slapped your face. I hit you so hard that your glasses fell to the floor, fortunately without breaking. You grabbed me by the wrists, twisting them:

"Have you really gone bonkers?"

"Excuse me."

"O.K. We'll do as you wish. We'll go to the very bottom of the matter."

"What bottom and where?"

"To the bottom of Hell!"

We drove as far as the Student Center for a hamburger, then he went to his office and I made my way to the library. Students were yawning over their books, the light was clear and artificial, spread enormously as during daytime, but now it had a strange emptiness, it appeared menacing and motionless on the arm-chairs, on the heads of the students, on the lazy cloud of cigarette smoke, on the walls, on the abstract paintings. The Art Department painters were semi-failures, and that's why they were professors. They had neither a name nor a face but, nevertheless, they managed to get their paintings hung a little everywhere, in the library or in the lecture halls. The only one who escaped this dreary fate was G.O. Shait since he had a certain public in the surrounding communities and countryside.

We had known very many artists but on this campus, (at least to me,) they all appeared to be plagiarists. Of course, it's not true. But one tends to belittle when one believes to know better. Or, perhaps, the judgment stems from the fact that we all know each other somewhat, even intimately, and therefore we do not respect each other anymore.

There are circles and circles of persons here, there are intrinsic ties, explicit ties, all inter-connected, all orbiting around the University, money, students, positions, promotions, the published book, the book that so and so has been writing for 30 years, the fundamental manuscript that poor Henry lost while moving from one place to another, hence a new delay in the process of promoting him to full professor, etc. Vanni Webes, the swaggerer of New York, who came to visit us one day, upon seeing the paintings in the library bluntly observed: "They are certified fakes. Your Art Department should seriously dedicate itself to fakes because at least there's a market for them."

This remembrance led me to examine those paintings more attentively, and I was especially struck by one of them. It depicted a vast blue sky, a variant of shadings of sky. It was so authentic that it looked like an enormous enlargement of a photograph. A tiny seagull was visible very, very high in the sky. The sea was not visible but I felt its presence instantly in the invisible depth and I was suddenly assailed by a nostalgic desire to leave, to live for a moment, or for ever, far from this library, from this city.

I drew closer to it and read the painter's name: G.O. Shait. So G.O. actually had something, aside from the cut-off hand, aside from whore mongering, aside from the drugs that he took. Simon had characterized him as a Judas in his film, G.O. evinced satisfaction with the characterization since he had no pretensions, hated polemics and what he yearned for most of all was to get out of the province and to make enough money to retire to his home at Tortola, in the Caribbean. The inspiration of this painting no doubt came from there. I tried to imagine Tortola to myself, to see myself in G.O.'s house which I would have rented and to re-live on that island the island of my dreams as a girl when I read a strange book, *The Virgin under the Lion*.

The heroine was a girl of my age, thirteen or fourteen. Walking alone on the deserted beach, she always thought that it would be mysteriously perfect to lose her virginity on that beach. And one day a fisherman emerged from the sea with two enormous shells. The girl thought that if she would stretch herself out on the sand and close her eyes, he would take her with the swiftness and naturalness with which he had taken those shells. The fisherman stops alongside her, she sees his bare feet and his legs, then she turns around and writes on the sand: "Knock on my window."

On the next morning, at dawn, the fisherman tosses a pebble against the window of her bungalow. She comes out and walks towards the beach. The man follows her. Then she stretches out on the sand, and the man does likewise, at first some distance from her and, after a little while, he moves directly alongside her. They don't say a word to each other, and the man mounts her. Then he goes away and she does likewise. It is only a dream, it is one of those dreams that the girl had never dreamt before. At any rate she was no longer a virgin, and this was very beautiful.

The book continues. Every morning, now, the man tosses a pebble against the windows of the bungalow. And every morning she goes down to the beach, she walks and walks, and the fisherman always follows her amid the dunes. When she stretches out on the sand to take the sun, he does likewise, then he mounts her like the first time because now the morning stroll has become a rite. When he is on top of her the girl has a vision of so many other girls like herself, whose image is reflected on the rocks, being possessed in silence by the lion.

I walked away from the painting vaguely dazed, vaguely in love with myself. I returned to my seat, then my eyes glimpsed the feet and legs of a man, and the man's hand between those legs behind a seat covered with books. I turned my eyes and saw the girl at a nearby table. She, too, was half-hidden behind a pile of books and to me she looked like Roseanne. She had not noticed the man and continued her reading. Roseanne is a statuesque brunette and her hair, divided into tresses, comes down to her shoulders. I thought that I had been right to accompany Simon. He had come to meet her and she was waiting for him in the library. It was as simple as that. She must have felt my eyes on her which were trying to recognize her because she raised her head from the book, looked at me, petrified, but when she saw the man she suddenly slammed the book shut and ran off among the aisles of bookshelves. She had seen the man who was masturbating while looking fixedly at her. And she had also seen me.

I followed Roseanne, at first at a normal walking pace, but then I too began running. On the stairs I sighted her read sweater and her black tresses, but then she went through a door leading to the underground passages. I followed her up to there, saw that she was still running as she was entering another door and when I lost sight of her, I turned back. I came to pick you up at the office and we went back home.

"You know," I said, "there was a man masturbating in the library as he watched a girl's legs. She was wearing a red sweater and two black tresses reached down to her shoulders. She resembled Roseanne."

"Did you talk to her?"

"She first noticed me, then the man, and now I don't know whether she ran off because of me or the masturbator."

"I've got to phone her," you said, suddenly. "Why, don't you believe me?"

"I'd like to confirm it."

It was, however, already late, we followed the discussions on Watergate on TV, we did not talk any more about the incident in the library. Then I went to bed, took a sleeping pill, totally unaware of what you were up to. I saw you only on the next morning, a Saturday. I was in your arms, we made love, you were inside me with the neatness of a knot and this was beautiful all over again, my eyes were closed and I saw myself on the beach of the island with the fisherman mounting me.[4]

---

[4] Although the Matthias-Bes relationship, already recounted by Vera, is not a product of Vera's fantasy, fantasy nevertheless plays a foremost role in many pages of her diaries.

Some passages, dated October 1965 (when presumably she and Simon were in British Columbia,) bear the title, "As I remember it."

I. A glorious, brief but glorious pre-puberty, nursery age, the best moments spent together with another body, as small as mine, but ambitious and indefatigable, a big and generous smile. Reciprocal advice during the moments of an irrepressible urge to urinate after many hours spent in an old and mouldy garage, the exploration of unknown cavities, the splits that gave no account of themselves, "Let me look at it again." Each discovery that had to be classified was excitedly divulged on the handle bars of the bicycles, at first in whispers, slowly growing into shouts of joy. This was followed by a very fast race around the walls of the school and then once more by a return visit to the old garage for the confirmation. Erotic symptoms? Certainly. But there was something vital and delicious in what we were doing.

II. In that old and mouldy garage, covered with ashes, with its dusty windows, small and trustful world little by little became more intense, intimate, two little private suns. Someone might be spying, but no such thing happened, a descent of paranoia on our shoulders, anxiety, then a call from the nearby house, the instant dissolution of the enchantment, "Pull up your pants!", a belt being buckled, one thinks of secret hours.

III. There was certainly envy, but that did not exclude delight. To piss in a bottle.
A mother, a man. He was fat and did not seem to be my father. We called him Prick. A father who smiled when I looked at him. Lamentations of cats in Spring. Lacerating lamentations that could make you faint. Then the hormones, we run with the first racquets, bursts of laughter. One hot summer night somebody calls me into a tent. Dark confusion, I run away. And if he had raped me?

IV. Baseball, roller skates, arid desert of people. Then pure air because a marvelous, virile, smiling man appeared, full of knowledge, and with eyes that sparkled. He gave, and came. Officially the principal of a high school, and I observed for four intense years, and I blushed, and thoughts flowered. Adrenaline flowed. And finally it focused as man. The thoughts remained inside me, only music went in and out, Coltrane, Parker, Evans, they said love and had my love, once again different hours at the violin, prolonging the sounds that only I heard, until a rainy day arrives, the sofa is soft, oh how I would let myself be taken now, the rain, the sofa, and nobody came, yes, nobody came, spring rain, how old must he be now? Thirty five, forty?
Warm is the color of two side by side.

V. Projection, desire, then something else sprouts. And I dive into it, each time it's an eddy, and I always ask for more. "You almost have no hair on your head." All the hair is on the strong thorax, and all the will is in that hooked nose of his.

17.

We had not made love for a few days, and my greatest fear was Roseanne's presence on the campus which distances you from me. But now, miraculously, our bodies were together as before, as always. I deluded myself that you were still mine, and we had the whole weekend during which to enjoy ourselves. We had dedicated Saturday, Sunday and Monday to love. I thought of transporting a mattress to the garage so that we could lie on it there, naked, amid the smell of the gasoline and the spiders. But that was a silly idea: I had no nostalgia for my childhood and adolescence.

Experts would say that we have perfected the art of prolonged coitus, because now you are able to stimulate me to the point where I could achieve three orgasms, at times four, in the space of four hours. The inside of my cunt, which I had always imagined to be reddish-violet in color, made of a soft, gelatinous substance, responded fully to the regular movements of your body. I often felt you soft and silken, delicate to the extreme, like the seagull in G.O.'s painting. But this time you were very hard, and I recalled the priapism of Vaffancu. Only now I laughed over it. I was happy. For a long time, now, you hold the center without oscillating.

Then I dreamed little of him, except for certain nightmares in which I was Lady Macbeth.

It's a misfortune that the breasts are so small that they cannot be contained in a bra.

But the eagle will spread her wings. Poor deluded girl! Fear of the gossip of the little city. Race towards the big city.

It's difficult to eye young men after what's happened. Because they could not and would not do what I would like.

We also perfected the art of the simultaneous orgasm, highly recommended by "Cosmopolitan." And that depends almost exclusively on your patience and on the control you have on your emotions. In fact I, too, have habituated myself to delay an orgasm in order to prolong the pleasure.

We reposed in the pleasing knowledge that the day was ours; there would be no visits, no disturbances, the phone was off the hook and the doors were locked. But then you said something that surprised me. "I'd like to make some lasagne today." You do make them very well and I do like them very much. You knead the pasta, then you cut it, and prepare the ragu and the ricotta, the eggs and the different cheeses. All the required ingredients were already in the house, but I didn't think about it. I thought, instead, of your going out, making the purchases, sorting them out, dividing them, opening the door—in short destroying the intimacy with activity. Moreover, usually, you make lasagne only when you have guests.

I intuited a plot on your part. Do you see where the loss of trust leads to?

"Did you invite Roseanne?"

"Roseanne?"

The description of Roseanne in the library with the man masturbating as he watched her legs, and I behind her, and you who wanted to phone her for a confirmation of my story, went through your mind and mine, simultaneously, like a lightening flash.

"Weren't you supposed to phone her?" I asked.

"Invite her, we'll have the lasagne together." "Are you sure you won't make any scenes?" "Very sure."

After all what unpleasantness could possibly happen? We would spend a tranquil evening as a threesome in honor of Pythagoras, and, thank goodness, without any further outbursts of rage and accusations. And that, I told myself, would have been of great benefit especially to her, Roseanne, in that she would no longer feel rejected or hated. But was it really true that I did not reject her, that I did not hate her?

"In that case, you phone her." "Oh, no, no. You must..."

You did phone her. You said that you would pick her up at 3:30 in the afternoon. I objected that it was too early, what would we have done all afternoon and in the evening? Was Roseanne quick- witted, urbane? I realized that my anxiety was making a comeback. I was silent and, finally, I talked to you about my fears.

"But wasn't that your idea?" Of course. Then you said: "What's done cannot be undone. The New System is in progress. And according to this new system Teng becomes Deng, and Nanking is Nanjing."

"Would you make love with me and to her at the same time?" I replied, actualizing what you have called the New System.

You laughed, vastly delighted, and asked: "Would you like to make love as a threesome?"

I recalled that time in the house of Anna and Punks with Anna and me stretched out on the waterbed together with Punks. It was a twosome, initially. And upstairs, you and Anna, were also playing a twosome. But actually there were four of us, it was a foursome. When Anna joined the game and you remained outside, the triad no longer functioned. After Anna's proposal you said, "The fourth player has remained home, sick". And this amazed me.[5] Both you and Punks rejected a foursome. According

---

[5] See Part One, *Simon's Diary*, p.76 of the manuscript. Simon refers to the Socratic Timaeus: "One, two, three, but where, my dear Timaeus, is the fourth of those who were yesterday my guests and are to be my entertainers today?"

Jung comments as follows: "He has remained in the realm of the obscure mother, delayed by the lupine voraciousness of the unconscious which would have nothing escape from its jurisdiction unless an adequate holocaust is offered."

In short, quaternity is a symbol of totality, a triad is not. According to alchemic doctrine, the triad designates an opposition in that it presupposes another triad, just as above presupposes below, light presupposes darkness, good presupposes evil. Everywhere, says Jung, opposition signifies a potential and where the potential exists there is the possibility of a development and of an event because the tension generated by contrasts aims at equilibrium.

"If we picture to ourselves quaternity as a square and we divide it into two halves with a diagonal the result is two triangles whose vertexes point to opposite directions. Metaphorically, therefore, one can say: if totality, symbolized by quaternity, is divided into two equal parts, two triads pointing in opposite directions would derive therefrom."

Jung brings into play *the theriomorphic symbolism of the spirit in the fairy tale*. In it appear the wicked Huntsman, the prisoner Princess and her White Horse that is transformed into a tripod because 12 wolves have wrested a hoof from him. The tripod attribute of the white horse is due to an accident that occurred at the moment the animal was about to leave the realm of the Dark Mother. Expressed in psychological language this would mean that when the totality of the unconscious becomes manifest, i.e., when it leaves the unconscious and passes over to the sphere of the consciousness, one of the four remains behind. detained by the *horror vacui* of the unconscious. The upshot is a triad that corresponds to an antithetic triad, in short a conflict ensues.

The archetype of the spirit is always expressed in the form of an animal. The function of knowledge and of intuition is represented by a saddle horse. This indicates that even the spirit can be possessed. The Three-legged White Horse is the property of the diabolic Huntsman, whereas the four-legged horse is at first the property of the Witch, of a *mater natura* who prefigures the primitive, "matriarchal", so to speak, state of the unconscious, wherefore it alludes to a psychic constitution in which the unconscious is faced only by a weak, non-independent consciousness. The Four-legged White Horse demonstrates his superiority to the three-legged horse because it can command the other.

Since *quaternity* is a symbol of totality and totality plays an important role in the world of the images of the unconscious, the victory of the quadruped being over the tripod being is not surprising. Jung recalls that the alchemists called this problem the *Axiom of Mary*.

"With the alchemists we can clearly see how to the divine triad there corresponds a lower triad (similar to Dante's tricephalous devil.) This consists in a principle which, thanks to its symbolism, betrays an affinity with evil even though it is not exactly certain that it does not express something other than evil. Rather everything suggests that evil, that is to say it's current symbol, belongs to the family of these figures and represents the dark, the nocturnal, the infernal, the chthonic. The Below in this symbolism is in antithetical correspondence to the Above, that is, it is conceived as a triad like the Above."

In this study, *op.cit.* Jung accommodates everybody because his definitions of the Trinity and of the Triad are many and varied. To the trinity he adds the quaternity and by so doing he reverts to the enigma raised in the Timaeus dialogue. In short, there exists a problem of the three and the four.

The characteristic of tripod and quadruped is obviously irrational, but they are important for the analysis of myth and of dream. Now the characteristic of tripod, as the property of an animal, signifies an unconscious masculinity, immanent in feminine being. To it corresponds, in the true woman, the *animus,* which, like the magic horse, represents the "spirit." In the *Anima,* on the other hand, the triad does not coincide with a Christian representation of the Trinity, but with the "lower triangle," the lower triad of the functions that constitutes the so-called "shadow." The lower part of the personality is mostly and primarily unconscious. It does not represent the entire unconscious but only its personal section. On the other hand the Anima, insofar as it is distinct from the *shadow* personifies the collective unconscious. If the triad is associated to it as a saddle animal it means that the animal "rides" the shadow that is to say, it behaves like an incubus and in this case it possesses the *shadow.* But when the triad itself is a horse, it has lost its dominant position as a personification of the collective unconscious and, as a horse belonging to the Princess A, the hero's bride, it is "ridden", i.e. possessed. Like the Princess B. The triad is transformed by enchantment into *The Three-legged Horse.*

Jung explains the matter as follows:

1. The Princess A is the Anima of the hero. She rides, i.e. she possesses The Three-legged Horse, the shadow, the lower functional triad of the bride-groom. This means that she has confiscated the lower half of the hero's personality. She has grabbed him on his weak side, as often happens in ordinary life, because wherever one is weak one needs support and completeness. Woman is at her right and proper place at the weak side of man. This is how we would have to formulate this situation, were we to consider the hero and the Princess A as two ordinary persons. But since the story is of a wondrous character and unfolds principally in the magic world, the interpretation of Princess A as the Anima of the hero is certainly more just. In this case, the hero, through his encounter with the Anima, escapes the profane world like Merlin thanks to his fairy. In other words, as an ordinary mortal he is one who, as the prisoner of the wondrous dream, sees the world dimly, as through a fog.

2. The matter gets notably complicated as a result of the unexpected circumstance that the tripod, in turn, represents a feminine being, i.e., the entity corresponding to the Princess A. This is the Princess B. The latter, in her equine form, would correspond to the shadow of the Princess A (hence to her triad of the lower functions.) But the Princess B is distinguished from the Princess A in that, unlike her, she does not ride the horse but, instead, she is contained and magically transformed in it and for this reason she has fallen under the domination of a male triad. Hence she is possessed by the shadow.

3. Now the problem arises: whose is the shadow that possesses her? It cannot be the shadow of the hero because it has already been possessed by the hero's Anima. The fairy tale tells us that it is the Huntsman, the magician who has bewitched her. As we have seen, the Huntsman has a certain connection with the hero because the latter, little by little, puts him in his place. We could

to Jung, Oneness is simultaneously a Triad, and this is linked with femininity. But I didn't know its opposite, namely that three as an unequal number, is masculine. And Jung translates the triad directly as maleness. Punks, Anna and me, okay. Anna, me and Simon, okay. But why Roseanne?

---

therefore arrive at the supposition that at bottom the Huntsman is none other than the hero's shadow. But this conception is opposed by the fact that the Huntsman represents a considerable power that not only extends to the hero's Anima, but goes much further, indeed as far as the regal brother-sister couple of whose existence the hero and his Anima have no presentiment whatsoever and which also crops up suddenly in the fairy tale.

The power that goes beyond the sphere of the single one has a *super-individual* characteristic insofar as the latter is understood and defined as the obscure half of the personality of the single one. As a super-individual factor, the *numen* of the Huntsman represents the dominant element of the collective, thanks to its characteristics: Huntsman, Sorcerer, Raven, Magic Horse, Crucifixion, i.e., suspension at the top of the tree of the world. Hence the reflection of the Christian conception of the world in the sea of the unconscious logically assumes the features of Wotan. With the figure of the Huntsman we encounter an *imago dei* because Wotan is also a god of the wind and of the spirit wherefore the Romans opportunely called him Mercury.

Perhaps at this point it would be well to set Jung aside and stick only to the facts as narrated. In them there's neither nobility nor degradation, if we except the intellectual sickness of ordinary persons, with links to symbols and dreams, who in a moment of their magic life have wished to personify themselves in the mythic roles of the Princess/Bride and of the Hero/Huntsman.

18.

You went out to fetch Roseanne and came back sooner than I expected.

I had expected that you would have lingered in the car to gossip with her, at least for awhile, especially since you had my approval. Instead, I realized, (and this was another surprise,) that there is only a relationship of quiet, amicable fusion between the both of you, and that neither of you play games — like mailing recondite allusions or formulating phrases to fit occasions.

Roseanne struck me as a normal student, deferential but not distant. And I must admit, for the first time, that your figure suggested to me the image of the professor in slippers, cordial and relaxed, talkative and spontaneous, one more to make gentle fun of as the archetypical academic rather than one to admire as a male, or seducer. You were homespun and alien to arrogant airs, and often amusingly and pleasantly jocose. With just a few touches you had managed to create the right atmosphere, so much so that I no longer felt like a stranger, or defenseless, vis-à-vis Roseanne. A strange calm came over me. We prepared the lasagne together, chattering, laughing, exchanging jokes and quips. We seemed to be old friends, of the kind between whom everything has been already said and everything has been experienced in common. The kind of friends whom (apart from Punks and Anna) we have never had.

I felt like kissing and embracing Roseanne and if the moment suggested it, even to disrobe before her, to let her see how I was built, slim and sweet, sister and mother. Now she had a strange fascination for me. She had undressed and she had laid down with you, and yet it seemed to me that both of you had had hardly gazed each other.

Her anatomy aroused my curiosity. I observed the curves of her body, the big mouth, the housewifely arms, and I tried to imagine what her effusions and reactions during the love act would be like. The thought excited me, and from it I distilled a pleasure alternating between languor and aggressiveness. A forgotten image took shape before me, but it was not distinct or authentic and that image could have been a configuration of you and me. Do you remember the trip to the city of San Gimignano, years and years ago, when you were the guest of your publisher in Siena? A 12th century fresco, attributed to Niccolo di Segna, stamped itself on my consciousness. It was a nuptial scene. The bride and groom were seated in a tub of water; her right hand rests on his shoulder, washing it, while he places his left hand between her legs, washing them, and none of them seems to be saying a word to each other. They just look at each other. On the left side, some distance from them and not looking at them, is their handmaiden, arms outstretched, as if to protect them from strangers. I had a sudden desire to make love with you in front of Roseanne (the handmaiden,) in a tub even here in the kitchen, savoring the voluptuous smell of the gravy simmering in the pots. And, instinctively, I unbuttoned my blouse, my breast emerged in all its whiteness and I felt I was leaving pink bruises on my neck as I touched it.

Then I said: "Yesterday a girl in the library fled from a man who was masturbating while looking at her."

I looked at Roseanne, our eyes met. "The girl fled along the underground passages and I followed her. I thought I knew her but she vanished in the tunnels. "

"Why did you follow her?" you asked.

"I really don't know,"

Then Roseanne, blushing, said:

"I was that girl."

"That's what I thought," I said.

"I ran as fast and as far as I did because a woman was following me. But if I had recognized you, I would have stopped, and I would have broken into tears. "

"Why would you have broken into tears?"

"I felt a hatred for that man."

I went up to her and I embraced her. She was soft, very soft but tense.

"You know, Roseanne... I had planned to hate you. But now I can't anymore. Do you believe me?"

"It does one good to be forgiven... you're a good girl."

"No, I'm exclusive. This is my not so good side. Instead, it would be necessary to share."

"Share what?" you asked, looking up from the gas-range.

"Love, darling!"

"How about sharing a game of frisbee in the meanwhile?"

"And the lasagne?" Roseanne added.

"Let's go," and I accompanied her towards the garden. "We have the whole afternoon and evening before us. I'm really very glad that you came, you know that, I hope?"

"Me, too."

The afternoon slowly evolved into evening. We had played frisbee on the wet grass, joking, laughing, kidding each other. And you were the silliest of all, Simon. Two women were enamoured of you and you try to make yourself look ridiculous. At a certain point Roseanne, over-heated, flopped down on the wet grass and said that she had seen the god Pan running through the woods.

"The god who?"

I, too, flopped down on the wet grass and rolled around in it.

"Shall we undress him?" I suggested to Roseanne.

"Let's!" she agreed.

You had the round dance in mind. Matisse's Round Dance, you said. But this required that all three of us be nude. And as we were going through the motions of the round dance in the rain we blocked you, tearing off your shirt and your shorts, leaving you naked under the rain with your hands protecting the shadow between your legs. Roseanne and I went back to the house, padlocking the door, and directing obscene gestures your way and making ugly faces at you from the window. We let you in the house only when we noticed that you were shivering.

"I'm going to bed," you said. "Is anyone going to follow me?"

Together we followed you to the bathroom, we rubbed you dry very thoroughly. You were laughing, excited.

"But what are you two doing to me... what are you looking for?"

We were pretty much wet ourselves by now, but Roseanne did not want to undress.

"I'm alright, but I'm hungry!" she said. I went into the bedroom and slipped on my pajamas. "Roseanne," I called out. She came in, helped me arrange my hair, and then I said to her, "Do you know that Simon wants the both of us?"

"No, I don't believe that," she replied. "You'll see."

The lasagne were delicious despite the can of red peppers that you had added to the gravy, thinking they were peeled tomatoes! We were seated on the rug around the low glass table; enjoying the food and the wine, the candlelight and the music. We had also done lots of drinking. And now a warm feeling of pleasure and satisfaction enveloped us lovingly like a blanket. You had also lit the fireplace. The music was night jazz, soft and hyper-scrutable. The rain still beat against the window panes, but it was so cozy inside! Eyes closed, I stretched out on the rug and, once again, I surrendered myself to my dreams.

On the deserted beach in Tortola, in the Caribbean, there was a girl of my age in a bikini.

She said to me: "Uranus has entered the realm of Scorpio. For the next fourteen years we will have an increase in homosexuality."

"No, I go under the rainbow," I replied. "I'll become an hermaphrodite."

"Impossible," she said. "You're too much of a whore. You will never be able to love a woman."

"I'd be able to do anything", I said. "See? I'm water."

"No, you're Spring."

"Look," I tried to make her understand, "my personal history is simple. My father is not my father, but a man who my mother married in order to carry out certain roles. My mother conceived me on the high seas with a sailor who later died. She once showed me his photograph, dressed in officer's uniform. At first she said he was her cousin, a distant cousin, and later she told me that he was my father. A strange, distant father. And then one so young! If I looked backward, however, I saw Prick in his sandals, big around the midriff like a pregnant woman, but he was tall and bent, wore glasses and was always looking for a book. I didn't have girl friends when I was growing up. The faces that I knew were those of the Catholic nuns of New Canaan. But often I didn't go to the nursery school, preferring to sit on the station platform watching the incoming and outgoing trains."

"But you already had a body," she said. "And sex is hidden precisely in a train."

"No, no, it sits on the handle bars of bicycles," I said. And I added, "But that wasn't love. My kind of love is something that involves the whole body, not only a precise point of the body on which to draw, into which to enter with the pencil—I also dreamed of the other person (there was another person) who also had a pencil and who began to draw and who then put that pencil in that center which was me."

"But of what love are you talking about? I'm Roseanne, Roseanne, do you hear me?"

I took her hand and I placed it on my breast. It feels as light as a wing, and when it stops I feel it's like something dead.

"Love is in dreams and sex is in life," I said, resting my hand on her hand that was resting on my breast. "And in life no sexual act is similar to another sexual act. I'm evolutive, giving and receptive."

"I'm contemplative," she said, and she opened my eyes with two fingers. "Do you see me?"

Her face was directly over mine. We kissed. Then, with a ready laugh, we looked at you next to the fireplace, in your very serious yoga position, watching us as if we were objects in a museum.

"I feel like some ice cream," I said. "Do we have any ice cream?"

"Sorry, no," you answered from your distant corner, shaking your head.

"I'll go get some," Roseanne volunteered.

Outside it was windy, it was raining and it was cold. It seemed that spring had no intention of arriving this year. But she went out taking the key to our car. Why had I asked for ice cream? Why did I let her go, and not Simon? I wanted to punish her. But I didn't want to punish her. On the contrary! Yet I was satisfied by her departure. I was almost patronizing Roseanne. Perhaps she loved me. I mean to say that perhaps she also loved me. And this gave me relief, a sense of belongingness.

But from the void came your voice.

"You know that this kind of talk is damaging to me? The more you insist on this threesome, and the more I dwarf myself. I become the fourth player."

"Weren't you the one who first looked around for a threesome?"

"Number three stands for dissolution, darling. Mine of course."

"You make me feel guilty," I admitted.

She came back soaked, but visibly pleased to have done something. Perhaps she had felt a real need to estrange herself from herself, to change her body and the thoughts in her brain in the rain and to think things over, as well. I took her by the arm and accompanied her to the bathroom, I rubbed her down with a towel, dried her and then left her alone by the mirror where she began to comb her head.

"Hurry up," I said. "The ice cream is waiting for us."

We ate the ice cream around the fire, and we smoked another cigarette. Billie Holiday was recounting her sad story in a blues number. We were all getting bored, so I proposed to re-accompany Roseanne home. But I added, "You can also sleep here... in the small room." I blushed. And I understood that she understood, in fact she darted a glance at the door of the small room.

"No," she said. "I'm waiting for a phone call from my father." So I put on my overcoat and we escorted Roseanne to the dormitory. "There'll be another night," I thought to myself. The three of us exchanged kisses in the car as if she were going away for ever, as she herself put it. "It was a beautiful evening, thanks."

That night we slept in the small room, on the old mattress. It was a dream-filled night for me. One of them seemed to be a continuation of the strange dream on the Tortola beach. Now the girl on the beach was Roseanne, and I was Bes, her mother. You were also there, Simon, but suddenly your tiny shadow began to move, lengthening itself, and you became the fisherman, tall and proud. He reminded me that Matthias always calls me Bes, but when he mounted her and me, together, he had an amputated hand and I immediately remembered the stumped hand of the dream in New Canaan, but now the hand caressed my pubes and a whisper in my ear told me to do the same with the other girl, the girl in the bikini. Only the voice was the voice *of* the bear, yours. But, apart from this, what is strange is that while you were mounting us you didn't call her intimate recess a cunt, but a *temple*.

I wonder why.[6]

---

[6] This last paragraph is interesting because the dream is of a Jungian character. Evidently the fusion of Matthias and G.O. with the archetypical figure of the fisherman, which at the same time contains Simon, or his "voice", are elements of Vera's unconscious. The ancient hero, Matthias, has become the new hero, G.O. albeit still under the control of the standardized hero, Simon, who by making a distinction between words and their content, almost philosophizes in the manner of an old man, like the old man of the fairy tale, or of the father, he who knows much and is capable of discernment.

The dream is also interesting because it excludes Simon from the threesome relation—his voice becomes that of the fourth—and at the same time it consummates the threesome, in the symbol, with the participation of the fisherman who here has the same functions as the huntsman. Fisherman/Huntsman also become a synonym of *Stranger*.

Re-reading these *Diaries*, June 25, 1981, I note for the first time the recurrence of names, adjectives, attributes, descriptions of physical aspects, mutabilities of persona and personalities who, in some way, have something to do with the phenomenology of the psyche of the fairy tale. Not everything corresponds, yet everything corresponds. It depends on the reading.

Jung explains that in dreams it is the figure of the father from which originate persuasions, prohibitions and counsels. The indivisibility of this source is often emphasized by the fact that it consists only in an authoritarian voice that pronounces definitive judgments.

The word, *father*, in its various transformations in the relationships, recurs on p. 46 when Vera asks Simon, *"Whats my lover like, daddy?"*, and when Simon tells her, *"One of these days you'll abandon daddy and you will become Eve"*; on p. 45 when Simon calls Vera *"dear baby"*: *"It also applies to you, dear baby — once the primary trust is broken — that the father will catch you in his arms — life is born*; on p. 50: *"You've married your daughter... "*; on p. 125: *"I believe that Dress, jealous and displeased, must have been wracked for many nights and days by the crazy notion that the stranger Simon was none other than her Italian lover who had died at sea at the outbreak of World War II, and that now, transformed, he had come back to her in the guise of Simon in order to retrieve his daughter by marrying her, and this relegate Dress to an unsmiling old age and to her wierdish widowhood. "*

On page 152 Vera calls Simon, *"Father Confessor"*, and on p. 38 Simon writes, *"With a fatherly air, I remark... "*; on p. 43 and in the pages that follow, Simon recounts the fairy tale of the Son and of the Father. Hence in most cases it is the figure of an *old man* who symbolizes the "psyche" or "spirit" factor.

The word *old man*, by itself or in relation to the word *boy*, appears on p. 13. It underlines also the relationship *father/daughter* with a tinge of incest. *"The only thing that still interests this old man, exiled from all affections, exiled from himself, exiled from the great causes that enjoin participation, is the wild journey into the sex of this princess fourteen years his junior, on which he drunkenly feeds in a parody of incest. He's a child."* On p. 45 and following: *"Now there's an old man who is dancing in a room..."* At times this role is performed by a "real" spirit, that of a dead person.

The word *spirit* and the word *mercury* recurs an infinite number of times in the text and in the footnotes, so much so that I am quite familiar with them. References to the "dead person" as reincarnation or real spirit are found on p. 45 and in a footnote on p. III: *"Simon believed in the divine. Therefore he also believed in the stars, in the seasons, and in death that recurs in life. He believed to have had three lives, and all in a total form, in that they involved birth and death...* More rarely, we find grotesque figures similar to *gnomes* or to sapient and speaking *animals*. On p. 42 is recounted the fairy tale of the *Dwarf* and the *Young Girl*; on p. 165 we come upon the adjective "gnomish", and on p. 200 Simon *"dwarfs himself"*. *"The more you insist on this threesome and the more I dwarf myself, I become the fourth player."*

Now there is a kinship between "dwarf" and "gnome", Dictionaries define the gnome as an "earth-spirit, of small stature and deformed in appearance," and the dwarf as "a monstrous man because of his smallness and perhaps because of an alteration of his endocrine glands." Simon was short of stature, he did not classify himself as a dwarf, but it could also suggest that idea, it did not suggest itself because in general he looked normal, but actually he was lengthened by the boots that he constantly wore, and these had high heels. Nor was he deformed, but his optical affliction, glaucoma, at times made him strabic, indeed blind and deformed.

Jung, however, decidedly accepts gnome as synonym of dwarf. The forms of dwarves, he says, are found primarily in the dreams of women, hence it seemes logical to him that Barlach in *Der tote Tag (The Day of Death)* attributes to the mother the figure of a gnome with a "bearded arse," just as Bes is associated with Karnak's mother-goddess.

The spirit, or psyche, can also present itself to the two sexes in the form of a *boy* or an *adolescent*. For women this figure corresponds to the so-called "positive" *animus* which indicates the possibility of taking a conscious spiritual position. For men, this figure is not that univocal: it can be positive, and it has the significance of the "higher" personality of the *Selbst* or of the *filius regius*, as conceived by the alchemists. But it can also be negative and in this case it indicates the *infantile shadow*. In both cases the boy represents a certain spirit or psyche. The old man and the boy go together.

This couple also plays a notable role in alchemy as the symbol of Mercury, lung, again, says. It is Vera who on p. 168 declares: *"I have loved Mercury, this fantastic elf, this youthful, this elderly seducer who suffused me with animation. Now the animation has flown away, and I've become a rag...*

It is beyond doubt that culturally Vera was influenced by Simon, and in the specific case he is always the one who, albeit jokingly, identifies with Mercury.

On p. 39: *"I'll be Mercury. All alone and thrice one. Because it is I who impregnates, generates, gives birth, devours, kills... even myself."*

And on p. 41 he becomes an *"elf"* for Vera in that Simon says, *"Okay... I'm Pithagoras, I'm Nijinsky... I can dance for you."* The *"elf"*, i.e. the *gnome*, is linked to the dance in the popular culture; and Mercury himself, as spirit, is a dancer and a satyr. On p. 115 Simon, sarcastically, calls himself *"scientist and satyr."*

Even more illuminating is the fact that Simon, among his favorite Latin poets, had also translated Horace and one of his Odes (X-Liber Primus, CARMINUM) to Mercury, titling it "Ode to my great uncle," since Horace writes, *"Mercuri, facunde nepos Atlantis."* He had it framed in a little painting among the many little paintings in his office, now surely the property of Anacleto Zinghelli who inherited all of the scientist's literary remains. What I remember of the discussions, however, is that the *Ode to the great uncle* calls Mercury *ingenious* because he has civilized the mores of humankind with the gift of the word and with the use of the gymnasium, he calls him *inventor* because he takes and hides anything and everything that strikes his fancy as, for example, Apollo's heifers, a lordly being who at that moment was without his quiver but who, nevertheless, burst into laughter at the prank. He also taught guile to the wealthy Priam, allowing him, under his guidance, to get out of Troy and escape the enemy occupants of the city. Thus we also know him as *professor* and as *artist*. The great uncle places only pious souls in the sacred chairs, he has a small group of friends whom he keeps in a state of harmony by using his *"virga aura"* (golden rod), and he is loved by the gods who dwell in the supernal and infernal regions alike. Zinghelli had lent Jung to Simon after he had read this Horatian translation, and the result was a course on social anthropology which Simon had given during 1972-73. (See footnote 22, first part of "Simon's Diary".).

But what compels attention in the aforementioned passage is that reference to Bes, gnome, associated with the mother-goddess. Often the onomasticon does not reveal its mysteries yet there are at least two names in this text, Bes and Shait precisely, that assume a surprising importance in the light of the Jungian interpretation. Vera is called Bes by Matthias and by his wife, Sue, but never by Simon or by others. A personal document of Vera's found among Simon's manuscripts reveals that her middle name is B. I've discovered that B stands for Bless, so willed by Ms. Dress in thanksgiving for the miraculous way in which she succeeded in conceiving her daughter. It was later deformed into Bes by Matthias, since in general lovers give their women pet names that have a meaning only for them. But I presuppose that Matthias called her that way because Vera had come to him (just as to her mother) under the aspect of a benediction.

As regards the name Shait, it is not a traditional patronymic in the family of G.O. Shait. Shait was born as Guy Oliver Shy, which he had legally changed into Shait without realizing the seriousness of his action. Simon was the first to analyze that name for him, making it derive from the Arab word *Shaitan,* which in Hebrew means Satan.

Jung observes that the Arab philosophers consider *Shaitan* an Arab word. They see it as a derivation of the root *sh-t-n,* whereas some prefer the root *sh-y-t.* Preferably it is thought that the Judeo-Christian Satan is of Arab origin. In Hebrew, however, *Saitan* is also the name of a serpent.

"With the enormous differentiation of late-Hebrew angelology and demonology, the imaginary world of the Hebrew religion receives a polytheistic feature which must have made it easy for it to absorb the primitive demonism of the pre- islamic Arabs," writes Jung. "Even the name of the serpent is, perhaps, not exempt from the influence of the very precocious assimilation of Satan as the serpent of the earthly Paradise."

From time to time in his rage as the offended person, Simon calls his friend "painter-hero" (p. 29), "anti-hero" (p. 46), "little satan Shait" (p. 101), and again on p. 47 there is a reference to the serpent in the Garden. Simon: *"Eve is already pre- formed in the Garden, and the serpent already exists in the Garden."*

Vera: *"Is Shait the serpent?"*

Also singular is the fact that recurring common words in the test such as *old man, boy, stranger, raven, princess, huntsman, fisherman* come to assume amazing meanings. The singularity lies also in the fact that these words are interchangeable: at times it seems that they describe both Simon and G.O. Shait. In a flash of intuition Vera actually considers Simon to be a "counterfigure" to G.O. (p. 46). If we were to interpret these *Diaries* as a fairytale, the designation "old man" becomes of primary importance in that the old man appears in fairy tales as a "sage" or as an ambiguous elf, a malign figure who, out of selfishness, does evil for evil's sake. As the archetype of the spirit, in the form of man, gnome or animal, the old man always presents himself in a situation in which perspicacity, intelligence, good sense, decision, method would be called for. At times, he is the "white sorcerer" and at other times he is the "black sorcerer." He is identified with the *sun,* he carries with him a tub which he uses to roast a gourd, he has a positive, favorable character that points to what is above, but he also has a character that points to what is below, a character that is in part negative and unfavorable, in part simply chthonic, but neutral in its broadest aspect.

His very figure as a dwarf *a priori* involves a restrictive dimension. As a handicapped being because of the loss of an eye, tom out of winged malign spirits, he has lost his sight and his perspicacity, and has entered the demoniacal world of darkness. He is damaged by it, in fact, he recalls the fate of Osiris who lost an eye through the malign look of a black pig, Seth. In another fairy tale, he appears mutilated in a leg, in a hand, and in an eye, and he reawakens a dead man with an iron club. By mistake he is killed by those whom he has often resuscitated, and along with his life he loses his entire fortune. It is ironic that Charlotte Shark would metamorphosise Simon in the skin of the "*uncatchable wild lion-tailed macaque with a tufted tail and a bushy mane who is finally killed with a shot from the carbine of the character symbolizing Envy, who is in the service of Death...* (p. 67)

Often in these texts the archetype of the spirit is expressed in a *bestial* form, the old man is a malefactor and a sensualist, and generally exhibits human aspect and behavior, "nevertheless his magic qualities together with his spiritual superiority," observes Jung, "hint at something extra-human, super and sub-human, in good and in evil. His animal aspect does not indicate a devaluation, since in many respects the animal is also superior to man."

Nevertheless, the animal, he adds, in his complete unconsciousness, always remains the symbol of that psychic sphere of man that is hidden in the obscurity of bodily instinct. Jung cites a famous fairy tale in which there are pigs, ravens, princesses, heroes, huntsmen, three-legged horses and four-legged horses, and also crucifixion and salvation. In it figure pagan and Christian aspects. It is rather complex, even if Jung defines it as "childishly simple." It points to, however, on the one hand and with rare evidence—to the contradictory character of the archetype of the psyche and, on the other, to the play of antinomies "which has as its only great purpose the higher development of the consciousness."

I have dwelt at length on this footnote in order the better to clarify in my own mind the "bourgeois" bestiality of these diaries, and to extract some "edifying teachings" therefrom, as I state in my introductory remarks.

19.

We had Roseanne over for supper last night too. It was a last meeting before her return to Utica. I phoned her. She was un-decided.

"I've got to tell you about a dream I had. You were in it."

"Me? Why me?"

"So you're coming?"

"Okay."

In the last few days I had been almost totally obsessed by the idea of a *menage a trois*. I felt a rancor towards myself and towards Simon. I felt him obstinately distant, uncommitted, still vaguely diffident and fearful of my unforeseeable reactions. And, above all, I felt that he no longer trusted me. He was afraid that I might lock him definitely in a situation which he would bitterly regret later. He thought that I was blackmailing him, and it was true. I was blackmailing. And, for my part, I was staking everything.

I was nervous Monday, Tuesday, and all of yesterday. Yesterday, after accompanying you to Senator Key's house for a consultation on university matters, I found myself again alone at nine in the morning with no desire whatsoever to work on my thesis. I decided to clean the house again, figuring that some physical work would distract me, by tiring me. It's curious, but in this last crisis-ridden month I've cleaned the house so many times that sometimes I think I've become a slipshod housekeeper.

I had stopped at Anaconda Plaza, at the drug store, to get a supply of cigarettes. And as I often do when I've got time to kill, I stopped to browse at the paperback book shelf. It's incredible how much stuff is being put out by the publishing industry, especially in the matter of books dealing with sex. We Americans are innocent and this is why we want to inform ourselves on everything, for fear of being left behind. For many of us psychology, especially, remains the frontier of mystery. And I was trying to fill that lacuna. At last I found the book I was looking for. It was an anthology of letters written to a well-known magazine, *Sex Forum*. Frank and confessional, the letters covered a great variety of erotic experiences, from lesbianism to sperm-swallowing. It had an index so I immediately looked up the term *menage a trois*. It was there, but it explained nothing. It suggested another text as reference. Disappointed, I was about to return the book to its place when my attention was drawn to the word *troilism* which I did not know but which described exactly that type of threesome experience which had been in our consciousness since last Saturday night.

There were letters *pro* and *con* troilism. I thus discovered that my reactions, during Saturday night, were neither unique nor abnormal. The *voyeur* element is shared by all those who enjoyed this type of encounter. It is sexually and mentally exciting, especially for that mind in search of a renewal of routine living.

According to the doctor who edited the collection, there exists in us the unconscious satisfaction of watching other persons make love. It is a satisfaction that derives, so asserted the doctor, from the repressed desire, that has never surfaced before, to spy on our parents in their performance of the sexual act. Often the participants themselves become even more sexually excited when they know that a stranger is present, spying on them. The mirror in a room or on a bed often assumes the personality of a "third". Indeed to see one's own acts in the mirror corresponds to one of the properties of the *voyeur*.

I bought the book and went back home. I was so excited by that reading that I wanted to make love instantly, in front of our looking-glass, never used before for this purpose. But you were far away, discussing who knows what with the state legislators... so I masturbated in front of the mirror, deriving a savoury relief from it. I thought of the man in the library, and I thought of Roseanne. Did Roseanne masturbate? Did you ever masturbate Roseanne? Would you have masturbated me and her at the same time? If so, how?

I impulsively phoned Roseanne, and I invited her. Then I set to work with a brush and a pail of soapy water, listening to pop music.

You were supposed to phone me around ten o'clock, but the hour passed and there was no ring on the phone. I told myself that the work you were doing had required more time than foreseen and I tried to forget you. I continued with the house cleaning operation, cherishing the moment when I would stretch myself out in the bathtub. Eventually two o'clock rolled around, and then two-thirty, and the usual fears re-surfaced. I myself had accompanied you to the place of your appointment, but then was it really true that you went there and not elsewhere? And what if you were with Roseanne? Certainly you were there when I phoned, and perhaps you had both made fun of me, of this fidgety and police-like wife. I was seized by a sudden rage, I beat my fists against the wall. But then, suddenly, you called at three and asked me to come pick you up. I got a glimpse of you from the car, you looked sodden and exhausted in the wind that was beginning to blow harder. In fact, you yawned during the ride home.

"This has been one of those days that I call lost forever," you said, with a tired smile. "All I want to do is sleep."

"I invited the Holy Spirit to dinner."

"Roseanne?" you made a sudden movement. A new life flowed through your quickened body. You no longer yawned.

Then, almost suddenly, you sat back again, depressedly, and in a lamenting tone you said, "But why, why Vera?"

"I thought it would please you."

"No, I'm fed up... I'm fed up with dragging myself in shit, in troubles, in body games. I'm fed up with eating, drinking, fucking morning, noon and night, rancid lectures, mean-spirited colleagues, passive students, cold hearts..."

"The meeting with Senator Kay must have really depressed you."

"It sure did. There was a lady who looked like an owl, in an empty and dusty room with old registers and piles of papers. When I was seated with the others, she stood up behind me, observing my neck. She was so fat and worn-out that I felt my own flesh falling apart. I thought of my eyes, I thought of cigarettes producing cancer, I thought I had syphilis, I thought of a little room in a hospital and of my son Sandro, in Italy, whom I would have urgently set for, whom I would have begged to bring me a pistol. A pistol for his father, a coward in the face of illness."

"Would you use it?"

"Maybe..."

"Who was that woman?"

"Everybody called her Mrs. Immortality. She built, after raising money here and there and everywhere, the Public Library of Anaconda, and she has also placed my books on its shelves. She has been the favorite guest of governors and senators. She was also an old flame of Herbert Hoover, an adviser to Cardinal Spellman... she's a three-time divorcee, and two of her husbands committed suicide following the divorce. As she was observing my neck, I wondered just where the magic might reside in Mrs. Immortality's grotesque body."

At home I made him a strong gin-tonic, which he promptly gulped down. After which he had another, took a shower, and changed his clothes. Then the book caught his eye.

"What's this?"

"It's a gift for you. In it there's a word, troilism, that made me buy it."

You leafed through it lazily, then you threw it into a corner. I realized that you had already read it.

"At what time is Roseanne coming?"

"You have to go pick her up."

"Now?"

"In a little while, yes."

You went out, unwillingly. I, instead, began to amuse myself. I prepared the chicken, I drank another gin-tonic, and when you both came into the kitchen I said, and with an exuberance that surprised me, "How punctual you both are!" I embraced both of you, kissing her first, on the mouth, and then you. And you said:

"Look at that! If I had kissed her you would have accused me of performing an illegal act!"

"Why didn't you then?"

You first kissed me, then her. And Roseanne, shrugging her shoulder, said, "I've read that polygamy is legal, at least in some areas of Idaho."

"But not anal sodomy," I said. "That is prohibited all over America."

I realized that, trying to be witty, I had made a stupid and senseless remark but one that, at the same time, established the limits of "our" polygamy. But your face darkened. Making some excuse, you went into the bedroom, adding that we should call you when dinner was ready. Or, did you simply want to leave her alone with me?

We sat down at the kitchen table, drinking gin-tonics. Roseanne was wearing a dowdy dress, a bit babyish, which was fashionable among students. Nevertheless she was very well-built, athletic without being hard. An ideal stewardess type! I asked about her interview with TWA and she replied, "Depressing." And I asked about her family, about her father and mother, and about the boy she was planning to marry. She had even bought a trousseau. But then the marriage never took place. Why?

"Because of my virginity," Roseanne said. "I was afraid."

"Me too, but of my mother."

"I was afraid of my father."

This was followed by a reflective pause, then Roseanne added: "No, it's not that exactly. I wasn't afraid of him, but of his trust. He always had such great trust in me, in that matter. Every time I came back from somewhere his eyes x-rayed me. He spoke very little. What did you do with Sinbad? Did you enjoy yourself? Etcetera. And I knew the answer that he wanted."

"Do you love your father very much?"

"He's super."

"More than your mother?"

"I also love her, but he's super." I didn't understand. Then she added, "When we were little, my sister and I, she always attacked him. But my father always was silent, patient..."

I studied her.

How different Roseanne would be today if she had followed her impulse, if she had given herself to Sinbad instead of respecting the paternal law! She would have never entered my life. She would be a mother and wife now. Instead, she had reduced herself to the experience of the mature man, stealing. But hadn't I also done the same? I had decided to loose my fake virginity with Simon, knowing very well that he was married with two children. And then dragging him along with me, as I could not have done that with Matthias. Are we women rapacious? Nevertheless, I still insist with myself that I did not steal Simon from Billie. He loved me. He had wanted it. He wanted, more-over, to remain in America. In fact, he had used me precisely for this purpose. Or do I imagine all these things in self-justification? I don't know. I know only that I would not have him taken away from me by Roseanne, because I would have left him first. Perhaps this is why I wanted the threesome relationship, so that I could build an alibi for myself. And in this way nobody would have robbed from anybody. Hell, of course, would welcome us with joy, but together.

Then, without looking at me, she said: "I'm sorry over what happened between me and your husband."

"Do you love him?"

"I don't know... and you?"

"I don't know, either. The difference between you and me is that I'm his wife, and this makes it more a matter of pride than of love. But I believe I still love him..."

"I'm sorry. You are a good person."

"No, not at all. At first I felt offended. Now I'm no longer offended. On the contrary, look, I'm glad that we've talked about it."

"And the dream?"

"Ah, the dream!" And I blushed. "Okay, I'll tell it to you. I was on a beach with you and him, and he made love with you and then with me. Isn't that horrible ?"

"No," she said, and smiled. She reached out a hand and took mine. "You know," she said, "one time I also had a dream. I was with him and he was with another woman. I don't remember her face, but certainly it was you. And I was happy, I swear, and in harmony with the whole world."

I got up. The chicken was ready now. All that remained to be done now was to kindle a log in the fireplace, and wake up the pascià in the other room.

I said: "You go call him."

She laughed.

"If I go alone, he'll grab me instantly. If we go together he'll grab us together..."

"You know him so well."

"No, I don't. But I do know one thing. When he wants something, there's no stopping him..."

We entered the room on tip-toe. You were sleeping like Duke Alexander de Medici in Guicciardini's description.

"Lord, are you sleeping?"

Uttering these words, stabbing him with a dagger (a long-stemmed carnation which I had taken from the looking-glass,) and passing it from one side to the other of his body were all one and the same action. The duke, after receiving so grievous a wound, rolled backwards on the bed and, thus rolling, he slipped down from the rear of the bed and attempted to escape towards the door, shielding himself with the book on troilism which he had taken with him. But Roseanne dealt a knife-thrust to his face (it was the broken stem of another carnation,) and slashing one of his temples she cut a great part of his left cheek. Meanwhile, Vera, who had pushed him back on the bed held him there on his stomach by pressing down him with all her might, while keeping a hand over his mouth to prevent him from shouting. So the duke, helping himself as much as he could, bit her so hard and angrily on her forefinger that Vera, who by now had saddled herself on him completely, could not strike him with the flower-dagger so she called out to Roseanne for help. Roseanne ran here and there about the room, and being unable to wound Simon without wounding Vera first or, at the same time. At best she could pierce only the straw mattress. But finally she took recourse to a knife which she happened to have on her person (it was a hairpin) and grazing the duke's throat with it, she jabbed at it again and again until it was properly cut. After he was dead, she inflicted still other wounds on him as a result of which he shed so much blood that it flooded almost the whole room. What was noteworthy in all this was that for the whole time that Vera held him firmly underneath her, and for the whole time that he saw Roseanne run from the front to the rear of the bed, and vice-versa, exploring ways to kill him, he never complained, or made an attempt to shake her off his back; nor did he make any effort to release the finger that he had lovingly seized between his teeth.

Finally, exhausted after that unexpected orgasm, I said: "Lord, are you dead?" And I ran to the bathroom to wash up.

20.

We sat down on the rug to dine.

As a scientist, Simon, you tend to perceive reality in symbolic terms, attaching great importance to details. You know very well the difference that exists between the formal atmosphere created by sitting around a dining room table and the informality resulting from sitting crossed-leg on the rug near the fire, as was your express wish.

The food was tasty. Roast chicken in a stew of peeled tomatoes, garlic and parsley, and *risotto alla Milanese,* suffused with saffron. We ate slowly, enjoying everything, talking of usual and casual things. Roseanne asked you why you were so interested in watching the TV without the sound. I replied: "According to him, a comic film assumes form on the screen... and we ourselves can provide the missing dialogue." "Curious, I must say," she commented. After the meal was over, I quickly cleaned up, piling the plates in the washing machine. Usually I washed them right away, but now I wanted to stay with you and her, without leaving you alone for a minute. When I returned I found you both stretched out on the Peruvian stole, sipping wine, silent, gazing at the fire. You had put Coltrane on the record player, but very low, absorbtive. The sensual flows of the other Saturday were not yet present, despite the kisses on open mouths that had ushered in the evening, and despite the battle on the bed that had taken place a short time earlier which you had defined as an attempted homicide on the part of both of us, your women.

Now I was looking for a triggering cause, and finally I said: "I bought a new dress, do you want to see it?"

You jumped up, surprised.

"A new dress? But when did you buy it?"

"When I went shopping with Kate, do you remember that day she came to your office and when she commented that she very much liked my choice?"

You didn't remember. Yet Kate had made a terrible *gaffe* because the choice of the dress was a secret. I wanted to prepare you before telling you about it, waiting for the right moment. And you, distractedly, replied: "Yes, the jacket is really beautiful." But you were referring to an ensemble that I had bought two weeks before. But Kate understood and together we laughed about the risks of life when even secrets of no real importance can cause apprehension and misunderstandings. You, on the other hand, had initiated a new economic plan for the household budget, and I was afraid of an angry outburst.

I said to Roseanne: "It's a white jersey, very sexy, you'll like it too."

"Can it be seen?" she asked, and, together we stared at you.

"Oh, let's all take a look at the very sexy jersey."

"Shall I bring it out here and try it on?"

"Put it on."

Appy, I went to change, taking off my shirt and pants. I undressed completely, leaving on me only my panties. They were soft and thin, a strip of silk at best. You yourself had advised me to buy them. And even though at first I had felt insulted by your suggestion, figuring that you wanted to dress (and undress me) as you had probably done with other women, I was now satisfied with bikinis. A woman, I told myself, must always try to appear sexually fresh to her man, if she wants to keep him in bed over the years. It was now 13 years that we had been sharing a bed together. I also removed my bra in order to slip on the new dress. It was truly stupendous, very daring, chic and designed deliberately to set a woman's body in bold relief. Made of a close-fitting texture, the dress wrapped itself around the body, emphasizing the curves. The most notable detail was the open-neck, so low it was useless to wear the bra. I did not see myself as a Scarlet O' Hara, but that dress did so much for me that I could have competed with any other girl, including Roseanne.

When I came into the living room in barefoot, aware of being sexually desirable, I saw you both on your knees in front of the fire, you with your arms on her shoulders and she with hers on yours.

"Here I am for you... Am I disturbing?"

I felt the scratch of jealousy return, but I didn't want to spoil everything, now.

"It's really cute," Roseanne said. "It looks very well on you."

You got up, lighting a cigarette. And finally, with a worried expression on your face, you said:

"So this is the dress?"

"Don't you like it?"

"No, that's not it."

"It's one of the few occasions when having tiny tits is an advantage."

"I can see that very well. But with that kind of an outfit, you're looking for a lover. You didn't buy it to keep a husband."

Roseanne and I protested.

"So you don't like it."

You laughed: "I'm wondering why you said that it looked good only on tiny-titted women. Wouldn't it look good on Roseanne?"

Such a remark would have irritated me on any other occasion. Roseanne herself interjected: "Are you crazy? There's nothing more personal than a dress."

"Okay. But didn't we agree that, at least tonight, each one of us was entitled to do what he or she pleased? If you don't want to try it on, Roseanne, that's entirely up to you."

Roseanne looked at me, questioningly. "He's right," I said. "Let's put a fashion show on for him."

I had another sexy outfit which I had bought last year for the trip to Italy and which you, Simon, considered so provocative that could lead to a street riot. I proposed that I wear that one, and Roseanne the other. Roseanne agreed and this gladdened me, the evening was unfolding in the desired direction. So we went into the bedroom carefully closing the door behind us, even though at this point such a precaution was rather silly. I took off my dress, shamelessly displaying my body, totally naked except for the bikini. I observed her to see if she was observing me while she slowly undressed, but I was also curious to see the body of the girl with whom you had made love. Her legs were robust and nervous, like those of a ballerina. Roseanne did take dance lessons. Her body was very beautiful, shapely, full and hard, whereas I was fragile, bony and slim, almost diaphanous. The only way I could show off an attractive body was to preserve its slenderness to excess, while Roseanne, with the years, would have to face the perils of pregnancy which leave certain zones of the body flabby, while puffing up others.

I put on the dress that you had considered too far out for Italy. The gown was long and pleated, made of printed silk. Its novelty consisted in the top piece, a small pea-colored jersey held together by two laces, one around the neck, the other around the waist. Inside it I appeared nude. And Roseanne put on the new dress I had bought. It looked good on her. The whiteness of the material contrasted violently with her dark almost swarthy complexion.

We came into the living room on tip-toe, as if flying on a gangway, offering ourselves to your eyes and your judgment, summarized in your comment: "I was right, it doesn't go well only with tiny tits."

Roseanne protested: "But I'm not big-titted!"

You drew closer to us to kiss Roseanne's breasts, and then mine.

"See, Simon," I said, "you're confused, you don't know what you want."

"It's true. Abundance blinds me, like the food, so I end up eating nothing at all."

We returned to the bedroom, again carefully closing the door behind us. Roseanne got back into her own clothes so quickly that I barely noticed her putting on her bra and her panties which were long, white and girlish-looking like laced-edged shorts. They masked the whole lines of her body. I, instead, dressed myself slowly, perhaps in order the better to be observed by her, or maybe because I sensed that you would be coming into the room. I was lounging between the chest of drawers and the bed, when you came in; I saw you from the mirror. And I noticed that when Roseanne was about to put on her dress you tore it out of her hands.

"It's hot here," you said. "Why don't you stay as you are? We can relax next to the fire, and even imagine we're on a beach."

Roseanne surprised me by instantly consenting to the proposal without uttering a word. She returned to the living room in her over-sized panties, and I did the same in my bikini. We stretched out on the Peruvian stole with you, fully dressed, in the middle, scrupulously avoiding to touch us. Then, suddenly, pulling on the elastic band around Roseanne's panties, you said: "Why don't you take them all off? Let's imagine we're on a nudist beach. I was on one in Senegal, nudity quenches desire."

"No, no," she protested. "The panties are a must to me if I want to survive this night."

I laughed, because it was true: pure like a virgin on her nuptial night!

"I'm going to take my shirt off at least, do either of you mind?"

"You can take everything off, if you'd like," I said, and I closed my eyes.

You were next to me and her, in shorts yourself now, with one hand on her, the other on me. Then you pulled my hand towards the center of your body, and I immediately noticed that you had a semi-erection. Then you also drew her hand to the same spot, and her hand grazed my hand and your erection.

But she withdrew her hand instantly, as if scorched.

"You really don't want to take everything off?"

"I'm fine the way I am, thank you," she replied, in an irritated tone. Then she turned around and lay down on her stomach, hiding her head between her arms. *"I've read that polygamy is legal, at least in some areas of Idaho." "But not anal sodomy. That's prohibited all over America." "You two do whatever you please, I'm going to sleep."*

You stared at me. "Do you want to?"

"Yes."

My body, my mind and my nerves were excited to a fever pitch. I was conscious of the fact that something very strange was taking possession of me. I wanted you to make love with me, but at the same time I wanted you to start off with her. In fact, you turned towards her, laying a hand under her belly, trying once more to pull off the elastic band around her panties. But she stirred, visibly annoyed, pressing her body even harder against the Peruvian stole and her hands even more closely against her head. Then, discouraged, you again stretched yourself out between the two of us, and said:

"The same rite is being repeated after so many years. I was ten years old when for the first time I perceived that a girl was made for love. This girl used to sleep beside me in the hay-loft in Selimo during the thrashing time in our countryside. Worn out, the men and the women slept and snored in the darkness of the hay-loft, but she and I held out breaths. When I whispered to her to take off her tiny underpants, she said, 'Pull the lace.' Despite the darkness, I found it immediately, it was a chance. I mounted her, but remained absolutely still. I didn't have a hard-on, I had nothing. It was as if I were on a bridge, and she was the water. Then I realized that I was afraid. What if those around us should wake up? They could have killed me with their pitchforks. I dismounted her and fell asleep. On the next day, in the sunlight, I avoided her eyes and she mine, but we flirted which each other by playing hide and seek behind the trees. We had tried to do something so much bigger than ourselves that in the light of day we were ashamed of ourselves, though knowing that henceforth we were bound to each other by a secret."

Then you got up, slipped off your shorts and threw them into the fire. I glimpsed your semi-erect prick, and I saw the flame. You were wholly bent over the flame, as if you wanted to immolate yourself. I shouted, "Come back here between us, have you gone crazy?"

Roseanne also turned around and saw you nude.

"What are you doing?"

"Get up," I told her, "give me this!"

I gathered up the stole and I threw it over you, pulling you away from the fire.

"I'm going to bed," you said, and you disappeared in the bedroom.

Roseanne and I remained alongside the fire. I took her hand and pressed it. We remained thus alongside the fire, silent, until very late, until the coal in the fireplace turned to ashes. I began to feel cold. But it was also a feeling of fatigue. So I said to Roseanne, "Let's go see the scoundrel."

We went into the darkened room and slipped under the bed-sheets, she on one side of you, I on the other. Your body gave off a smell of burning.[1]

---

[1] Page 10 of this text (Part One, "Simon's Diary") already foresees the book's end, which is the marital relationship between Vera and Simon, and even the upshot of the disaster. Simon writes: "*Although sex is the most unreal of fantasies, it gives one joy and repose, it is another life at the portals of death. Our sex life, however, is poisoned by social monsters, by boredom, by porno-fantasy and by luke-warm blood. Vera knows this, but she always demands more, and now she is projected towards regions unknown, and all that is left for me is to await the new unknown. It will be a shattering event, but even that will pass...*"

The following year, 1975, Vera and Simon recognize that their marriage has been incestuous, and that it is necessary to break it up, put an end to it... They were father and daughter, and at the same time brother and sister. She abandoned herself completely to the interests of G.O., her hero, and Simon, who at this point definitely becomes the huntsman, the sorcerer who has bewitched her and who, at the hero's command is thrown to the ground and trampled by the horses.

Simon often called Vera "princess," and called Roseanne "my princess." By degrees the sorcerer takes the place of the hero and it is possible that Simon actually feels re-born and assumes the figure of hero in Roseanne's eyes. That he called her "my princess" is explainable in terms of the unconscious, that new part of fascination that tends towards what is above, the higher. Jung would say that in this case Vera is Princess A, and Roseanne Princess B. The latter, in her equine figure, corresponds to the shadow of Princess A. But Princess B is distinguished from Princess A in that, unlike her, she does not ride the horse, but it is contained and magically transformed into one and, in consequence, she falls under the dominion of a triad. Hence she is possessed by a shadow.

If things had taken a different course, there was the possibility that Simon/Hero would have married Roseanne, and Guido/Hero would have married Vera. It was impossible because Vera, at first, threatened to kill her and Simon if they ever should marry, and when she was sure that she could crucify the Raven she began her deep association with Shait.

Roseanne wrote furious letters, ordering the couple to stop plaguing her over the phone. One letter, dated "Monday evening after your call", began: "Will you please stop calling me up? My parents are always sitting 'near' when you phone, and I have to explain to them why you call so often." "...and you Vera, as regards the way we took leave of each other, I, for once, left without rancor or resentment. Two things did displease me: (1) the fact I had occasioned another quarrel between the two of you; (2) your threat to kill Simon and me if we ever got married. This really upset and frightened me because I was completely out of touch with what was being said and above all because you were not joking: to think that you can consider yourself capable of killing really shook me up."

That letter also says: "... and you, Simon: - please forgive me if I told you things that hurt you. I tend to be brusque and even ironical with you, but only because I know you can take it and that it can also do you some good. The fact that we are so attracted to each other sexually is at once unfortunate and marvelous. But your possessiveness turns me off..." "Simon and Vera: - I think that we have subjected the idea of a *menage a trois* to a grave test. One must always avoid comparing sexual experiences if there's a third around because it seems to me that the right to make love as a twosome should be respected with discretion. Love and sex aside, I should like to have a companion with whom to share my life and to whom I can give everything, knowing that he loves me as I want to be loved. I don't know whether I have what it takes to live with more than one person, male or female, I would like to have children (one or two of my own, the others adopted,) married or otherwise." "I am finishing writing this letter today, Tuesday, June 12. I just received a letter from TWA and I get the impression that it is a much more obliging and courteous company than others to which 1 applied. Farewell."

After Roseanne's renunciation because of Vera's threat, Simon dedicated himself to making Vera happy, following her step by step in her love affair with G.O. And just like in the fairy tale, Simon did the same thing: He immolated himself for the person he loved. I am overwhelmed by the boxes of notebooks, as I said at the beginning of this commentary. It is only of interest to cite some excerpts from Vera's *Diaries*, 1974-75, to recapture the amorous and seductive nature of this woman.

In connection with a party in G.O's house, Vera writes: "I got myself up meticulously, then I put on the violet dress that fits me tightly and sets my figure off flatteringly. I dressed myself up having Guido in mind, trying to make myself as beautiful as possible for him... and, in fact, as Simon confirmed, I was really sexy... Guido and Phedra greeted us at the door - friendly, comical kisses on the cheeks. Guido had wanted to kiss me on the mouth but I turned my head lightly, so our kisses were lost..."

"I: - I must ask you a terrible question, Simon. May I? Is it so terrible for you to know that I'm about to get involved in an affair with G.O. Shait? No, you replied. And there was nothing else to say. I hope that everything will go smoothly within this frame of our mutual understanding. But it won't be easy. Simon wants me to remember. It is important to him because we have arrived at an agreement: he will leave me my freedom, but he will still give me the security of his love only if I will be honest with him for he, too, has chosen the amorous road of the truth.

"He asked me, 'You want me to get mad at you, right?' And he said this with hostility. But this wasn't what I wanted. When I'm angry I rebel. I go along my own way, with regret, but never accepting authority without comprehension. In fact, I have chosen the only way for conquering my love, in my unique selfish way, and what I really wanted, and still want, is naught else but this experience with G.O. Shait.

"I have had few experiences in my life. I am deeply, so deeply attracted by him, in every way, in my senses, in my body... He's Dionysius perhaps because he's so alive, so vital, and I don't want to lose anything. I believe that Guido knows this and he's correct when he said, 'In loving another, one will truly arrive at loving himself.'

"I want this experience, and I am seizing the opportunity. I only hope that I shall not lose everything, and by this I mean Simon. I know that Simon is the man that I love in the deepest sense, because we have exchanged so many things, and we have grown together in mutual understanding, in feeling each other's presence without the need of words. But I want G.O. and I don't want to lose Simon.'

'After all, I'm not a very clean person, and I have so many defects,' G.O. says.

And I: 'Tell me about your defects. I like to know the defects of others. It makes me feel superior.'

And G.O.: 'Very seriously, I'm a vain man, I've often thought about it and I've confirmed that it's true, but probably not dangerously so, I'm not dangerous. I greatly appreciated that line by Simon, *I spend my life in profile.*'

'I, too, was vain in many ways, G.O. We are so alike and probably that's the reason why we are attracted to each other sexually...'

G.O. says, 'I'm selfish, too.' I've also thought about this, whether it was really true, but aren't we all selfish in our own way? Each one of us has his or her own way of betrayal and concealment. The shortest way is to admit it, as Guido has done, and I love him also for this frankness.

G.O. says, 'I know that we feel good when we're together... we have some defects, we have certain virtues... It is true, or am I mistaken?'

'It's all true, you know?' I reply.

And he, 'But I'm afraid to change the things around me because afterwards where does the friendship end up?'

'Simon lets me go...' I say.

And he, 'He's doing something that I would never do if I truly loved... Does Simon love you?'

'I think so. I think that it's for this reason that he lets me go. May I ask you a question? Would you come to bed with me?'

'There's nothing else that I would want more at this moment than to make love with you. But I'm afraid to change things around me. I like very much to be with you but I'm afraid that if things change I would suffer from it later... I don't want you to leave my life.'

'Do you want me as a lover?'

'No. I've Patty already. I'll have to find a way to tell her the truth so that we never see each other again.'

I became frightened, but he said, 'Don't worry. If there's one thing that unites us, this thing is called nature. Everything could be against us, but nature is with us.'"

The letters and diaries of that time are composed, on the one hand, of anxiety, on the other, of love. They are accounts of petty reciprocal vendettas between Simon and Vera, of G.O.'s desire to be understood and absolved by Simon. But in one of his scattered notes Simon wrote: "... this s.o.b. of G.O. is my P.L.O."

At this point the figure of the son, Daniel, is resurrected. He is entirely on his mother's side and seething with vengeance as regards Simon, his father.

A letter written by the youngster (always the first in his class and bound for Yale in about a year) reads: "... I'll never be able to forget what you once told me about my mother. Once you were in a drunken stupor you told me that G.O. Shait had painted a picture showing him licking my mother's cunt. Isn't this the word that you used, cunt?!! I wanted to shout, I wanted to cry, I had never heard so vile a word in all my life. But you uttered it -you filthy, corrupt pig! No, to call you a pig is to insult pigs. To think that I am related to someone who was able to use a word of this kind! I spit in your face. For me you are dead. And I will tell everyone that you are dead. And when you really die, I'll open a bottle of Dom Perignon to celebrate the glorious occasion. You are a swamp from my aspect. You fancy yourself one of the greatest scientists of our time, but you are absolutely a pig, devoid of any emotion whatsoever. When you will have been swept away from the face of the earth the angels in heaven will sing *hallelujahs*..."

Unfortunately, Daniel is still too young. He does not know yet of Blake's *Marriage of Heaven and Hell*, of Blake's been born the same day and month of his rejected father. Let us return to Lung's fairytale to wind up our narrative: As an introduction, Lung poses this question:

"The legend of the original sin contains a profound teaching: it is the expression of the obscure feeling that the emancipation of the consciousness of the Self represents a Luciferine act. From the very beginning, universal history knows of a quarrel between the feeling of inferiority and arrogance. Wisdom seeks a middle point and expiates for this boldness with an ambiguous affinity with the devil and with the beast, and therefore suffers from the possibility that this may be badly interpreted morally."

The fairy tale:

As *the young man is tending his pigs in the woods, he discovers an enormous tree whose branches are lost in the clouds. "How would it be if you looked at the world from that height?" he tells himself. He spends the whole day climbing up the tree, without even reaching the foliage.*

Evening is drawing on and he must spend the night on the trunk of a branch. He resumes the climb on the next day; at noon he reaches the leafy branches and towards evening he comes to a village built in the midst of the branches. The village is inhabited by peasants who welcome him and offer him hospitality for the night. On the following morning he continues his climb. Toward noon he arrives at a castle wherein dwell a young girl and he learns that from this point on one can climb no higher. The young girl is the daughter of a king, being held prisoner by a wicked sorcerer. The young man remains with the princess and is allowed to enter all the rooms of the castle. But his curiosity is stronger than the prohibition; he opens the door to the room and inside he finds a raven affixed to the wall by three nails, one of which pierces its neck, the other two its wings. The raven complains of a terrible thirst and the young man, moved to pity, gives it water to drink. At every sip a nail drops to the floor, and after the third sip the raven is free and flies away through the window. Hearing this the princess panics and says: "The raven was the devil who had bewitched me. It won't be long before he'll be back to capture me again!" In fact, one fine morning she disappears.

Now the young man sets out to look for her and a wolf comes towards him. In the same way he finds a bear and a lion who give him some strands of their pelt, just as the wolf had done. The strands of pelt are magic gifts by means of which the young man may call the wolf; the bear and the lion to his aid at any moment. Moreover; the lion reveals to him that the princess is a prisoner in the immediate vicinity, in the house of the huntsman. He finds the house and the princess, but learns that flight is impossible because the huntsman possesses a white horse with three legs, who is all-knowing and who would unfailingly alert the huntsman. Nevertheless the young man attempts a rescue of the princess, but in vain. The huntsman catches up with him but lets him go because once when he was a raven the youth had saved his life... So the huntsman goes off with the princess. But the youth enters the house, furtively, when the huntsman is in the woods, and he persuades the princess to flatter the jailer so as to wrest from him the secret of how his white horse has achieved its sapience. She succeeds in obtaining this information at night and the youth, who has been hiding under the bed, learns that at about an hour's distance from the huntsman s hut lives a witch who raises enchanted horses. Whoever succeeds in tending her fillies for three days can, as a reward, select himself a horse. At first she had given twelve lambs to the twelve wolves, who lived in the woods around the farm, in order to sate their hunger and thus prevent them from carrying out a raid. But she did not give any lambs to the huntsman. The wolves had followed him as he rode off on his horse and at the point of passage across the border they managed to wrest a hoof from his white horse. And this is why the horse has only three legs.

The youth hastens to the witch and offers his services on the condition that she give him a horse that he himself will select, but also twelve lambs as well. An agreement is reached between them. Then she commands the fillys to escape from him. She gives him an acquavita in order to put him to sleep. He drinks it, falls asleep and the fillys run away. On the first day he recaptures them with the help of the wolf, on the second day he is assisted by the bear; and on the third by the lion. Now he can choose his reward. The witch s little daughter points out her mother's horse to him; naturally he's the best one and also a white steed. He asks for it. But he hardly leaves the sable when the witch punctures the four hooves of the horse and sucks the marrow of its bones. She makes a cake with the marrow which she gives to the young man for his journey. The horse is exhausted but the youth gives him the cake to eat and the animal re-acquires its primitive strength. He leaves the woods unharmed after having pacified the twelve wolves with the twelve lambs. He goes to fetch the princess and they both ride off together. The three-legged white horse again alerts the huntsman who quickly goes into hot pursuit of them and very soon catches up with them because the youth horse will not break into a gallop.

When the huntsman draws near; the three-legged horse shouts to the other; "Little sister; throw him off!" The sorcerer is thrown to the ground and trampled by the two horses. The youth then places the princess on the three-legged horse and then both gallop up to the father's kingdom where they celebrate their wedding. The four- legged horse begs the young man to cut its head off along with that of its companion because otherwise other disasters will strike him. In a twinkling the two horses are transformed into a magnificent prince and into a marvelous princess who soon thereafter proceed to their "own kingdom". At one time, they had been changed into horses by the huntsman.

This is the fairy tale of the book and it is really uncanny how every thing, more or less, coincides.

A final paragraph in which Jung comments on the fairy tale could help us to arrive at a conclusion.

"Leaving out of consideration the theriomorphic symbolism of the psyche, what is particularly interesting in this tale is the fact that the function of the consciousness and of intuition is represented by a saddle horse. With this it is indicated that the psyche, too, can be possessed. Thus, the three-legged white horse is the property of the diabolic huntsman, while the four-legged horse at first is the property of the witch. Here, on the one hand, the psyche is function, that can change proprietors like a thing (horse); on the other hand, however, it is also autonomous subject (sorcerer, as the proprietor of the horse). When the young man obtains the four-legged horse from the witch, he liberates a spirit or a mode of thinking of a particular species from the dominion of the unconscious. Here, as in other places, the witch signifies a *mater natura*, the primitive "matriarchal" state, so to speak, of the unconscious; wherefore there is an allusion to a psychic constitution in which, in the face of the unconscious, there is only a weak, non-independent consciousness. The four-legged white horse shows himself to be superior to the three-legged white horse because he can command it. Since *quaternity* is a symbol of totality, and totality plays an important role in the world of images of the unconscious, the victory of the four-legged being over the three-legged one is not wholly unexpected."

I sink in the face of these conclusions but I can still add something. Persons tend to make confessions when their lives are at the final point. And they do so with boldness or humility in order to attest to themselves that they have passed through this earth and that they have taken from it what they wanted, and have distributed what they had on it. This is why the diaries are biblical; they make persons think of so many things, above all of death. Because they have embellished it with love.

If I were to write a novel of "my own" on the characters in these diaries, I would have to add a third part that would describe them in the flow of time, in terms of the fates that befell them. I shall not do so because this novel in diary form is not a novel as such but a treatise on education, a bitterly satiric essay purposely planned as a surreal fairy tale and which precisely through artifice must also present itself as fastidiously erudite and as the bearer of many implications, of a real character, in substance. My footnotes have taken the place of narrative sequence. Therefore I shall note several additional things:

VERA: On p. 66 of an autobiographical novel still unpublished called CONFITEOR, written by Simon in Detroit, Michigan, during the famous July 1967 uprising in the city's "blind pigs" Vera Jones is mentioned, as Simon's wife, with her true name of Guendalisa Jones, while Vera - eventually her middle name - was left out. In footnote 7 (Part One, "Simon's Diary") I wrote that I had again seen Vera and G.O. Shait on February 28, 1980. It is an important footnote, and deserves re-reading.

Today is July 9, 1982 and all I know of Vera and of Shait - neither of whom I have not seen again - are only rumors that have reached my ears primarily through Anacleto Zinghelli. Vera has abandoned Shait to follow Mathias, now retired, in Bath, the New England town that is mentioned in the diaries. She is waiting for a divorce from Shait. Her son, and Simon's, Daniel, is a frustrated genius at Yale, where he has been allowed to attend courses discussing ways of dispelling the father-complex. Dress has also gone back to the old house in Bath, the house in which Patrick, the never accepted husband, was born and grew up.

SHAIT: Epiphanically, he realized that his true vocation was to return to Phedra, the mother of his children. But she insisted on remaining in Texas with her new husband, and on having him as a partner in their Art Gallery. Shait resigned from his teaching post, drawing a minimum pension, and went to live next to Phedra in El Paso. Apparently, he acquired a degree of notoriety in that city because of some forged paintings sold by the Gallery. The forgeries were quickly judged as more appealing and pleasing than the originals. G.O. served a few months in jail, but in Texas everybody still buys Shait's forged paintings, especially the Vermeer's.

CHARLOTTE: She is a prominent figure as the head mistress of a fashionable girl's school in Florida, with military academic criteria, of which she is the founderess. One of the courses, the least famous, provides the girls with training in anti-terrorist and anti-rape tactics, also with the help of hundreds of rock doves or roach birds or flying rats, known as flamingos.

ANNA: She had a job teaching at the University of California at Los Angeles, and was living on a beach house in Malibu. One night, the house went up in smoke, and she died in it. Later, we learned that Anna Madison's house was set on fire by a 26-year-old illegal immigrant from Columbia, a drug trafficker, who claimed he had been repeatedly "humiliated" by the woman, during love making, and finally "discarded" as lover with a small check in a pink envelope, as a thank you.

RAFAEL: The gentle virtuoso flutist was considered to be, at least until recently, the most discreet person in Anaconda. He kept cultivating *gaviotas* and

English tobacco, obviously, while his studies continued to be appreciated by specialists in his field, even though they now would appear seldomly, and still trigging off old vendettas.

His motto was, as one shipwrecked person said to another, *"En el fondo, el mar es bueno."* In fact, poor reckless Rafael! He was "forced" to retire (and he did, and even left the country) in order to escape a law suit for sex harassment, in which was stated that Professor Rafael Oviedo de Bernalbe had "engaged in pervasive and regular sexually discriminatory conduct toward" a female student.

Rafael was from Pontevedra, Galicia, but he never lived there. Cattle and hog raising was his family trade, and that also lended pay for his studies in Salamanca, Oxford, and Florence. His true country, however, for some mysterious reasons was Vatican City. And eventually he went back there. There? Of course, for many souls in Anaconda **there** is a place meaning only, somehow, **where**?

ZINGHELLI: He seems to be a man at peace with himself after the tragic incident of swallowing a dental bridge, fortunately restored to him later in one piece through the anus.

He is no longer so harsh in his judgment of others and in his oratorial presentations. Evenhandedly, he keeps trying with some success to administer his position as scholar and influential Jesuit dissident, comforted by a new wife, twenty years his junior, and also very gracious and affectionate.

He corresponds regularly with Simon's Italian sons, Bernardino and Alessandro who, convinced that a meritocracy has no place in Italy's universities and its scientific community, turned, to the United States, unconsciously following their father's steps. And being highly talented decided to stay here permanently.

Dino, now 22, studies film-making at New York University, New York City, and he has also cut a couple of records with his new- wave group known as DUST/GANG. Alessandro, now 25, after obtaining a summa cum laude degree in political science at the University of Rome, *La Sapienza*, won scholarships for further studies with the SAIS center of Bologna, then in Washington, D.C., an advanced international program of the Johns Hopkins University, from which he is seeking a Ph.D. Sandro is already the author of a couple of books dealing with Europe-America politics and economics. In a recent letter to Zinghelli, he expressed his trepidations and uncertainties regarding the rightness or wrongness of a diplomatic career.

He also asked: "Do you have any definitive idea about my father's fate?"

Zinghelli smiled, sadly. Yet he never believed, most probably, in Simon's death, claiming instead that he was anonymously working either alongside the founder of liberation theology, Gustavo Gutierrez, or in the barrios of Lima, Peru. One day he presented me with a postcard from Condevilla in Lima, with a handwritten quotation from Isaiah 42:6-7, proclaiming a vision of justice:

I, the Lord, have called you
for the victory of justice.
I have grasped you by the hand;
I have formed you
and set you as a covenant for the people,
a light for the nation,
to open the eyes of the blind,
to bring prisoners out from confinement,
and from the dungeon
those who live in darkness.

Anacleto Zinghelli was asserting that the calligraphy on the postcard, in green ink, was Simon's. I didn't recognize it. And, actually, I didn't want to know. Nevertheless Zinghelli was putting the finishing touches on a large monograph on our colleague, avoiding to cite the year of his birth and that of his death.

He used to repeat: "Who knows if he was ever born, who knows if he ever died?"

By quoting John Russell on Meyerhold the Director, he once said of Simon that "he was the complete professional, and he was never the same, year by year, month by month, or week by week. There was virtually nothing that he could not do in the anthropological field of research and higher education. He knew exactly what he wanted, and exactly how to get it. He had an extraordinary and distinctive speaking voice. He was a prodigious mime. He knew how to set the stage of his work, how to light it, how to make silence seem louder than speech, how to enroll the best advanced students of the day as equal partners, and how to make grants work for him and the University as it never worked before. He reinvented himself, throughout his life, in such a way that there is no one of the many books he wrote by which he can be judged. God have mercy on him."

But mistakes are at the very base of human thought, embedded there, feeding the structure like root modules. If we were not provided with the knack of being wrong, we could never get anything useful done. We think our way along by choosing between right and wrong alternatives; and the wrong choices have to be made as frequently as the right ones. We get along in life this way. So the hope is in the faculty of wrongness, the tendency toward error. The capacity to leap across mountains of information to land lightly on the wrong side represents the highest of human endowments.

These remarks by Thomas S. Crane, quoted from Lewis Thomas, were read in memoriam of our good friend and patron, John O. Crane, who died May 16, 1982, in Woods Hole, Massachusetts.

These remarks are for us too.

Many of the academic brains of the so-called Rockefeller Years have left Anaconda, others have aged in their university chairs, and other still have simply vanished in the suburbs. Among the left-overs is also Carmen Cara, along with a few others of the old gang. The text mentions me now as Carmen and now as Cara, and once also as Carmen Cara. It is in Zinghelli's rigmarole that I am remembered as "... *the great Carmen Cara, incontestably a Capricorn to the depth s of his lawyer's soul.*"

My full name is R. Carmen Cara, but no one ever paid attention to that R. It stands for Rex.

I am Simon's attorney, I handled his divorce from Vera, the division of his property, his last will and testament, the monthly allowance that he has to pay to Daniel until he reaches 21. And I am also in direct touch with his Roman children, wherever they may go.

I teach Administrative Law for evening students which are broadcast over TV on the following morning to around 163,000 students registered in the Anaconda university system. We are an immense political city, the academic level is excellent and there is a concentration of disciplines in which some names still stand out in the sciences, in agriculture, in medicine, in literature, in the fine arts. What is lacking is a cultural tradition, and there are ongoing attempts to give the university one, by cutting and adding and by grouping hundreds of programs in the cuts. Humanistic studies have become the least representative thanks to capricious deans, highly and exclusively motivated by ambition. Anaconda is fearful in its tranquility. It crushes hundreds of individuals twice a year, regularly: during the Christmas and summer vacations, when a great number of students and academicians are roaming around the world in connection with their research work. They come back, and they suddenly realize that they have a year of life left, that the equipment has been carried off, along with their books, their laboratories, their students, and their colleagues. Candidly, a dean once said to the members of the Council of his college, "Yes, at least twice a year we exercise in panic."

New faces appear in the Inner Circle with unobjectionable credentials, but equally desirous of working at a salary lower than that offered to "the best ones" who were hired from more prestigious universities during the Rockefeller Years. With 64 autonomous colleges, the Anaconda system, which is controlled by four major centers, is the most massive and, at the same time, the most bemired of the academic systems of the United States. This system captures its prey by pouncing upon it with teeth and, at the same time, winds its immense body around that of the victim, compressing and suffocating it. The Anaconda system swallows its victims whole so as not to leave all too tell-tale traces behind.

I myself was never uncomfortable or unhappy there. Were I to receive offers to go elsewhere, I would refuse them. I am the attorney of the system, at times in order to defend it and, at times, to babble about it, and I am in possession of its legal archives. The collective commitment is to salvage the salvageable, and for my part a first testimony of the commitment is the recuperation of these Diaries.

I live in my office, usually, and I am alone. Once a week, when I'm not traveling, I meet with a lady who has a beach house in Winthrop, Massachusetts. She's a widow, and her children live far away.

Author's Note

Today is Thursday, March 17, 1994, St. Patrick's Day—a day almost 20 years after this glossed novel was written. I'm kind of frightened about the passing of time. Every year I have to pen out, with tears, names of friends from my Address Book.

And a couple of months ago was the turn of dear R. Carmen Cara who, like Molly O'Neill, was a well known lover of mycology: the spy, in a word, of a precious cup that could belong (if surveying a patch of autumn wood or the tender underbelly of a spring field), to a domestic white mushroom or to a shiitake, to a *cremini* or to a *portobello*, to a *porcini* or to a *chanterelle*, or ... to a poisonous one.

Ms. O'Neill observed, quite recently, that "gathering mushrooms takes wit, instinct, knowledge and a certain raw cunning." And Carmen had all those quality. Apparently, he was poisoned by mushrooms that he had picked up in the garden's greenhouse of his Dark Lady of Winthrop, Massachusetts: in reality a modern, practical garden's greenhouse in a garden a la Voltaire.

Yes?

Let us cultivate our garden.

These are Monsieur de Voltaire's last candid words. Or did Carmen pray, like Baudelaire, O Death, old captain, comfort us with poison... Did he, or...? Well, do you care?

I don't know, Sir! I don't know!

He might very well have had a final danse macabre with his Dark Lady, why not?

> Au chant des violons, aux flammes des bougies,
> Esperes-tu chasser ton cauchemar moqueur,

Et viens-tu demander au torrent des orgies
De rafraichir l'enfer allume dans ton coeur?

Do you have hope that violins and candlelights
Can make nightmarish revelries depart,
And do you come demanding orgiastic rites
To quench the fire of hell that burn within your heart?[1]

O.K., I understand.

Did you then, well, let me ask you... did you ever meet Mr. Spence, the trial lawyer? He once said that you cannot decide when you're going to fall in love. He said just that. You cannot decide when... when what?

He spoke of seduction. But he was right, anyway, and so right that during the years you, I, kept repeating to myself: O you, shall I make public your every pleasures, *mon coeur mis a nu?*

And still I couldn't decide.

Oh, Love!

Did you say, Love?

Then one day Mr. Spence talked to me through an apologue. It was Friday, October 15, 1993 the day in which I also discovered that my friend Rudolf Nureyev died of AIDS, January 1993, and that Simon's son, Daniel, now living in Manhattan as a concert pianist and composer, was infected with H.I.V. positive, the virus that causes AIDS!

An article about him on the ASCAP Newsletter, the American Society of Composers Authors and Publishers, to which I am a member, led me to him. I phoned him from Selinsgrove, Pennsylvania, (a place where also Lorenzo Da Ponte lived for awhile,) and screaming he said, "Do you think I've a chance, Giose?"

Again, I was frightened.

---

[1] See Charles Baudelaire's "Danse Macabre" in *Les Fleurs Du Mal. The Fowers of Evil,* trans. by William H. Crosby (BOA Edition. Ltd., Brockport. NY, 1991) 184-5.

Immediately I sensed a very sore head, a headache, and a pain inside. It was emotion, I believe. But I couldn't clearly know at first if I were suffering of dehydration like when, sometimes, playing tennis with somebody like Andre Agassi, or of guilt: a deep pain on account of him, Daniel, and of his misfortune, as if I were directly responsible of it.

No. It cannot be it!

And the book? What did you say you call it, *A Glossed Novel?* C'mon, coward, tell him. Its called *The Three-legged One.* A Glossed Novel by... A book designed for sarcasm, parody of mores and moral in exchange for a few Bergsonian laughs, almost just like (not quite) the other one you wrote in English, *Benedetta in Guysterland. A Liquid Novel* by...[2] To amuse whom, yourself? Well, then, tell him. Didn't you write the truth, this time? Well, yes, always, every time I start writing something I deal with... How do you call it, Truth? Well, yes, and I hope you didn't forget what you said in a speech at the University of Bologna, April 9, 1984, claiming that your "literature is almost all autobiographical in nature: novels, poetry, literary criticism," etcetera, with that making clear, crystal clear that any form of autobiography tells the truth. Is this the truth, the whole truth?

Hell, no!

Wait!!

What Philippe Lejeune, the greatest student of autobiography (after James Olney, of course,) can say at this point? Does he deal with I, You, He?

Well, listen:

> The identity of the *narrator* and the *principal* character that is assumed in autobiography is marked often by the use of the first person. This is what Gerard Genette calls "autodiegetic" narra-

---

[2] See Giose Rimanelli, *Benedetta in Guysterland. A Liquid Novel* (Montreal: Guemica, 1993).

tion in his classification of narrative "voices," a classification he establishes from works of fiction. But he states quite clearly that there can be narrative "in the first person" without the narrator being the same person as the principal character. This is what he calls in broad terms "homodiegetic" narration. We need only continue this reasoning to see that in the reverse order there can be identity of the narrator and the principal character without the first person being used.[3]

No, Daniel! I wrote a book of lies, Daniel, because just like all writers I'm a born liar. Yes, oh yes, we're a bunch of liars ... and that, well, in order to make a lousy buck or to recount the pain, the truth?

Both, perhaps. But I know only the pain, a little like Baudelaire who recounted the pain, and a little like Voltaire who recounted the scorching truth.

But why, please tell me Daniel, why is there so much variation in the time it takes to develop AIDS after infection with H.I.V. positive? Are you positive? And is it true that the average period is considered to be 10 years, though some people progress to AIDS within a year or two?

Oh Daniel, Daniel! Forgive my ignorance, the summer reading has left me tickled pink, but just now somebody from the hill across the Susquehanna River, pardon, from bigot Susquehanna University is telling me that AIDS was discovered in 1981 whoooooosh, didn't I know?—a year in which this book was already all written down notwithstanding the dates at times confusing given by loyal Carmen, dead now, and so much so that I could finally get back a manuscript—this one—that he kept hostage for so many years.

And I came also to know that today as today there are in the world about 14 million people infected with the virus, and by the

---

[3] See Philippe Leejeune, *On Autobiography,* trans. by Katherine Leary (University of Minnesota Press, Minneapolis, 1989) 5-6.

year 2000 — will I still be alive? — the infected will be between 30 or 40 millions. Is it true, Daniel? Oh, Daniel, will you be alive? I'm crying, Daniel, and would you want to know why?

"No! Don't, please! I stopped doing it, I stopped crying and crying and now I'm just frozen!"

"You mean, Daniel... You mean, you're scared?"

"Well, Giose, do you think I'm deliriously happy? Of course I'm scared. In fact, I'm scared to death! No, I'm a liar, a little like you, Giose. No, not even. I glow in the dark like a Kellogg's New 15 oz. size RICE CRISPIES Low in Sugar and Fat Free... I mean like the Kellogg's AstroBall that zings before your eyes with only two proofs of purchase. Oh, yeah, the Kellogg's, Giose, that also zips!"

"Zip the zipless? The ups and downs?"

"Who the hell I know? In reality, I don't know. Also because I decided to play only, from now on, with what glows in the dark, as a matter of fact you too, Giose, try to throw it down, I mean the AstroBall, and watch it take off in another direction, but watch out, read carefully the Instructions! Which way will your crazy cosmic AstroBall bounce?"

"Who knows? It's like sickness, isn't it?"

"Not at all! But keep the faith high. I'm learning. Send me your book, will you?"

"I will."

"How do you call it? *The Three-legged One?* And what's that? Anyway... The AZT apparently deters transmission of H.I.V. from mothers to newborns, and that's good news, it explains a kind of decline in the frequency of dementia among my fellow patients, although only two, of dozens of antiviral substances - the DDI and DDC – have so far happily joined the AZT with full licensing."

"I don't understand."

"Certainly. It's Greek. But we're now waiting for a D4T... What am I saying? Nonsense, Giose, since it's Greek for you. In

reality, no one knows, yet, how to fend off H.I.Y. And since—
again *since*, since like *sin*—since there are no magic medical
bullets, it seems that progress can come only inch by inch. Scary,
uh? Yeahhh! But I'll manage, Giose, I'll manage... Do I make any
sense to you?"

"To me? Oh, yeahhhh! Yankee Doodle had a hat, Daniel. And
now I feel I'm in no land. But, I guess, I too - just like you - have to
try to manage, uh?"

"I like that verb, *manage!* Bye, Giose."

"Bye, Daniel."

And we said good-bye with raised hands in the fog, just like
two people on the opposite banks of the river. And somehow I
was now at peace with myself. So I went back to Mr. Spence's
apologue, perhaps to give myself an extra dose of Kellogg's.

"You have to break the horse," he said. "If you take a horse
and say, 'Come this way,' the horse will balk. So you just keep
pulling on him gently. And he'll try to run away from your
questions. But you keep coming back until he answers. Then you
pat him on the side of the neck. And you pull him again. And
once you've got him leading, you get him to admit things that are
important to your case."

Our case?

Yes. *Veritatis splendor.*

About The Author

Giose Rimanelli was born in Italy on November 28, 1926, of an Italian father and a Canadian mother. He gained international fame with some of his novels during the Fifties, translated in many languages and also made into movies and radio plays, such as *The Day of the Lion* (1954), *Original Sin* (1957), *Third Class Ticket* (1958), *A Social Position* (1959). To his narrative activity he has added poetry, professional journalism, theater and literary criticism, both in Italian and in English. As for poetry, Giose has primarily engaged himself with Latin and Provencal poets whom he has translated, eventually leading him to the rediscovery of the dialect of his native Molise with the great songs and ballads of *Moliseide*.

He has lived for many years in both United States and Canada, teaching Italian and Comparative Literature in major universities, writing and doing extensive researches about the two countries. He was for awhile (1953) chief editor of the Italian/Canadian weekly *Il cittadino canadese* of Montreal, and out of that experience he published the best-selling *Third Class Ticket* (1958). And while he was teaching at the University of British Columbia (1963-65) he did research for *Modern Canadian Stories* (1967), which for many years was adopted as a standard textbook in Canadian schools.

Giose considers Canada his "sentimental" motherland. In 1977 he donated his correspondence and a bundle of his still unpublished manuscripts to the Fisher Rare Book Library of the University of Toronto, for future studies. He is SUNY-Albany Professor Emeritus.

OTHER BOOKS
by Giose Rimanelli

Alien Cantica (1994)

Benedetta in Guysterland (1994)

Moliseide (1990, 1992)

Arcano (1990)

Time Hidden Between Lines (1986)

Molise Molise (1979)

Italian Literature: Roots & Branches (1978)

Graffiti (1977)

Poems Make Pictures Pictures Make Poems (1971)

Tragic America (1968)

Love Monks of the Middle Ages (1967)

Carmina blabla (1967)

Modern Canadian Stories (1966)

The French Horn (1962)

Lares (1962)

Tea at Piccasso's (1961)

The Sneak Craft (1959)

A Social Position (1959)

Third Class Ticket (1958)

Original Sin (1957)

The Day of the Lion (1954)

Tiro al Piccione (1953, 1991)

VIA FOLIOS

A refereed book series dedicated to Italian studies and the culture
of Italian Americans in North America.

Published by BORDIGHERA, INC., an independently owned not-for-profit scholarly organization with no legal affiliation to the University of Central Florida or John D. Calandra Italian American Institute, Queens College/ CUNY.